Days

of

Watershed

Pivotal Faith That Shapes Our Lives

R. J. Graves, Jr.

This is a work of fiction. Names, characters, places and incidents are products of the author's imagination or are used fictitiously. Any resemblance to actual persons, living or dead, or to events and locales is entirely coincidental.

Cover design by: BETIBUP33 Designs

DAYS OF WATERSHED
Pivotal Faith That Shapes Our Lives
Copyright © 2018 by R. J. Graves, Jr.
Published by R. J. Graves, Jr.
Edited by Susan C. Graves
Pensacola, Florida 32503

Visit us at www.facebook.com/rojocci
www.therojoccipapers.com
ISBN-10: 0-9984073-4-8
ISBN-13: 978-0-9984073-4-0
Christian Fiction
$13.95 USD

Printed in the United States of America.

This book is dedicated to Mom and Andree.
Thank you so much for the kindheartedness
and genuine love you have expressed
toward me over the many decades
we have known one another.
I love you both and I'm so grateful
that we are so close,
if not geographically, then in our hearts.
I hope you enjoy and are inspired
when reading this story.

Acknowledgments

Several people have helped me with many aspects of this book, none more than my editor, Susan C. Graves, whose tireless efforts and extreme attention to detail have continued to amaze me. Heartfelt thanks also to Betty Graves, Mike Parker, Kathy Coker, Sarah Whipps, Bob Cornwell, and Dr. Frank Osborne for their most helpful input and encouragement during the many revisions.

Although I may have inadvertently left others out of these acknowledgements, I am, nonetheless, very grateful for their inspiration and support too.

watershed; (waw-ter-shed), noun 1. The land or region draining into a river, lake, or ocean. 2. A turning point; an important period, time, event, or factor that marks a change, transition, or division.

"'What do you want Me to do for you?' And he said,

'Lord, I want to regain my sight.'"

Luke 18:41

ONE

The air in the courtroom was suffocating. From where I sat on the witness stand, the cloud of cigarette smoke hung a few feet above my head, adding to my increasingly gloomy disposition. Two enormous ceiling fans turned their paddles ever so slowly through the thick air as if complaining of the effort. Glancing out at the faces, all of which were staring back at me, I dispassionately responded to yet another probing question, accusingly posed by the defense attorney. Though I never looked his way, I could sense the piercing glare of the defendant with each of my condemning responses. I'd never been called to testify in a murder trial before. The atmosphere was tense. My brow wet. My throat dry.

Leaning forward toward the microphone to give my answer to his final question, my torso shifted under the bullet-proof vest, revealing to me the extent of hot sweat that had accumulated within its impenetrable cocoon. On the many occasions I had testified in court, I had learned to keep my answers short and to the point. I was confident, I had accomplished this in this proceeding as well. Having been dismissed by the judge, I stood, adjusted my neatly pressed uniform, and proudly marched back to my seat in the courtroom, knowing the defendant's eyes would follow me across the room. Although I loathed his threatening demeanor, I refused to be intimidated by it. I sat stone still and unwavering in my bearing. My mind, in an effort to defend itself, wondered how I had arrived in this courtroom amidst this distressing situation. Gazing out the partially opened window, I contemplated my life. My thoughts drifted to a period of time, several years ago, when everything began to change.

In those days you couldn't buy a job. The well had dried up. The orchards were barren. Not only had the low hanging fruit disappeared, but there wasn't a speck of fruit on any of the trees. In some cases, the trees themselves had vanished. It seemed stranger than fiction to me, a transplant from the East Coast to this Promised Land among the giant redwoods and white granite peaks. You see, within minutes of disembarking my cross country flight I knew I would absolutely love living here. I could feel it in the air. It was lighter, fresher, sunnier, and decidedly more prosperous. My birthplace may have been in one of the original thirteen states, but I was somehow reborn in the American West. Being only twenty-two years of age, I had arrived at my heaven on earth. But a mere three years later, here I was unemployed, discouraged beyond words, and with almost nothing to show for myself. My wife of less than two years was a school teacher. But her meager salary could not support the two of us. Besides, she didn't draw a paycheck during the summer months. For us, the 1970s were ending in one long, dying fizzle.

By the autumn of 1979, I had hit rock bottom. For several years I had been a journeyman carpenter, a moniker I had proudly enjoyed wearing. My friends and I had felt fulfilled in our chosen professions. We had been hard working, clean cut, highly skilled craftsmen who jogged every morning, played golf on Saturdays, and attended church services twice on Sundays. Holding positions of leadership at church, we also taught evening Bible studies during the week. We were intelligent but knew our place. We were proud but in the best sense of the word—we took pride in a job well done. It mattered greatly to us not only what the finished product looked like, but also that precision and quality were accomplished during the assembling process.

All of us were Baby Boomers and perhaps a dying generation of those who thought the character of an individual was more important than the appearance. We were young and strong, yet vulnerable because none of us had been able to save a nest egg, a buffer for times like these. We hadn't even considered that we may need one at some point. So here we were, unemployed for the first time in our lives. It was bewildering. It was disheartening. It was dismal.

Have you ever been unemployed? There's not just the loss of income to deal with. It also brings a lack of support for the life you have chosen to live. For most, it's an identity crisis, an absence of part of your personhood. For instance, when unemployed what do you call yourself when meeting someone? From what perspective do you enter a conversation with friends and family? How do you spend money when you're not making any? The questions you consider are endless . . . and quite fruitless.

After many unproductive weeks of applying for anything within my skill set, in other words, working with tools, I was near despair. Shortly thereafter, I submitted one application after another for jobs completely outside of anything I had ever done before. Finally, along with the gasoline rationing of those days, my number came up. I was hired for a position the likes of which I had absolutely no prior knowledge or experience. It was with mixed emotions I showed up on that first Monday.

"Take this to the uniform store after work today," stated my new boss, Mr. Lawson. Being a self-important man with an overbearing demeanor, he was obviously very proud to be the manager. He didn't seem malicious, but arrogance oozed from every pore. What he lacked in friendliness, he more than made up by being direct.

"Is that what you wear for your first day at a new job?" he questioned with a frown. "Tomorrow arrive in a button down collar or don't bother showing up."

Mr. Lawson was tall and wiry with an uncanny resemblance to my high school principal, which was so distracting that the only response I could muster neither defended my position or explained it.

After clearing my throat, I replied, "Yes, sir, I'm sorry, Mr. Lawson. I thought maybe a nice polo shirt . . ."

"What gave you that idea? We dress to win—everyday! Understand?" He paused, waiting for my acknowledgement, then continued in a slightly subdued tone. "Now, for today you'll just have to go out in 'less than success' attire."

"Yes, sir. Again, I'm sorry, I just thought . . ."

"Too late for that now," he chided. "For today and the rest of this week, you'll be training with Mac. He has been our top salesman for several months. Mac will show you what it takes to be a winner."

With a wave of his hand, he directed my attention to Mac, a fifty-five year old, stocky man of medium height with a flat top haircut and the tiniest goatee I had ever seen. After exchanging greetings and the customary assessment of my qualifications by my reluctant mentor, we clambered into his work van and headed for the first client of the day, a small factory that manufactured widgets of some sort. Making the turn out of our company parking lot, Mac got right to the point.

"Boss says you were a carpenter? Hard work, eh? Well, listen up, selling and servicing first aid kits can be a good life. And there ain't no heavy lifting neither. Hey, look at me," he coaxed in his mildly diminished Brooklyn accent. "I've got a nice house in Uniontown, a new car every four or five years, and my second wife don't hate me because I make my alimony payments on time."

"Second wife?"

"Yeah, I'm on my third one now, but I'm still paying the second," he chuckled, shaking his head.

"Uh, how's it going with the third one?" I hesitatingly asked.

"What? You writing a book or something? Eh . . . ask me next week, and I'll let you know." With this last statement, he glanced in my direction as he flopped his wrist over the steering wheel. I noticed he was wearing a gold watch and a pinky ring to match. Mac was definitely aiming to impress. But who? I wasn't sure.

Trying to change the subject, I asked, "So how long have you been doing this?"

The only two words I heard of Mac's response were "Seventeen years . . ." before my mind began drifting while I gazed out the side window. This job was a far cry from being a skilled craftsman. How could I ever take pride in this kind of work? I felt cheap, like I wasn't performing to my potential. Still unable to focus on my trainer's continuous ramblings, I contentedly daydreamed; my mind refusing the fight to remain in the conversation. I was a journeyman carpenter, not a band aid salesman. I wanted to cut complex angles on rafters and hipped dormers; layout and build beautiful, curved staircases with flying balconies; and finish a redwood, lap-sided house with exposed rafter tails, Dutch gables, and custom columns on the front porch. You know, I wanted to do something productive, something substantial, something meaningful that would actually contribute to the Gross National Product.

It wasn't so much my position in a company that mattered to me. Rather, I was more concerned about what I was producing. To me, it mattered that I matter. I had a need, a passion, to do a thing profitably and to do it well. I wanted to eventually design and build homes and commercial buildings. And I had thought I was well on my way until this slump in the construction industry hit. Now my dream was on the ropes, if not dead altogether.

Fading out of my reverie and back into the ongoing noise, I tuned into Mac's monologue. Yes, he was still talking. He hadn't even noticed whether I was listening or not. I'm not sure he even cared. It appeared to me he just liked to talk. His "to be honest" was repeated so frequently in his statements I began to wonder if this implied that his other comments were untrue. It seems more likely to me that when someone declares "I'm just being honest" they are actually very opinionated and enjoy spouting their opinions without a care as to whether the listener is interested in hearing them or not. This was most decidedly the case with my short-term trainer, Mac.

He was a nice enough guy in a middle-aged, cynical, and bitter kind of way. Or maybe I was just reading too much into his comments because of his accent and my own depressed disposition. I glanced over at him and nodded, giving the impression I was still paying attention. He grinned back at me as he continued his soliloquy. Without a pause, he pulled into a parking spot at the doughnut shop.

"First stop?" I inquired with my own brand of subtle sarcasm.

"Yeah, first lesson too."

17

"What's that, Mac?" I loved the way those words sounded together and decided right then and there, I would be using that combination frequently.

"Caffeine and sugar," he confided frankly. "Always keep topped up. You have to appear before your clients as a high energy guy. They'll buy more product from you if they think you're working hard for them." His wry grin widened his round face.

"So doughnuts?"

"Yeah, first stop every day is for caffeine and sugar. What are you having?"

"Uh, I'm not sure," I replied as I peeked past him to our reflection in the front window. His form completely obscured mine.

"Go ahead, I'm buying," he pressed as he caught a glimpse of the prominently displayed tray of apple fritters. "Never mind, two of them apple fritters and two medium coffees," he blurted to the person behind the glass counter.

"Just a small milk," I stated apologetically. "I don't drink coffee."

"Milk?" he mocked. "Kids nowadays."

A tiny factory where they produce a gadget for folks who like to walk was our next stop. Apparently, once you don this little device it will record the amount of steps you take and accurately calculate how many calories you burn while doing so. It is all housed in a tiny plastic case smaller than a wallet. Shortly after we arrived, Mac opened their first aid kit, which hung upon the wall in the lunch room. Our company sold several types and sizes at differing prices. I can't recall all the model numbers, but suffice it to say they were like shirt sizes: small, medium, large, and extra-large. This unit was a medium. He showed me how to clean the interior of the painted, metal kit using the moist towelettes in a box on the upper shelf within the cabinet. He also advised me to be sure to use the customer's product, so they would need more of the item sooner. Instructing me on how to organize everything in the box, he then filled out the order form for the missing items.

Once we were finished, we walked down the hall and entered the manager's office. Evidently, he was not having a good day because he immediately barked, "What do, you clowns, want?"

"Hey, Gene, how you doing today, my friend?" asked Mac with more enthusiasm than I had heard out of him since Mr. Lawson had introduced us. Mac thrust out his hand and exclaimed, "You're looking good. How was your weekend?"

"Terrible . . . and don't call me your friend," he snapped back giving Mac's hand a half shake. "Now, what do you want?"

"Gene, I want to introduce you to our new salesman, Nicolas Roberts. He just started today, and you were the first client I wanted him to meet."

I stretched out my hand and smiled, "Hi, Gene, nice to meet you."

"Yeah, great, how much this month?"

"Uh . . ." I glanced at Mac, who gestured for me to show Gene our order form. I quickly handed it to Gene.

"What the . . . fifty-six dollars?! For what? Band aids and ointment? This has got to stop. I'm calling an employee meeting right after lunch. They must be using band aids to fix their hammers."

"Their hammers?" I inquired sheepishly.

"Yeah, the ones I'm going to break over their heads." Mac chuckled.

I shook my head.

Gene slammed the form down on his desk and signed it. Then he thrust it back at me without even glancing in my direction. I grabbed the paper, pulled his copy off, and laid it back on his desk. "Thank you, sir. You have yourself a nice day."

Mac and I gathered the needed supplies from his van and walked back into the factory. After we finished restocking the kit, Mac showed me how to wipe down the exterior and exclaimed a final admonition,

"A clean kit is a kit that will get used. Don't ever forget that, kid."

Once we were back in the van and headed down the road, Mac reinstated his lecture and my training. "Well, kid, how's it feel to make your first five dollars and sixty cents?"

"What?"

"Yeah, we make ten percent on every service. Seven percent on any kit we sell."

"I think I'll focus on service then," I mumbled.

"Bad attitude. Sales are where you'll make your money. Service is just the bread and butter. Sell one kit for a hundred dollars, yeah it's only seven bucks, but now you have something to service every month until you retire. Got it?"

"Yeah. Thanks."

"Look, kid, these are your clients not mine. Your territory has maybe eighty-five units out there needing service. It's your job not only to expand that number but to devise a sales plan and a schedule for servicing. For example, Gene's kit needs servicing about every four to five weeks. We just closed a sale for fifty-six dollars, so you can figure on about that amount every month or so."

"Okay. But that doesn't seem like much," I interjected with a tone of concern.

"It's not. But you do that number times eighty-five customers, and you have a pretty good start toward your monthly goal. Let's see . . . about forty-eight hundred bucks."

"What's the goal?"

"Your goal is ten thousand in sales and service each month."

"Ten thousand? Dollars?!"

"Yeah, you can do it, kiddo. And when you hit ten thousand, your total percentage doubles, twenty percent across the board. See what I was telling you? It's a real good living."

To prevent a sarcastic comment from leaping out of my mouth, I promptly turned my head to look out the side window of the van. What Mac didn't understand was that I had been making a really good living when I was a carpenter. I brought home more than twice what he was declaring as a "real good living". Plus, I had loved my work and had taken a great deal of pride in what I had done. Now, here I was selling gauze and aspirin to bitter old men like Gene.

"What's Gene's problem anyway?" I asked, trying to divert Mac's attention to someone other than myself.

"Gene? Oh, he's typical. Why?"

"Typical?"

"Yeah, most of our customers are like that. You should see him on a bad day."

"Great," I murmured.

Mac glanced in my direction but didn't say anything.

Sure enough, he was right. At every stop we made that day, and every day that week, the majority of the customers were grouchy, angry, bitter people who evidently hated their job, hated buying first aid items, or hated life. Most of them could probably be classified as "all of the above." My first day ended with a stop at the uniform shop to get fitted for my new uniform.

Asking my name, the rather impatient gentleman began taking my measurements. He called out the numbers to the lady behind the counter, who recorded them on an order form. "Six foot-one," he began. "Waist thirty-four. Inseam the same. Chest, forty. Neck and sleeve, standard."

After filling out the paperwork, the cordial lady brought me a sample uniform to try on. I reluctantly put it on in their private dressing room. Then, I looked at myself in the mirror. I couldn't believe my eyes. I was mortified. I loathed it. I looked like I sold popsicles to little kids waiting on street corners. Sure, I had seen Mac and the others in their uniforms earlier in the day, but somehow I hadn't pictured myself looking like this. Obviously, my desperate need for an income had temporarily impaired my judgement. That is, until I saw my own reflection. Hastily changing out of the uniform, I handed the items back to the lady behind the counter. Her knowing smile said it all. Within seconds, I slinked out of the shop feeling completely humiliated.

Though the week riding with Mac seemed to drag on, Friday afternoon finally came. Shortly after lunch, we headed back to the office. On our way, Mac explained that everyone arrived early on Friday afternoons, so they could restock their vans. He also confided that he thought Mr. Lawson wanted to be sure no one tried to leave early for the weekend.

Upon our arrival, Mac left me alone to restock his van. Assuming he had other responsibilities, I jumped right to the job. Just as I was completing the last few items, he walked up and slapped me on the shoulder.

"Lawman wants to see us in his office," he declared, rolling his eyes.

"Who?"

"Our boss, Mr. Lawson," he stated plainly.

The meeting lasted no more than two or three minutes, but the point Mr. Lawson made came across loud and clear. The less than eighteen hundred dollars of product I had sold this past week was entirely unacceptable. And if I wanted to stay employed as a first aid salesman, I would have to perform at a much higher level, or I would be looking for a job elsewhere.

Mac threw his arm around my shoulder as we walked down the hall after our dressing-down chat with Mr. Lawson. "Well, kid, you impressed the tar out of Lawman," he laughed. "Great job. Bet you can't wait to get started on Monday, right?"

"Yeah, that was kind of rough. Is he always that cheerful?"

"Oh yeah," he chuckled. "He's almost as friendly as old Gene down at the factory. Well, have a great weekend and don't forget to pick up your uniforms. You want to see Lawman's bad side? Show up here Monday morning without your uniform."

Carrying the unwieldy box packed with shirts, both long and short sleeved, five pairs of pants, and a single windbreaker type jacket, I lumbered across the threshold of our front door and dropped the enormous carton on the floor of our living room. Upon hearing the thump, my dear wife, Kristina, stepped out of the kitchen and began questioning me as to the contents of the box. She's quite the curious one when it comes to anything I may possess. Some husbands might call it nagging. I call it being inquisitive. I love my wife, but there are times when she can press my buttons and send me into the realm of being unreasonable. Thankfully, these moments are few. Normally, she is rather quiet. Many call her centered. Not a tall gal, she stays fit, can hold her own in a discussion, and enjoys doing so. Her reddish blond hair is short and almost always in a ponytail. And when she looks at me with those deep green eyes, well that's almost always the beginning of the end to any argument or the start of any interrogation.

"What in the world is that?" she questioned with wide eyes.

"Stuff from work."

"What's inside?"

"My new uniforms."

"Really? Let me see what they look like."

"Nah, they make me sick to my stomach, and we haven't eaten dinner yet."

"Ah, come on, honey, try them on for me. Please? Go on, let's have a fashion show."

Having been married for awhile, I knew it was futile to continue to say no to her. So I lugged the carton into our bedroom and put on my new uniform. As soon as I had turned the corner into the living room, where she was waiting on the sofa, I knew the show idea was a mistake.

Try as she might, she couldn't hold back the snickers and eventually broke into a full blown guffaw as I stood in front of her with my eyes lifted toward the heavens, utterly embarrassed.

"What are those stripes down the sleeves for, Nicky?" she chided playfully to my further humiliation. "Oh," she mocked, "And the stripes down the leg of your pants change color to match your shirt. How cute!"

"I despise this uniform and me in it," I lamented while slightly jeering myself, knowing how ridiculous I must appear.

"Awww, you look so handsome . . . well, in a boyish, popsicle-man kind of way."

I immediately started pulling at the shirt tails. "I can't wear this thing. It is so demeaning."

"Honey," her tone was much more sincere now. "It's a job, and it pays. And as you well know, we need the money. So you might as well start to have a better attitude about it."

"I'm a Journeyman Carpenter, not a salesman. I hate the thought of telling our family, friends, or anyone else that I sell butterfly bandages and antacid for a living. This really stinks."

"Hang in there, honey. Try not to let this ruin our weekend, okay?"

The following week was incredibly busy. I not only had to sell and service kits, but I also needed to figure out the location of each customer and how often they required servicing. I was yelled at seven times, threatened twice, and firmly admonished by one client to never return—EVER! I wasn't a total failure, however, as I sold enough to avoid getting barked at by Lawman. Plus, I learned a valuable lesson Tuesday morning after having caught a glimpse of myself donned in full regalia: avoid all possibilities of reflections from mirrors and windows.

At the end of the month, my sales totaled over ninety-six hundred dollars. Lawman called me to his office and gave me a short pep talk, the version of which only he can replicate. The following month I bumped just over ten thousand in sales. But it was during my third month of wearing my popsicle-man costume that I stumbled across a treasure trove that finally put a smile on Lawman's gruff face.

After I serviced the extra-large kit in a truck repair facility of a garbage collection company, the General Manager literally grabbed me by the shirt sleeve and pulled me into the empty lunchroom. Once he shut the door, he asked me in a near panic and low whisper how long it would take me to get a first aid kit for each one of his trucks. I asked him what size he was interested in purchasing. He responded that price was not nearly as important as the urgency of their arrival. Then he pointed to the medium size kit on the brochure I had pulled from my back pocket.

"I can have them here by next week," I stated confidently.

To this he urgently replied, "Order me four hundred and eighty-seven of those medium size ones and get them here ASAP! No, check that . . . make it an even five hundred kits. I'll need some extras because these employees of mine will tear them up or lose them. Yeah, order five hundred. Are you sure you can get them here by next week? I've got OSHA crawling down my neck."

"Who?"

"OSHA! The Occupational Safety and Health Administration. And if they find out I don't have any first-aid kits, there will be a huge fine to pay."

That month I was top salesman. With a total of more than fifty-seven thousand dollars in sales, I was labeled somewhat of a hero. Lawman hardly mentioned anything except the obligatory "Keep it up." It was a bit discouraging until I received my monthly paycheck. This was a real boost to our finances and certainly helped us make ends meet that month. However, sitting down in the living room of our little two bedroom house after dinner, I confessed to Kristina that I absolutely hated my job.

"Why, Nick?" she asked with a puzzled look on her face. "You seem to be really good at it."

"No, that trash truck deal was just God's great mercy. I really can't stand this."

"Is it the uniform? I wouldn't worry about . . ."

"Yeah, well, that's part of it," I interrupted. "But there's so much more. Customers fuss at me at almost every stop. Selling little nickel and dime items is something I utterly despise. And I have no pride in my work whatsoever."

"Well, a little humility isn't such a bad thing," she smiled, sliding her hand over my shoulder as she sat down next to me on the arm of our recliner.

"It's not humility. It's humiliation."

"Oh, come on now, honey."

"Yeah, I know. I just wish I was back working as a carpenter. Or, at least doing something other than this job. I don't know what, just something different," I complained.

"Like what?"

"What?"

"Like what? What would you want to do if you had your choice of all the jobs on earth? What would you want to be? Anything at all, what would you choose?"

"Uh, I don't know. I mean, it doesn't really matter what I *want*. It's more like what I *have to do*. So why even entertain the notion?" I shrugged.

"Come on, Nicky, what is deep down in that heart of yours. What would you really like to be? What would be your ultimate job?"

"Well . . . a Park Ranger. I guess if I could do anything. that's what I'd really want to do with my life. But that would never happen. I don't have any experience with forestry, police training, or anything like that."

"Doesn't matter. If that's what you're supposed to do, you'll get a job as a Park Ranger," she affirmed as she kissed me on the cheek. "Now, do you want some dessert? I made a strawberry pie."

"Sounds good."

"I'll bring it in here."

"Well, it would be an incredible miracle," I muttered to myself. "Those Ranger jobs don't grow on trees you know. Uh, no pun intended."

"I heard that," she chuckled from the kitchen.

"I will say this though," I proclaimed in a louder voice, "if I were ever to get a dream job like that, it would be a major turning point—a real watershed chapter in my life. I would feel like I had arrived, honey. I mean, really arrived. I'd never quit that job."

TWO

The following month I walked into the main office of the Independent Tapwater Service Municipal Utility District, or ITSMUD, to bring my account up to date, so we could take showers in the morning as well as other aquatic conveniences. Taking a chance that I might get a sale, I meandered down the hall to the Purchasing Department. I introduced myself to the purchasing manager in hopes of convincing her to buy a kit or two. To my delighted surprise, Mrs. Atmore, the senior manager in charge of companywide purchasing, was very interested. Before I left her office, we had worked out an agreement to supply a large kit for each of their service facilities, which totaled fifty-three, and one small kit for every car, truck, tractor, bulldozer, and crane the District owned. It was an order for a staggering one thousand two hundred and seventeen units. Her only condition was that we break the billing into three separate invoices, one for each of the next three months. My commission, just from this sale alone, was a whopping six thousand-one hundred dollars for each of the agreed upon three months.

After shaking Mrs. Atmore's hand and thanking her profusely, I walked down the corporate corridor with a lightness to my step and feeling happier than a dog who just found a meaty bone. Passing by the Human Resources office, I caught a glimpse of something on the job announcements bulletin board. It stopped me dead in my tracks. All thoughts of my recent mega sale flew out the window. My mind couldn't believe what my eyes were seeing. The sheet declared:

<u>Job Opening</u>
Watershed and Recreation Ranger I

Immediately tearing the sheet from the bulletin board, I hastened through the open door into the Human Resources office. The affable gal behind the counter asked if she could help me. I handed her the paper I had brought in from the hallway.

"How do I get this job?" I asked with a polite smile.

"Well, first you have to fill out this application and meet the minimum requirements for the position."

"Okay, then what?"

"If you meet our requirements, then you'll be notified of the date to take our written exam. It's held on a Saturday usually two weeks after the posting closes."

"When does the posting close?" I inquired, attempting to seem interested but not overly anxious.

"It closes by end of business this Friday," she replied.

"That's the day after tomorrow. I have to have my completed application back here by then?"

"Yes, sir. And a word of advice: I would get a date stamped receipt in case you have to prove you submitted before the deadline."

"Really?"

"Yes, just in case, since you'll be so close to the last day."

"Okay, thank you very much. That was really kind of you. Have a nice day, and I'll see you real soon."

"Thank you. You too," she nodded.

I turned to walk out, but just before leaving I swung around. "Uh, pardon me."

"Yes, sir?"

"You mentioned there is a written test."

"Yes, sir. It's about three hundred questions long."

"How do you study for something like that?"

She grinned as she reached down behind the counter. Pulling out a study guide the size of a small phone book, she handed it to me.

"Wow, this thing is huge. Thank you and wish me well," I chuckled nervously.

"Oh, you'll do just fine," she smiled back.

"Really? Why do you say that?"

"Because you're only one of three that even thought to ask for the study guide. See you Friday."

In my haste to tell Kristina about the Ranger job that evening, I almost left the study guide at work. Halfway across the parking lot and headed for home, I remembered and rushed back to retrieve it from my work van. After dinner, I filled out the application's numerous sections. Then I opened the study guide to begin my personal Ranger inculcation. The first few pages were all about ITSMUD. I discovered they owned, maintained, and operated more than four hundred and sixty thousand acres, including seven massive drinking water reservoirs held back by expansive earthen dams. To maintain these lands and lakes, the District employed a staff of fifty-three Rangers, most of whom were stationed at Watershed Headquarters. This facility, stated the study guide, was along the shores of the second largest reservoir just outside the town limits of a little burg known as Olive Grove. There were five other postings where a Ranger could be assigned. These were the District's recreation areas; each one housed an interpretive center, snack bar, boat rental facility, and launch ramp.

The more I read the study guide, the more excited I became about the job. I determined I would memorize as many pages as possible before the written exam. I wanted to be ranked number one when the scores were posted. The further I delved into its many chapters, the more I discovered the test would be based on seven sections: 1) General information about the District and its lands 2) Criminal Law 3) Fish and Wildlife regulations 4) Wildland firefighting 5) Operation of heavy equipment 6) General knowledge of construction tools and techniques 7) General rules for dealing with people using the parks. Frankly, it was quite overwhelming, but my desire to land the job overcame this as well as the many obstacles I had yet to face.

A week after I had submitted my completed application, I received a letter in the mail from the Human Resources Department at ITSMUD stating that I had met the minimum requirements for the written exam. The test was to be administered the following Saturday morning at a high school not twenty minutes from my home and would start at precisely eight o'clock. There was a solemn warning included that anyone arriving after seven forty-five would not be admitted. I immediately determined I would be the first in line, thereby reducing the chance of missing out on this once in a lifetime opportunity. Beginning that very evening and continuing through the week, I spent every available moment either studying or praying that I would score high on the exam. If it were possible to twist God's arm to get this job, that's precisely what I intended to do.

Leaving early that morning, I arrived at the high school at seven a.m. and was rather dismayed to discover that many of my fellow test takers must have had the same goal in mind. In fact, finding all the parking lots full, I had to park four blocks away along a neighboring street. By the time I walked to the school and found my way to the registration table, it was seven twenty-five. Handing the registrar my letter, I received a test booklet and an answer card. Before turning to find a seat, I asked her how many people were taking the test. My heart sank with her answer. There were five hundred and ninety-six of us. She further diminished my hopes by relaying that the District was only hiring two candidates from among these hundreds of hopefuls.

The test was timed, lasting a maximum of three hours. I was surprised to finish in less than ninety minutes. I looked up and glanced around. Everyone else was still working. I took this as a sign that I must have somehow carelessly raced through the questions. I was certain I couldn't have been the first to finish, so I rechecked every one of my answers. There were only two, or maybe three, of the two hundred and eighty-five questions I wasn't absolutely confident that I had answered correctly. By the time I had verified my responses again, I surveyed the room and noticed several people were heading to the registration table to turn in their completed tests. I followed suit. A receipt was provided, and I was advised that they would notify me of my ranking by mail within two to four weeks.

I left the high school that morning toting a bucket full of heavily guarded optimism. In other words, I felt positive I had scored high on the exam, but I was also equally convinced that nearly half of my competitors had done so as well.

Two and a half weeks later, I was standing in our kitchen when Kristina handed me a letter and queried in a sing-song voice, "Guess what came in the mail today?"

Looking at the return address and fearing it was bad news, I asked her to open it and read it to me. She obliged, but before she started reading I snatched it back out of her hand. "Sorry, honey, I just need to know."

"Well, how'd you do?" she asked cheerfully.

"Not good," I replied tersely. "I'm number five."

"That's fantastic, Nicky," she cheered. "Wow, number five out of four hundred applicants. That's amazing. Great job, honey!"

"It was five hundred and ninety-six, but who's counting? Besides they're only hiring two, so I missed it by three positions. Well, that's that. I guess I'll be a band aid salesman forever."

Kristina pulled the letter from my limp grasp and placed it on the countertop to read. "Hey, it says here 'Congratulations' that doesn't sound like a bad thing. And look, they're requesting you call the HR Department to schedule the next step in the hiring process. It's called a physical agility test. They say it could change your ranking. Nicky, you should do this. You're very athletic. I would guess you'll do better than anyone out there. You should give them a call."

"Yeah, I will on Monday. Today I'm just too discouraged."

"Nicky, you scored above all but four people. So maybe your expectations are just a bit too high, don't you think? Now, come on, where are you taking me out to dinner to celebrate?"

I telephoned the HR Department the following Monday to schedule my physical agility test. Three Saturdays later, I stood in line at one of the District's recreation areas, awaiting my turn to drag a fully charged firehose up a one hundred foot hill. It was a timed event, as were all seven of the tests. The second challenge required lifting three, eighty pound bags of dry concrete mix onto the tailgate of a truck and then placing them on the ground again. Next, came a peculiar test where I had to splice a barbed wire fence using a splicing tool and pliers. The following event involved lifting a fifty pound trash can to shoulder height and then dumping the contents into a trash truck.

On the final three tests, I felt fairly confident I would be able to score high, meaning I thought I had a good chance of completing the events faster than most of my competitors. I shoveled sand from a pile into five burlap sacks, tied them tightly closed, loaded them into a wheelbarrow, pushed the wheelbarrow across the parking lot, and stacked them neatly atop one another. The next test I knew I would ace. Each person had to drive a six inch long nail into an eight inch by eight inch timber using a small sledge hammer. I pounded the nail to its full depth in just three blows. The test administrator clicked her stop watch with a shocked look on her face. Then glancing at me with her mouth agape, she breathed, "What?!"

"Journeyman Carpenter," I stated proudly.

She nodded her head and pointed me toward my final task.

Six fellow applicants were in the line ahead of me when I arrived at the final test site. It was located on the docks of the reservoir. Looking toward the front of the line, I saw a young lady struggling to drag an aluminum rowboat up onto the dock. The boat, half submerged, needed to be placed upside down on the dock before the task would be considered complete. With a click of the stopwatch and a call from the administrator to stop, the gal had been unsuccessful. I watched with rapt attention as each of the remaining five participants in front of me failed as well. It wasn't until I was next in line that I realized the secret to accomplishing this task.

Examining my test identification card I had handed him, the administrator asked if I was ready. I nodded. He clicked his stopwatch and with no emotion shouted, "Go." I dashed to the bow of the boat and pulled it upward. This motion allowed the water to run over the stern thus emptying the majority of the water out of the vessel. It was nearly standing straight up in the air when I twisted it over and landed it upside down on the dock with a loud bang. The administrator stopped his watch. He chuckled and asked me to help him get the boat back in the water.

"What's so funny?" I inquired with a nervous smile.

"You're the only one today who figured that out."

"Well, that's good," I smiled again, this time with confidence.

"No, not really," he stated plainly. "Now, everyone who observed your technique will do the same thing. But, I will say this, I think you set a new record. Good luck. I hope to be working with you soon."

"Thanks, me too!"

Three weeks later, I opened another letter from ITSMUD indicating my ranking had improved to number four. I was to telephone the District's HR Department as soon as possible to schedule an oral interview. Although a bit crestfallen that I wasn't ranked in the top two, I was encouraged that I had moved up one place. The interview was scheduled the following week during my lunch hour. Knowing I wouldn't want to be caught dead wearing my work costume in an interview, I brought a change of clothes.

Arriving early, I sat in the waiting room after signing in at the desk. I curiously watched as one by one each of three candidates enthusiastically walked in one door and after several minutes, dejectedly plodded out another door. This was disheartening because I imagined whatever or whoever was behind those doors would chew me up as well.

I didn't consider myself a prime selection for one of the two positions available. I had no Ranger training, no law enforcement background, nor did I possess a degree in any related field. Soon my name was called. I entered the room and before long discovered why the others wore long faces when exiting. Seated at an elevated table at the far end of the room were five police officers of varying rank. It was a very intimidating sight, like being pulled over for a traffic violation and turning around to see five police cars with lights on and sirens blaring.

About fifteen feet in front of the table, facing the officers, stood a single chair. I was instructed to sit in the chair. I promptly complied. No sooner had the soft fabric of my khaki pants touched the hard surface of the rigid chair, than the first question came from one of the officers. Before I could finish my reply, another question came from a different officer, then another, and another in rapid succession. This continued for five to ten minutes. I lost all sense of time as one question after another was fired at me. Sometimes it seemed as though my answers were making them angry. Two of the five officers even shouted at me. It felt more like a criminal interrogation than a job interview and was terribly intimidating. Fortunately, having experience in dealing with angry customers on a regular basis, I was able to remain relatively calm and did my best to answer all their questions to the utmost of my ability. As quickly as it had started, it was over. Afterwards, they each started talking to one another and completely ignored me. I sat quietly for a few seconds until the HR lady, who had led me into this lion's den, directed me to leave . . . through the other door.

I didn't hear a word from ITSMUD for more than three weeks. I was getting discouraged, thinking I didn't possess the qualities they were looking for. Arriving home from work late one day, I noticed Kristina was waiting at the door with a smile that lit up her face. I soon discovered she was delighted because my paycheck had arrived, revealing that I had achieved another top sales month. We both were relieved because we needed the money. She had graduated from the local university a couple of years ago and had been hired as a third grade teacher by a Christian school in a neighboring town. We were thrilled for the extra money to help not only with her school debt but our household bills as well. Evidently, her monthly paycheck was in the mail too. It was a banner day for the little Roberts family.

After hugs and kisses and a promise from me that we would do something special to celebrate, she handed me yet another envelope. The return address was the HR Department, ITSMUD. Taking the envelope from her hand, I sat down on our sofa. Kristina joined me. It was the first time in this multi-step process that I was absolutely unsure as to how I had performed. I was both apprehensive and excited as I contemplated the contents of the envelope. Would I be disqualified, perhaps dropped a few positions in the rankings, or would I remain the same? At that point, I had no hope of moving up a single step. I hesitatingly unfolded the letter and Kristina, looking over my shoulder, began reading it out loud.

"Congratulations! You have successfully completed the oral interview. Your ranking is number four."

She continued to read, but I wasn't listening. My heart sank as the sound waves hitting my ear drums indicated I was still number four on the list. Who was I kidding? I wasn't going to get this dream job. I was doomed to a life of selling ointments and receiving endless criticisms from angry customers, all the while having to wear an outfit which more closely resembled Bozo the Clown's than that of a "sales professional" as Lawman told me to call myself. All I really wanted to do was go back to work as a carpenter. I wanted to return to having a sense of pride in a job well done, not drive around all day in my colorful van hoping and praying that none of my friends would see me. Yeah, it was paying the bills, and the last couple of months we even had some money left over. For that, I was very grateful. I mean, very, very grateful. But couldn't I have the bills paid doing something I enjoyed? A job where I wouldn't feel embarrassed to stop at the bank or the grocery store on the way home? A job that at the end of the day I could be proud of what I had accomplished?

My mind slowly faded back to focusing on Kristina's voice as she finished up her animated recitation of the ITSMUD letter. She placed it in her lap with a slap and asked, "So you going to call him?"

"Call who?" I asked.

"The captain of the Rangers, Captain Cross. Weren't you listening to me, Nicky?"

"What?"

"Nicolas Harrison Roberts."

"I'm listening, Kristie. I just wandered off for a second."

"Well, it says right here that you're supposed to call him to schedule another interview. This time the meeting will be held at Watershed Headquarters."

"Call who?"

"Captain Cross, Nicky."

"Really? Let me see that?"

"Honey, didn't you hear anything I was reading to you?"

"Well . . ."

"Honestly, Nick. Sometimes I really wonder what's going on in that head of yours. Now, go change your clothes. I told the Nussbaum's we would meet them at seven o'clock at La Tia's Mexican Restaurant for dinner. We'll have our celebration tomorrow."

The next morning I used a payphone after my first sales stop to call Captain Henry Cross and set up an interview time for the following Wednesday afternoon at three o'clock. I tried to get the last time slot for the day, but another candidate had already snagged it. My interview would be the second to last of all the potential Rangers they would interview for the two available positions. I was slightly disappointed I wasn't going to be the final one interviewed but happy for moving one step closer in this already lengthy hiring process.

Making me promise to make up the time off, Lawman agreed to allow me to leave at noon on Wednesday. I rushed home, changed my clothes, and headed for the Watershed Headquarters in Olive Grove. I arrived about twenty minutes early and was greeted by a gregarious woman, who called herself "the dispatcher." After a few minutes of mostly one sided conversation, I learned her name was Jill Garrett. She was the radio dispatcher for the Rangers. Rather the talkative one, Jill kept me calm as I waited for the captain to lead me down the long corridor.

Before long, the door opened at the far end of the hallway that led from the reception area, which doubled as Jill's radio dispatch office. A short, wiry, uniformed man in his mid to late fifties preceded a younger man, dressed in a coat and tie, as they walked toward the friendly dispatcher and me. When they moved past where I was seated, the uniformed man turned and stretched out his hand to shake the younger man's hand. He thanked him for coming and closed the door behind him. Watching as he turned toward me, I could see his half smoked cigarette had an ash as long as the unburnt portion. With a squint of his eyes, to avoid the smoke, he introduced himself.

"Captain Henry Cross. You must be Nicolas Roberts?"

"Yes, sir. Friends call me Nick though."

"Okay, Nicolas, come on back here."

"Good luck," called Jill as I left with Captain Cross.

"Thank you," I smiled and gave a quick wave.

Captain Cross opened the door at the end of the hall and led me into a large conference room. Seated at the table in the center of the room were several Rangers dressed in their ITSMUD uniforms. Captain Cross introduced each one, starting with the man at the head of the table, Chief Bill Bruckman. Chief Bruckman was the only person in the room, other than me, who wasn't wearing a uniform. He was dressed in suit and tie and had an amiable although very professional demeanor. I immediately liked him. There were also two lieutenants and six sergeants in addition to Captain Cross and Chief Bruckman. The Chief and the Captain were the only ones not visibly wearing guns. Captain Cross directed me to sit in the single chair at the opposite end of the table.

The atmosphere was much friendlier during this interview. They asked questions about my family, my hobbies, and if I would have a problem working nights, weekends, or holidays. A few of them were particularly interested in my carpentry background. I was also asked if I could operate any heavy equipment. I told them I felt comfortable on a backhoe, bulldozer, and a front-end loader, which seemed to please the entire group. When I mentioned I was an avid rock climber, two of the sergeants perked up, asking several questions regarding my experience. The whole interview lasted about thirty minutes and ended when the chief nodded toward the captain. Everyone stood, so I did too.

Two weeks later, I received an ITSMUD letter in the mail announcing that I had successfully completed the interview, and my new position in the rankings was number three. The following two months I endured a psychological evaluation, which lasted an entire day and involved answering more than six hundred questions of a most peculiar sort; an oral examination by a clinical psychologist, whom I was sure needed some therapy himself; and a physical exam, which was replete with more prodding and probing than I had ever experienced. It had been six months since I had walked into the Human Resources Department carrying the job announcement I had torn from the bulletin board. And it was two weeks before Thanksgiving when the phone rang that evening.

"Hello?"

"Is this Nicolas Roberts?" The voice on the other end was so distinctive I knew precisely who it was.

"Yes, sir," I boldly answered.

"This is Captain Henry Cross, Watershed Headquarters."

"Yes, sir, Captain Cross. How are you, sir?"

"You still want this Ranger job?" he inquired in his abrupt style.

"Yes, sir, I sure do."

"Well, if you want it, it's yours."

THREE

Although I tried to give him my two weeks' notice, Lawman fired me on the spot. I turned in all my uniforms and sales book. He had the Payroll Department write my final paycheck immediately. Of the nearly nine months I had worked at the first aid company, I had been the top salesman five of those months. Mac called me later that night to wish me well. We had an enjoyable conversation. Mac, like many people I have met over the years, had a good heart. He wanted to do right by folks. However, most of the time something inside of him prevented him from doing so. Just before we ended the call, I thanked him for all of his help and encouragement.

"You'll go far, kid," he reassured before hanging up the telephone. "You're a natural born salesman."

The Monday before Thanksgiving 1980 was my first day as a Watershed and Recreation Ranger I. Uncertain of how long it would take me to drive to Ranger Headquarters in rush hour traffic, I left the house with plenty of time to spare and pulled into the parking lot rather early. I checked my watch, jumped out, and strode toward the building.

Captain Cross, in a manner only he could perfect, made it his job to put me right at ease. Stepping through the front entry door, I found him leaning on the counter by the radio, squinting at me through the smoke of his nearly consumed, unfiltered cigarette, which hung precariously from the corner of his mouth. His uniform looked sharp, neatly pressed with the gold Ranger's star shining in the glimmer of the florescent lights above. While holding a hot cup of coffee in his left hand, he extended his right hand to welcome me.

"Good afternoon. What's your excuse?" he accusingly questioned with a wry grin. The long ash hanging from his cigarette unceremoniously dropped to the floor as he spoke.

"Afternoon?" I asked defensively as I glanced down at his foot, which seemed to instinctively grind the ash into the wood planks. "I'm forty minutes early, sir. I mean, we start at eight o'clock, right?"

"Well, some of us do," he declared with his patented brand of sarcasm. "And some of us get here on time. Today, you're on time," he declared with a wink. "Coffee?"

Normally, I would never drink coffee, but on that first day as a Ranger, standing there in the entry with Captain Cross, I heard myself respond, "Yes, sir." That was a day of firsts, including the first time I had ever filled out an FBI background investigation questionnaire. It was nineteen pages both front and back and loaded with questions. Some were regarding things about myself I didn't even know the answers to. I was then assigned to a senior Ranger named Phillip Williamson, so I could learn all the roads, trails, creeks, reservoirs, and geographical features throughout the District's tens of thousands of acres of wildlands.

Perhaps ten years older than I, Phil had been an officer in the United States Marine Corps before he came to work as a Ranger for ITSMUD. A no nonsense kind of guy, he had a soft side, but it rarely showed itself. Although my first day was filled with more paperwork than I had ever seen, my second day was spent out on the District lands with Phil and another Ranger, Robin Newman. Robin, or as he preferred to be called, Rob, had been hired as a Ranger three years before me. He rather enjoyed telling people he met for the first time that he was a farrier. When he told me this I asked the obvious question.

"What's a farrier, Rob?"

"I shoo horses," he stated plainly, setting me up for his usual antics, which he had accomplished countless times before.

"Why do you chase away horses?" I asked naively.

"So I don't have to polish their shoes," laughed Rob, slapping his hand on his knee.

"What?" I questioned, glancing at Phil who was shaking his head.

"I've heard this a hundred times, Nick," confessed Phil. "A farrier installs horseshoes on horses that's why he said he shoes horses."

"Oh, I get it," I chuckled. "Man, Rob, all kidding aside, that was really bad."

Our first day working together was indicative of the relationships I soon formed with these two Rangers, Rob ever the jokester and Phil the interpreter. The antics in the cab of our truck continued as we drove to a small valley to inspect an invasive breed of thorn weed called Purple Star Thistle. Apparently, if left unchecked, the weed would soon overrun this approximately half a mile wide by two miles long valley in only a couple of seasons. My inexperience became evident when I mentioned that I thought it was just a pretty flower. Phil and Rob both chuckled. Then, they explained some measures that needed to be implemented and determined the sooner the better. Phil told me the valley was slated to be the next ITSMUD reservoir.

The remainder of the day was spent traveling the numerous fire roads on the North End of the Watershed. Phil drove; Rob sat by the other window. And I, being the new guy, took my place in the middle of the bench seat. The four-wheel drive, pickup truck we rode in had been converted into a wildland fire truck. The constant chatter on the police scanner as well as the communications on the ITSMUD radio provided unlimited topics for conversation within the cab. The fire season was all but over. The main concern for violations in November was the potential for poachers. Phil had evidently acquired a keen eye for detecting even minute traces of these evasive criminals. At one point, he abruptly stopped our truck along a wooded ridge above one of the District's reservoirs. He had noticed a broken twig across the entrance to a barely discernable trail. Upon further inspection, some forty to fifty feet down the trail, he found two sets of differing footprints. Back in the truck again, he radioed the Ranger on patrol in that region. Within twenty minutes, two middle-aged men who had been fishing in a spawning area had been arrested.

"We're on work crew this month," explained Rob. "A Ranger should never approach poachers unarmed."

"Or without wearing our vests," declared Phil, thereby indicating the importance of the Ranger's bulletproof vest.

"Any of the Rangers ever been shot?" I asked, hoping for a particular answer.

"No, but we've had a few close calls. And the danger level seems to be increasing. In fact, Rob was patrolling the South End last summer when he heard what sounded like machine gun fire. He called for . . . well, Rob, why don't you tell the story?!"

"Yeah, it was getting late, just after sunset. I was slowly making my way back to Watershed Headquarters to call it a day when I heard gunfire. It sounded like a war had broken out. I immediately radioed for support, you know, cover. The closest Ranger was twenty five minutes out. Then Leigh, she's a Ranger stationed at the recreation area at Lafontaine, spoke up with an ETA of ten minutes."

"What's ETA?" I asked.

"Estimated Time of Arrival," replied Phil in a monotone. "We use a lot of acronyms around here. You'll also have to learn the Ten Code and the Phonetic Alphabet."

"What are those?"

"The Ten Code? Well, have you ever heard someone say, '10-4'?"

"Yeah, sure."

"That's the Ten Code. There's everything from 10-1 to 10-100, I think. We pretty much only use the more common ones like 10-20, for example. It's easier than asking

'What's your location?' or 10-9, which means someone wants you to repeat what you just said. Now don't confuse these with Code One, Code Two, or Code Three. Those are entirely different."

"What in the world are those?" I asked, not having a clue as to what he was talking about.

"Those codes refer to the urgency of your response. So Rob, when you heard Leigh was responding, what code did you ask for?"

"Code two. I needed her to come quickly, but I didn't want sirens because that would alert the suspects that we were heading toward their location," clarified Rob.

"So Code Two is fast but no sirens?" I asked.

"Yeah, well, kind of," explained Phil. "Code Two is lights, no siren. In other words, like Rob stated, get here as fast as you can but be quiet about it. Code One is no lights and sirens but make it your next priority. Code Three is lights, sirens, and get here now!"

"Okay, I got it," I smiled. "But what is this alphabet thing?"

"The Phonetic Alphabet. You'll have to learn this and the sooner the better. There are many words that sound or are spelled similarly. So we communicate almost everything on the radio by spelling it phonetically. Let's say I was calling in a suspect's name to check for warrants or a previous criminal record, and his last name was, uh . . . I'll just use Rob's last name, Newman. When I radio his name to Jill, she's our dispatcher, I would say, 'Nora-Edward-William-Mary-Adam-Nora'. The first letter of each word represents the corresponding letter of the alphabet, therefore spelling out Newman. It's much less confusing on the radio especially with letters like T, D, B, G, or when F, or S come up in a name."

"Yeah, or J, K, and M, N," added Rob with a grin.

"Well, you get the idea," concluded Phil. "It's much easier to hear and understand over the radio."

I must have had a confused look on my face because after a few seconds Phil chuckled, "Don't worry about it; I have a copy of all these things in my locker. We'll get you set up. Once you start using it, it'll become second nature. You'll pick it up soon enough."

"Thanks. I appreciate that."

"No problem. Now Rob, are you going to finish that story?" prodded Phil.

"Yeah, yeah, where was I?" asked Rob. "Oh, yeah, anyway, Leigh got there, and we decided to walk down the fire road toward the sound of the gunfire. It was a heavily wooded area, so we couldn't see very far down the curvy, dirt road. We came around a curve, and there in front of us, with their backs toward us, were these three guys dressed in full camouflage gear shooting up the woods like they had an endless supply of ammunition. I mean, whole branches were falling off trees, and shrubs were plopping over on the ground. Leigh and I both drew our weapons, and I whispered to her to triangulate."

"What's that?" I interrupted.

"It's where you create a triangle using yourself, your partner, and the bad guys as the points of each angle. It's the safest position for us and gives the appearance that we have them out numbered," Phil advised in his typically straightforward fashion.

"Yeah, so Leigh took up a position behind a large pine, and I knelt behind a log and a stump. We were, oh, about twenty to twenty-five yards apart. The bad guys were probably thirty yards in front of us. When they stopped to reload, we shouted for them to drop their weapons and put their hands above their heads. It was tense. I mean, real tense," expressed Rob with a serious look on his face.

"What did they do?" I anxiously inquired.

"Two of the three put their weapons down. The third was thinking something else though."

"Whoa!"

"Yeah, 'Whoa' is right. Leigh and I both shouted at him to put his weapon down immediately, or he would be shot. It was really scary, especially, when that guy started to turn around. But fortunately, two cops from the neighboring town of Mira Molina showed up just then. After seeing that all of us had our weapons drawn, and that they were pointing directly at him, he dropped his gun. That was a close one," breathed Rob.

"How did those other police officers know to show up?" I asked.

"They have these too," declared Phil, pointing at the police scanner mounted just above the District radio in the dashboard. "We all do. Every officer in every department in the entire area has a scanner. We all listen to each other, just in case. It was probably a quiet day in town, or maybe they heard the gunfire and wanted to help."

"Yeah, I'm glad everyone pays close attention to the scanners, particularly when something like what happened to Leigh and me out on the South End occurs," Rob acknowledged in a sober tone. "It was really fortunate those guys showed up when they did. It could have gotten really ugly in a heartbeat."

"Wow," I conceded with a shake of my head, "I didn't realize a Ranger could get into a situation like that."

"Well, to be honest," acknowledged Phil, "It doesn't happen very often. But our problem is, when it does happen the backup is so far away."

"What's backup?"

"You know, mutual aid, someone to cover or help you," confided Phil. "When something goes down on the North End, backup is anywhere from five to maybe fifteen minutes or so away, depending on where you're located. But if you're on the South End, like Rob was that day, cover can take upwards of forty-five minutes to arrive. By then, whatever went down would already be over . . . I mean, way over."

"That doesn't sound good," I opined, not really understanding that we were having a conversation regarding the Ranger's biggest concern with the law enforcement aspect of their job.

"It's not," replied Phil with a tone that evidenced an enormous amount of consternation. "It's terrible, and something needs to be done about this before one or more of us get shot . . . or worse!"

"Yeah," Rob chimed in from the other side of the bench seat. "That doesn't even address all the radio dead spots. There are entire square miles where you can't call something in on the radio. In fact, the situation I was telling you about with the three gunmen playing militia games, I had to radio that in from up on the county road. Once we hiked about a hundred yards down that fire road, we no longer had radio contact. Not a safe situation. If those Mira Molina cops hadn't shown up when they did, it could have been three against two . . . and the three all had automatic rifles."

"I've been here a number of years now," announced Phil, "and nothing has been done about it yet. In fact, old Henry, uh, Captain Cross, told me about a month ago that the District decided it was too expensive to install more radio towers, so we could get a better signal in these remote canyons and forests. That made me mad. This isn't some luxury item we want to make our lives more comfortable. It's an absolute necessity for the safety of the Rangers."

"Yeah, last Friday Henry told me that too," complained Rob as he shook his head. "That's just wrong."

"Looks like I got this job at the wrong time, you guys," I complained.

"No, Nick, don't think like that. Maybe having more Rangers will wake them up to our situation out here. It's not just a law enforcement problem. It's a public safety issue. I mean, suppose we notice a column of smoke coming out of an area close to homes. But because we can't radio our position or the location of the fire, we can't get help. Then, what if after an hour or so of fighting the fire we run out of water, and it rages up a hillside and burns down several homes? I bet we'd get some more radio towers out here before the following fire season. Don't you think, Rob?"

"Yep, that's all it would take is one major disaster like a fire, a shooting, or something where there is a major loss of property or life."

"I thought you guys had a union? Can't they do anything?" I asked looking back and forth between my fellow Rangers.

"Yeah, we do," replied Phil, "But they're a utility district union. They're not a law enforcement or firefighting union. Therefore, they aren't as attentive to us out here. I don't want to say they don't care; I sincerely think they just don't know how to care. That's all."

"I agree," nodded Rob. "I really like our union guy. He's visited Watershed HQ a couple of times and talked with us, but I really think he hasn't a clue as to what we struggle with out here."

"Like what?" I asked with vested interest.

"Like poison oak," lamented Phil. "That stuff is so nasty. We run into it almost daily. It's everywhere. When we're cutting fire roads, it's there; building or repairing barbed wire fence, it's there; fighting fire, it's there; chasing bad guys, it's there. Well, you get the idea; it's everywhere."

"What can the union do about it?" I asked.

"Get us some more time off," declared Phil. "I use more than half of my sick days every year because of poison oak. Last fire season, one of the State Rangers breathed in some smoke from burning poison oak and almost died. Two years ago, just weeks before his honeymoon, Rob got the nasty stuff on . . . well, you know, and had to get some steroids from his doctor to clear it up."

"Yeah," laughed Rob, "it cleared up the day before our wedding. So everything worked out okay."

"Rats," I fretted.

"What?" asked Phil.

"I'm almost certain I'm allergic to poison oak."

"Why do you say that?" asked Rob.

"Because I used to get horrible poison ivy rashes as a kid, so I'm guessing poison oak is just as bad."

"Worse," pronounced Phil almost with a sense of satisfaction that someone else would be blighted with this chronic Ranger plague. "Oak has a much more potent sap than ivy does. Man, sometimes all I have to do is look at it from fifty yards away, and I get a rash the next day."

"Bummer," I groaned.

"Yeah, it's a hazard of the job," conceded Rob.

"What are some of the other hazards of the job?"

"The sergeants," frowned Phil. "Well, actually only two of them."

"How many are there?" I asked.

Phil cleared his throat and glanced over at Rob, who was looking out the passenger window. "Well, seeing as how we're pulling into Watershed Headquarters, we may have to continue this conversation tomorrow. But suffice it to say, we have one chief, Bill Bruckman, he's a great guy, and one captain, you already know him. With Captain Cross, what you see is what you get. There are also two lieutenants. Both are pretty quiet, and you'll hardly ever have any dealings with them because old Henry is so hands on when it comes to the Rangers. Don't get me wrong, that's a good thing. Then, there are the sergeants, six in all. Two of them are stationed at Watershed Headquarters, uh . . . the sorriest two."

"What're their names?" I asked as I shut the truck door.

"We'll talk about it tomorrow. Just keep your head down, okay? You'll be alright," encouraged Phil with a nod of assurance.

On my drive home from work that day, Phil's words kept tumbling over and over in my mind, like a tennis shoe in an otherwise empty clothes dryer. The drying cycle ended thirty minutes later when I pulled my Jeep into our driveway. However, the tumbling started right back up again when Kristina asked how my work day went.

"I'm not sure. I mean, it was fine. I enjoyed getting to know the lay of the land and a couple of the Rangers." Not wanting to concern her, I decided not to mention what Phil had said to me about the sergeants as we walked across the parking lot at Watershed Headquarters.

"That's good, Nicky. Do you think you're going to like it there?"

"Oh, of course. What's not to like? It's beautiful out there. The three of us, Phil, Rob, and I drove all over the North End. Tomorrow we're headed down to the South End. I'm really looking forward to it. They told me the most remote areas in the District are on the South End. There's a place they call Ranker's Ridge, which is the highest point in the District's lands. They also mentioned a couple of small canyons that have waterfalls during the rainy season. So I'm really looking forward to tomorrow."

"Did you find out when you're supposed to attend the law enforcement school and the firefighting academy?"

"Kristie, first of all, it's called the Police Academy. Firefighting School is an entirely different training course. And, yeah, Captain Cross, who Phil told me everyone calls Captain Henry . . ."

"They all call him Captain Henry?" Kristina interrupted.

"No, I mean they just call him Henry. Apparently, no one addresses each other by their rank except in public settings. So Captain Cross is just Henry, and Chief Bruckman is just Bill, and so on. Anyway, Henry told me today that once I pass my six month probationary period they will enroll me in the next Police Academy. It's four months long," I moaned for emphasis.

"Four months? Where is it?" asked Kristina, incredulous that it would take so long.

"I don't know. I think somewhere over in the valley."

"Wow, Nick, four whole months. Do you have to live there in a dorm or something?"

"I'm not sure, hope not. I guess when I pass my probationary test, I'll find out."

"You have a test?"

"Yeah, Henry told me it contains about a hundred and fifty questions and covers everything that I'll be learning over the next few months. You know, stuff about the land, the reservoirs, the fire roads, the hiking trails, and some of the prominent features out there."

"Are you concerned about the test?"

"No, not really. I think it's more of an exam to see if I've paid attention to what the other Rangers are sharing with me each day. Henry gave me a set of maps and a copy of the Watershed Lands Master Management Plan. I'll study those over the next six months, so I think I'll be okay."

"Well, after you complete the Police Academy, then what?"

"If I graduate, which I'm hoping to do with flying colors, then I'll have a ninety day Field Training period that I must pass as well."

"What's that?"

"Henry says it's where I'll have a Ranger, called a Field Training Officer or FTO, ride around with me to see how I handle different law enforcement situations. He'll also help me if I'm lacking in any way. Phil mentioned to me today that the FTO scores a new Ranger on a daily basis. Then, at the end of the training period his total score has to average eighty-five percent or better."

"Ooh, that's sounds a bit intimidating."

"Yeah, I know. I have to pass it or my employment will be terminated."

"What are you saying, Nicky?"

"I'm saying, I'll get fired if I don't pass every one of those tests, or if I can't rate high enough on every one of those phases as a Ranger. If I do pass, however, I will be promoted to a Watershed and Recreation Ranger II."

"Wow, that's awesome, honey. More money too?"

"Yep, it's all pretty exciting, but it doesn't end there."

"What?"

"Then I have to attend Wildland Firefighting School. It's only a month long, but it's another element where if I don't pass, I'm out on my keister."

"Well, that seems pretty severe."

"Yeah, but once you are trained and on your own, you are the only law enforcement, firefighter, EMT, and rescue personnel for miles and miles out on the Watershed. It's a huge responsibility. So they want to make sure you know what you're doing, and that you're good at it. They need to be completely confident that you're impeccably responsible. They don't want you out there roaming around with a loaded .357 Magnum if you're some kind of psycho. That could spell disaster in more ways than one."

"What?" she asked with grave concern. "What could be a disaster?"

"I simply mean, my love, if a carpenter while he's nailing a beautiful length of wood in place inadvertently dings it, he cuts a new piece, replaces it, and it's no big deal. If a Ranger takes out his gun and mistakenly shoots someone, he can't just shrug it off. It's always a big deal."

FOUR

When I considered the qualities I thought a Ranger should possess, I was hopeful I was tailor-made for the job. Little did I understand at the time what it took to be a Ranger. However, from my earliest remembrances, I had always enjoyed being outdoors. Since moving to California, I loved to backpack, camp, and rock climb. I spent many weekends in Yosemite Valley and many a week in the High Sierras. It really seemed like I was born to be a Ranger. Yet without a degree in Forestry or a related major, I had thought the job was completely out of reach, so I had never even considered it. But here it was, six months after walking into the ITSMUD Human Resources department in my embarrassing band aid salesman uniform, and I was pulling my Jeep into the parking lot at Watershed Headquarters for my third day of employment as a Watershed and Recreation Ranger. I was nearly euphoric and over an hour early.

"Good afternoon, what's your excuse?" mocked a cigarette smoking, coffee drinking, Captain Henry Cross. It was a greeting I actually came to enjoy over the years. Often times I would reply with my own sarcastic remark, which seemed to amuse Henry. Actually, he had a very endearing side. Although to most, it was hard to find through his many surly facades. Sometimes he would make a harsh comment about something one of the Rangers had done with his classic "You can't fix stupid." Then he would turn to me with a wink and a grin, all the while squinting because of the chronic cloud of cigarette smoke hovering around his face from his latest unfiltered tobacco-roll with the two inch, droopy ash dangling from the end. These were always plummeting onto his neatly pressed uniform. Frankly, remembering the many times he had abruptly jumped up, hastily brushed off his trousers, and issued his unique string of curse words can still bring a smile to those of us who knew him well.

Getting to know my fellow Rangers wasn't the main objective of my early days at Watershed Headquarters. But as I worked with several of them in various settings and on different tasks, it became a pleasant by-product that remained after a long day's work out in the wilderness. They were men and women of the highest caliber. I found them surprisingly pleasant and hard working with a genuine love and concern for the health and safety of both the Watershed and the citizens that used its many tens of thousands of acres. Although my favorite Rangers, for the most part, worked at Watershed Headquarters, I hadn't met a single Ranger I didn't like. Albeit, years later that would change dramatically. But these were the early days, and I was relishing the honeymoon.

The remainder of November, as well as the rest of that year, we spent almost entirely repairing damaged fences, fire roads, boat docks, trail bridges, and the like. The rainy season had also begun and had brought with it many urgent needs that required the immediate attention of those of us at Watershed Headquarters. Additionally, the main concern that weighed heavily upon my mind was gaining and memorizing as much knowledge of the Watershed as I possibly could. Every night after dinner, I studied maps and guide books until bedtime.

On one such evening, as Kristina was sitting on our corduroy sofa watching *I Love Lucy* reruns, I was focused on scanning a topographical map of the Watershed. Being an avid rock climber, topo maps held a certain mystique for me, similar to a hidden treasure map for a pirate. You see, every serious climber wants to accomplish a first ascent, even if only at a local crag. It's a rite of passage, a badge of honor, an issue of immortality. It's no small task finding a rock face that has remained unscaled. All the major cliffs in Yosemite and throughout the Sierra Nevada mountains had been conquered. I needed a lesser known, if not altogether obscure spot. No wonder my eyes widened when I discovered a tiny section of the map where the elevation lines drew tightly together as one, indicating an extreme change in the lay of the land. This minute corner of the map entitled Ranker's Ridge might be just the answer to my first ascent prayers.

The following day, Phil, Rob, Steven Hildebrand, and I headed north from Watershed Headquarters in a crew-cab, pickup truck, hauling enough fencing materials to encompass a small ranch. Like Phil and Rob, Steven was a seasoned Ranger, who was taller than Rob but shorter than Phil and me. He was an avid cyclist, training nearly every day after work on the roads and trails throughout the Watershed. He loved competing in road races once or twice a month year round. Steven had extremely short gray hair that belied his age with a tiny goatee to match. He also had an endearing way of seeing humor in almost every situation. A quality I found as a new employee not only refreshing but somewhat comforting. We became fast friends.

The four of us were assigned to repair a two hundred yard section of barbed wire fence that had been destroyed by a flatbed truck, pulling a trailer full of four inch cast iron pipe. Evidently, the operator of the truck had failed to negotiate the outward slope of the curve on the road, causing both the truck, with its driver, and the trailer, carrying its load, to careen off the roadway. It had all slid uncontrollably down the hill and through the District's barbed wire fence. Fortunately, the driver had not been seriously injured. Unfortunately, our fence had been completely obliterated.

Phil, who almost always drove our trucks, skillfully steered the four-wheel drive vehicle off the asphalt highway and onto the dusty fire road. Rob and I sat in the backseat while Steven rode shotgun. I soon discovered the seating assignments on these work excursions were predetermined and gave evidence to the unspoken hierarchy within the para-military organization that was the Watershed Rangers. The senior Rangers either drove or sat in the front passenger seat. While the rookies and those with fewer years of service were relegated to the rear seats. However, if a sergeant was present, he was given the premier position of the front passenger seat regardless of who was in the vehicle. The higher ranking officers, including Chief Bruckman and Captain Cross, never rode in the work or patrol trucks. They had their own designated vehicles.

Gingerly pulling our truck off the dirt surface of the fire road, Phil slowly maneuvered across a downward sloping, dry field of waist high grasses dotted with manzanita and scruffy pines. The tiny pines were barely tall enough to see the daylight above the prevalent grass. Stopping at the bottom, we were able to view the damaged fence several yards up the opposing slope of the arroyo. Occasionally, we could hear a car or truck recklessly racing by on the road nearly a hundred feet above us. Truthfully, it was disconcerting as I realized the section of fence we would be repairing had been demolished because a truck had slid down the hill and landed exactly where we would be working. Especially since we could only hear, not see, a vehicle approaching. It gave me a strange sensation, like what U.S. Navy sailors assigned to submarines must feel when submerged. It was eerie.

Three of us walked down into the slightly damp creek bed and scrambled up the other side until we came to the destroyed section of fence. A tangled mess of wire, metal fence posts, truck parts, and vegetation lay before us. This was going to be a long and difficult repair. Just then, Phil called to me from several feet away.

"Hey Nick, stay out of that stuff. That's poison oak. It will eat you alive."

Gazing upward to where he was pointing, I observed that the fence needing to be replaced was strung right through a huge batch of the oily branches. It appeared there was no way to fix the fence without wading right through the middle of it. To my relief, Rob yelled from the back of the truck, "I got it. You guys get a start on pulling that steel spaghetti out of there while I cut a path, so we can install the new barbed wire."

"Thanks, Rob," shouted Steve. "Come on, you guys, let's throw all this down into the creek bed. Then we can haul it up to the truck when we're finished with the repairs."

Phil and I agreed. After donning our thick leather gloves and arming ourselves with pliers and bolt cutters, the three of us set about removing the damaged fencing. It was a daunting task. Before long, I realized why Rob had volunteered for the treacherous assignment of removing the poison oak. Wearing lengthy rubber gloves and using long handled snippers, he methodically cut each branch. Then, manipulating the snippers like tongs, he tossed the poisonous pieces into a pile a few feet away. He never so much as touched a single leaf, nor did he have to labor at doing so. Meanwhile, the three of us were straining and sweating in the December sunshine as we yanked and tugged on every foot of the entangled barbed wire. It was exhausting work. This was an invaluable life lesson I learned during my tenure as a Watershed Ranger—there is a never ending stream of labor intensive work to be done, and those who either don't have the skills or won't take the risk of a higher challenge will always be relegated to doing the more laborious tasks. During my first day repairing barbed wire fence on that hilly, danger laden terrain, I determined I would endeavor to volunteer for the more skilled challenges from that day forward.

Consuming most of the morning, Phil, Steve, and I had removed and relocated all of the damaged fence wire to the other side of the nearly dry creek. We had pulled some of the metal fence posts out as well. Just before lunch, Phil scrambled up the hill carrying a strange device that looked similar to a floor jack in an automobile repair shop. It had a flat bottom that he planted firmly on the ground next to the base of a fence post needing to be extracted. He then clipped a small camming piece attached to the extractor by a swivel. Once the instrument was readied, he applied intense downward pressure to the four foot long handle. In theory, the post should be lifted up and out of the ground. However, in practical application, there was much straining, grunting, kicking, and at one junction, throwing before the post was set free from its earthly bonds. As I observed the method, I considered it a rather thought provoking analogy.

Lunch time came as a welcome relief. We sat on the matted grass near the creek bed, under the shade of a lone oak tree. Rob appeared noticeably more energetic than the rest of us. It was clear he had chosen the easier yet much riskier job. Tomorrow would reveal just how careful he had been in removing the poison oak branches. The mood was quite agreeable as the four of us lighted from one topic to the next. Steve and Rob did most of the talking while Phil and I added our comments as we deemed appropriate. The main thrust of the conversation was the deep concern these three seasoned Rangers had regarding some rumors from the

ITSMUD Board about trimming down the law enforcement aspect of our job. This quickly evolved into a serious discussion. The three were in complete agreement that it would be absolutely ludicrous to attempt to enforce the rule of law on the Watershed without the proper tools to do so, in other words—without their guns.

Now, to some folks this may not seem like something to be overly concerned about. But to a law enforcement officer, it is a predicament of mammoth proportions. Not only are the ones who enforce our laws supposed to do so, but they are bound by those same laws to respond to certain activities. Oftentimes, citizens will flee when they perceive a crime is taking place. In contrast, the police cannot. They are obligated by law to respond. But how can they be expected to engage in a potentially dangerous situation without the ability to protect themselves and others? Are lesser weapons sufficient? How about pepper spray or batons? These were some of the questions posed during our afternoon lunch break under the oak tree.

The depth of knowledge expressed by these men in regards to human nature and instinctive response surprised me. It was apparent they were sharing from personal knowledge and experience. Interestingly, the setting and the subject matter seemed in stark contrast. In other words, here I was in the peaceful and tranquil surroundings of the great out of doors, engaged in an impassioned discussion with those of law enforcement backgrounds, the topic of which was the age old debate—guns or no guns. To me personally, having never considered the matter, it presented a disturbing dilemma, the essence being mainly a question of self-preservation. Or was it? Our country is a nation ruled by law. We have sworn some of our citizens to enforce these laws. For as a nation, we have determined that our laws must be enforced, or chaos would soon rule the day. But the men and women who are charged with the enforcing are human too. They have good days and bad days. They have hopes and dreams and the right to pursue them. Many are married; some have children. Yet unlike most of us, they go to work every day with the possibility that they could find themselves in situations where they're threatened with grave personal danger. And yet like none of us, they are sworn to confront it. Sitting by the creek, I realized these Rangers had a most unique perspective on the topic because they were all sworn police officers. All too soon, I would develop the same perspective.

Listening to their discussion, I began a similar debate within my mind. How much is too much? Is carrying a gun morally right? Is it a need? A want? The result of a fear? I recognized, for the first time since entering the ranks of the Watershed Rangers, that I too would soon be enrolled at the Police Academy. I too would be trained with an assortment of weapons. I too would be forced to make decisions I had never considered before. What would I do? Could I take a life? Could I actually shoot someone? Could I, with a gun in my hand, pull the trigger? Would my brain send the required electronical impulses down through my arm to my finger? I had difficulty wrestling with the proposition.

In our Bible Study class at church we had discussed the passage "He who lives by the sword, will die by the sword." What kind of life is that, I had pondered at the time? I had been confident, at least up until twenty minutes ago, that I wouldn't want to live a life that in any way resembled "by the sword." Now for the first time, in my less than thirty years on this earth, I had a job where the use of a deadly weapon was becoming a very distinct possibility. In fact, it was more of a probability than a possibility. And even more troubling, this was the first time I could recall that my faith came slamming up against my lifestyle in a vividly unquestionable way. A twinge of panic rose up within me, and beads of sweat began forming on my brow. In a vain effort to regain some semblance of internal peace, I gazed off at the mountains in the distance. It was slowly dawning upon my increasingly burdened conscience that I was, in a very real sense, approaching my own Red Sea where I wouldn't be able to go back. Yet the way forward seemed all too daunting.

"Let's see if we can at least get the posts in before we call it a day," proclaimed Phil as he stood up from where he had been eating his lunch under the tree.

"Sounds good," agreed Rob. "I have another hour or so in the poison oak, and then I'll be able to help with the posts too. I'm sure that will give us a good chance at replacing all the barbed wire tomorrow."

The topic of our conversation over lunch continued on the hillside as we resumed our fence repair. Although it was incredibly interesting, my anxiety was nearing a level that bordered on uncomfortable. I decided an immediate change in subject matter was needed. When the conversation paused, I jumped on the opportunity.

"Have you guys heard of Ranker's Ridge?"

"Oh, sure," replied Phil immediately. "It's down on the south side of the Watershed. Why do you ask?"

"Well, last night I was reviewing some of the topo maps Captain Henry gave me to study, and I noticed . . ."

"Captain Henry?" laughed Rob from the midst of the poison oak patch nearly fifty feet away.

"You mean just, Henry, don't you?" chuckled Phil.

"Yeah," I acknowledged apologetically. "I heard that everyone refers to Captain Cross as Henry, but since I'm new . . ."

"Man, I haven't heard anyone refer to Henry as Captain since that suicide in the woods off Bluff Falls Road last year," stated Steven, interrupting my effort at saving face.

"Yeah, that FBI guy was sure full of himself," asserted Rob. "He was so high and mighty and obnoxiously formal too."

"FBI?" I asked with concern that this conversation was heading right back to law enforcement rather than my feeble attempt at an apology.

"Yeah," panted Phil, trying to pull another fence post out of the densely compacted soil. "There was this hiker found dead just off Bluff Falls Road, who had a bullet in his head. The coroner ruled it a suicide, but the FBI had suspicions it might be a homicide because the dead guy was a member of a drug ring they were investigating."

"Whoa, all that happened out here?" I asked in disbelief.

"Sure," replied Steven. "When you are this close to a major metropolitan area, there are all types of crime that can occur on our Watershed." Then, pointing to the mountain only a couple of miles to our west he concluded, "There are millions of people living right over that ridge, and they like to come over here to do things they don't feel they can do over there."

Steven declared this like it was a well-known fact. However, to me it was a shocking revelation. I worked on pushing and pulling the next fence post as my mind wrestled with what Steven had just pronounced. I was beginning to understand, all too clearly, that in the very near future I too would be bound by law to respond to dangerous situations and apprehend those individuals that used the Watershed as an arena for conducting crime. Then came the thought that sent chills up my spine: suppose the bad guys had it in for me? Suppose they carried a lethal weapon? A knife? A club? A gun? What kind of gun? How big? How fast would it shoot? How many bullets per second could these miscreants shoot at me? How many bullets could I shoot at them? Could I survive a gunfight? Would I run? Could I kill someone? How could I possibly live with myself if I did? These were devastating thoughts for a young Christian who sincerely desired to follow the teachings of Jesus Christ. I mean, He does say I am to lay down my life for others, and the "love your enemy" commandment is a tough one—if you endeavor to obey it.

"So what did you want to know about Ranker's Ridge?" inquired Phil, now standing upright after tossing another fence post down the hill.

Relieved that the conversation appeared to finally be taking a turn in a more comfortable direction, I responded with a modest amount of enthusiasm. "I'm a rock climber. Are there any cliffs up there?"

"Sure," replied Rob. "But they're unclimbable."

"Why do you say that?" I asked, knowing there is no such thing as an unclimbable rock. It's just a rock that has never been climbed.

"Because Phil, Jerry Persons, and I went up there two years ago to try and climb the biggest cliff," confirmed Steven. "We couldn't make a go of it. It's too smooth. The cracks were so narrow we couldn't get our fingers in them. We tried several different spots up on the Ridge but didn't have the success we were hoping for."

"How high are the cliffs?"

"Oh," pondered Steven. "I think the tallest is about three fifty, wouldn't you say, Phil?"

"Yeah, between three hundred and three hundred and fifty feet," shrugged Phil.

"Really?" I smiled.

"Yeah," replied Steven. "But if Phil couldn't establish a route, what makes you think you can? He was part of Special Forces in the Marine Corps, and they're trained to go up and down cliffs like that."

"Well, I'm not claiming I can do it. I would just like to see it someday."

"We hardly ever go up there," confided Rob. He was still eavesdropping on the conversation from his job removing poison oak. "It's so remote, to drive there takes nearly two hours from Watershed Headquarters. Most of that time is spent on the fire roads. It's slow going."

"That's why we hardly ever go up there," declared Phil. "It's a simple math equation that adds up to eight hours. By the time we get to Double R, we only have four hours to do what needs doing before its time to head back to WHQ."

"What's Double R?" I inquired.

"Ranker's Ridge," stated Phil with a nod. "Don't worry, Nick, you'll eventually get used to all the Watershed acronyms."

Rob quipped, "And WHQ means?"

"I know that one, Rob," I interjected so as not to be deemed completely incompetent. "Watershed Headquarters, uh . . . correct?"

Everyone laughed, including me. However, I was even more relieved when the subject of discussion turned to the latest recipe for venison sausage. Evidently, Rob was an excellent chef. He mostly enjoyed preparing meals using his recent hunting trip acquisitions. Little did I know, he was an expert concerning all things venison. During deer season each year, he laid out a lunch spread at WHQ that was renown throughout the ranks. Have you ever heard of chicken fried venison? I hadn't either until Rob fixed up a batch one day at the picnic tables outside the old barn at WHQ. Surprisingly, it was rather tasty.

I was watching college football with Kristina in our tiny living room that weekend when I decided to delve into the deep philosophical questions posed in my mind by the conversation with the three Rangers. I had waited until I was sure our team had no chance of winning before turning off the television. Kristina sat cross-legged, reading a book at the far end of the sofa and looking as pretty as she did on the day we had been married.

"Honey?" I asked. "You got a few minutes?"

"Sure. What's up, my big, burly Ranger man?"

"Yeah, right."

"Okay, Ranger Nicky, what's on your mind?"

"Kristieee . . ."

"Sorry. I didn't realize you were being serious."

"Well, let me put it this way then . . . how would you feel about me if I killed another person?"

"You haven't worked there a month and you've already killed someone? When did you murder your first victim?"

"Come on, Kristina, get serious."

"Well, you said *another* person."

"I meant, how would you feel about me if I killed someone?"

"Are you planning to kill somebody, Nicky?"

"No. But I found out this week, while talking with some of the other guys at work, that there is a distinct possibility that could happen."

"Wow. Really?" Kristina leaned forward, her mouth agape.

"Yeah. It really bothers me. I've been struggling with these thoughts all week. I mean, this is as serious an issue as I have ever faced in my entire life."

"Maybe you'll never have to shoot someone."

"True. But I don't think it is something I should decide on the spur of the moment. I definitely need to figure out where I am in my heart before I'm ever confronted with the situation."

"Good point. So you're sure, as a Ranger, you'll have a gun and everything?"

"Yeah, of course. What is the point of having laws if you don't enforce them?"

"What laws?"

"I don't know . . . laws. You know, like Fish and Game laws, Criminal laws, Vehicle laws, Boating laws, and stuff like that."

"So it's not just in a box in your truck or something?"

"What's not in a box?"

"The gun."

"What on earth are you talking about? I'm wrestling with the major moral dilemma of taking a person's life, and you're worried about where the gun is located. Really, Kristie?"

"Without the gun, it would be difficult to kill the other person," she stated bluntly.

"Yeah, I agree. But I really need this job. We need me to keep this job!" I exclaimed with strong emotion, indicating how desperate I was feeling. "And whether I like it or not, guns are part of this job. I never had a moral issue selling gauze and bandages or even working as a carpenter. Do you understand how serious this is, Kristina?"

"Now just calm down, Nicky. We can work through this."

"Look, once I have completed my probationary period I am required, as a condition of continued employment, to attend and graduate from a Police Academy. After my successful completion of the Police Academy, I will be required to wear a Ranger uniform and among other things a gold star, a bulletproof vest, and a .357 Magnum handgun. Do you understand that I will be a full-fledged police officer? I'll be a cop, Kristina. The Watershed and Recreation Rangers are cops. They are the only law enforcement officers on the hundreds of thousands of acres out there. They also fight the fires, handle the medical emergencies, do search and rescue, weather readings, maintain the trails, fences, bridges, signage, and everything else. But most importantly, they keep the peace."

"Hey, Nicky," she inquired softly. "Can you explain something to me?"

"Sure, honey. What is it?"

"Why do they need guns to keep the peace?"

FIVE

Have you ever prayed diligently for something you were absolutely convinced you needed? At least when you were praying, you *thought* you had to have it. But with the passage of time, your certainty became tarnished, less clear. Then, once having obtained your heart's desire, you questioned whether you ever should have pleaded with God for it in the first place. This, regrettably, was my dawning reality. For less than two months into my dream career as a Watershed and Recreation Ranger, I was beginning to entertain these distressing thoughts. I was barely halfway through my probationary period, and I was having some very serious doubts about my new job.

This is a considerable problem for any new employee. When I also contemplated the sluggish economy and my lack of any other prospects, I truly believed I was out of options. There was no turning back unless I was willing to return to selling first aid supplies, which I couldn't bear to think about. Somehow, some way, I needed to reconcile my new job to my faith . . . or my faith to my new job. These weren't the same equations. Nor would they bring about the

same results in my career, my marriage, or in my life.
Astounded at my own depth of self-questioning, I continued
to wrestle with issues that sent shockwaves down into the
depths of my soul, way down where no one is allowed to
tread, let alone ask questions. Even my Lord hadn't been
allowed in this dark chamber where neither sunshine nor
moonlight had ever etched their shadows upon its fleshy
walls. Or . . . had He?

"I need this job! I need this paycheck!" I shouted one
morning while driving to work in my mobile prayer closet. "I
can't quit. We have no savings. We can hardly pay our bills
as it is. Plus, I'll never find another job. I just can't quit, not
now any way. How would we pay our rent, our utilities, our
credit cards? Surely the landlord would kick us out on the
street in short order if we were late paying him. What
would our friends and family think of us? What would they
think of me?!"

Shaking my head as I pulled into the parking lot at
WHQ, I decided that the only way to survive was to
reconcile my faith to my new job, not my new job to my
faith. It was an altogether devastating thought as well as a
chilling decision. But at this point in my life, my job had to
come first. It wasn't that I wanted it that way. Nevertheless,
it had to be. I felt I had no choice, no other option. I knew
the door to the dark chamber deep down within me had
been cracked open ever so slightly. Intensely uncomfortable
with the vulnerability, I shuddered as I walked slowly across
the lot to the building. It was the first time I could
remember since committing my life to Christ that I had ever
consciously decided to choose in favor of a circumstance and

not my faith. But this was different. This was my livelihood. This was real. I tried repeatedly to justify my decision. Regardless, I felt utterly defeated.

"Good afternoon, what's your excuse?" greeted the bantering, cigarette smoking, coffee sipping, Captain Cross.

"Hey, Henry," I mumbled. "How you doing this morning?"

"A lot better than you," he sarcastically snapped back with a chuckle.

"Why do you say that?"

"Because you and the crew are going up on Ranker's Ridge today. One of the helicopter pilots spotted a huge dadgum tree that must have fallen in that storm last weekend. He claimed it tore up some of our fence on one end and was hanging way out over the dadgum cliff on the other end. You'll have to take the ropes and safety gear, so you can get out on it with a chain saw."

"Why do you want to cut it up? Wouldn't it be better to let it decompose where it fell? I mean, it seems to me that . . ."

"Greenhorn," snickered Henry while shaking his head. Then squinting through the fog of his cigarette smoke, he gazed right at me and blurted out, "Kids. Them dadgum kids will climb out on that tree, and they'll have some stupid dadgum competition to see who can go out on a limb the farthest. The one who wins will be the same one whose parents will sue the District because he fell to his death when that limb broke clean off that dadgum tree that you didn't want to remove."

"Whoa. I never thought of it that way, Henry."

"Of course you never. That's why I'm the captain, and you're the dadgum greenhorn," he stated candidly with a wink.

Nodding my head in acknowledgement of his astute observation, a smile slowly broke across my face. I realized for the first time the secret to a good relationship with my superior's superior was to always remember that in his eyes I'm the dadgum rookie, and he's the captain. He's the sage and savvy, twenty-five year veteran leader of the Rangers. He's the boss; I'm the subordinate. He was telling me in his classic style that it was okay to joke and kid with him but to always remember my place and more importantly—his place.

Because I had learned to adhere to this early morning revelation, I always had a great relationship with Captain Henry Cross. He was demanding but liked to have fun as well. Seemingly quite unorthodox in his decisions, he was fiercely loyal to his Rangers whenever there was a problem with the District's Main Office, a citizen complaint, or even with the occasional visit from the news media. Some called him extremely old school, but he was the type of old school that stood by his word. And his handshake was as good as that word. If he told you "yes," then the answer was "yes." On the other hand, if he said "no," you would be well advised to leave it alone.

Within an hour, Phil had pulled the four-wheel drive, crew-cab truck around to the largest of the three rollup doors on the back of the WHQ building. Steven, Rob, and I loaded up the barbed wire fence repair tools and supplies while Phil grabbed two chainsaws, an ax, and a couple of machetes. Next, Phil drove the truck to the gasoline pump at the back of the massive storage barn behind the WHQ building while Steven and I gathered up the safety climbing equipment. Walking across the gravel toward the barn, Rob met us with what he considered the most essential item—a case of bones.

Bones, more commonly known as dominoes, is a game that nearly all of the Rangers on work crews played at lunch time. Now, I'm not referring to standing several of these little tiles on end, close together, and then flicking the first one with your finger, toppling them in succession. No, Bones is a game of math. The goal is to win by scoring the highest number of points using multiples of the number five. Each tile or "bone" has a number of dots engraved upon the two ends of one face. The grouping has one that is a zero/zero, then zero/one, zero/two and so on, all the way up to zero/six. This same pattern is etched on each bone with the largest number being a six/six. It actually is a mentally challenging contest and was a favorite among the work crews, who only needed the Bones and a level surface to play on. One clever Ranger had even devised a "Bones Board" that rested upon the tops of the front and rear bench seats in the crew-cab truck, creating a flat tabletop on which to play.

Considering the daily, mundane, labor intensive assignments, the game of Bones was a welcome reprieve from tasks that required little cerebral stimulation. In fact, the half hour lunch break sometimes extended to more than an hour because the participants were starved for an intellectual challenge. At first, this violated my conscience. As a carpenter, this would have been an offense worthy of termination. I had been reared by parents who taught the importance of giving your employer an honest day's work. And as a Christian, I knew the Bible encouraged me to do everything as unto the Lord. Cheating Him would never be anything my deep seated convictions would allow me to do. Unfortunately, over a seemingly short period of time, I was becoming pleasantly numb to the pricks within my conscience.

With Phil at the wheel, the truck banged and chugged its way ever higher on the rutted and rock strewn, fire road toward Ranker's Ridge. It had taken over forty-five minutes of paved road travel before reaching the gate. After passing through and relocking the gate, we started our bone jarring ascent. Twenty minutes later, Phil stopped the truck at the bottom of a particularly steep section of road. Steven, who had ridden shotgun, instantly hopped out to lock the hubs, so the four-wheel drive could be engaged. This would be my first time to climb up an exceptionally narrow, fire road with someone else driving. It was absolutely terrifying. To compound my fears, I ended up in the seat directly behind Phil and on the side that offered a full view of the steep drop-off no more than a foot or two away from our tires as we headed ever upward on this exposed section. At one point, I glanced at my rear seat mate, Rob. He was smiling from ear to ear.

"Now, you know why I was adamant about sitting over here."

"Thanks, Rob," I replied with a hint of sarcasm in my tone.

"If you think this is bad," laughed Rob, who evidently was having a difficult time withholding his glee. "You should have seen this road before we had the dozer up here last winter. It was really bad."

"Worse than this?" I asked in disbelief.

"Oh, yeah, much worse," chuckled Phil, his left arm hanging out the open window as his right hand steered this four-wheeled, bucking bronco around a hairpin curve.

"How much farther?" I inquired, trying not to sound like a scared child on his way to the family doctor for his annual immunization injections.

"This levels out in another quarter mile or so," declared Phil. "Then we travel about three or four miles across some rolling hills . . . then the bad part."

"The bad part?" I questioned loudly, my voice hitting an octave that sounded more like it came from a member of the Vienna boys' choir than a concerned passenger on this Watershed roller coaster ride.

"Yeah, the last mile or so up the face of Double R is a bit dicey," replied Phil frankly. "Don't worry. We've been up it several times."

"We?" I chuckled nervously, giving indication that I wasn't worried about the other passengers. I was worried about Phil and, more specifically, his level of driving ability on these steep and narrow, dirt roads.

"Yeah, we," laughed Phil, maneuvering the truck up onto the rolling hills section of this trip. "Granny Low and me."

"Who?"

"Granny Low," Phil stated with confidence. "It's the lowest gear in the four-wheel drive manual transmission. It can climb the steepest of grades with no trouble at all."

"Yeah," laughed Rob. "Phil swears this truck can climb straight up a tree."

As we approached Double R, Phil stopped our vehicle on a small knoll with a full view of the rock cliffs on the west side of the ridge. Steven jumped out with a pair of binoculars. Steadying himself on the hood of the truck, he gazed high up the cliff.

"Yep, I see it. It's hanging over the edge maybe thirty or forty feet. Looks to be that big oak you claimed was coming down one day, Phil. Here, take a look."

Phil held the binoculars up to his eyes and within seconds agreed with Steven. It was the same tree at the top of the cliffs they had feared would come crashing down one day. After a minute or so, he handed them to Rob who, after taking his turn gazing up at the cliffs, released them to me.

"That's magnificent," I whispered, so I wouldn't sound like a rookie.

"Yeah," agreed Rob. "It's a beautiful place that hardly a soul knows exists. Well, except for us Rangers and an occasional hiker. But it's so remote that not many folks venture up here."

"If I were to come here on a weekend, how would I get up here?"

"There's a Staging Area on the east side of the ridge, but the arduous hike is about five to six miles . . . it's almost all uphill," conceded Phil.

"Is that the shortest route?" I asked.

"Yeah, the way we came is a full twelve miles from the paved road, and with these steep sections it would be a brutal hike," advised Phil.

"Plus, you can't drive your personal vehicle on the Watershed since that surveyor got stuck out here three years ago," added Rob. "Really the only time we make the trip up here is when something comes up needing our attention. Like Phil mentioned the other day, this place is extraordinarily remote. There's just no easy way to get to it."

"Come on, you guys," asserted Steven as he hopped in the front passenger seat. "We've got another thirty to forty minutes to the top, so let's get going."

"Forty minutes?" I probed. "But it's right there."

"Yeah," agreed Phil. "But the rest of the way can be extremely dangerous and must be taken slowly and carefully."

We rolled along for several more minutes until we reached a tight left turn where a huge limb from an oak tree hung down unusually low, just a few feet above the road, which now appeared to be no more than a moderately wide hiking trail. Phil downshifted into Granny Low, and the truck lunged immediately forward at a pace I was sure could be matched by a slow crawling turtle. In fact, as this road narrowed even more, I considered getting out and walking myself. It was so steep that it was impossible, without great abdominal strain, to sit forward in my seat. Our truck creaked and chugged inch by inch up this hazardous path. At several locations, the slant of the road tilted precariously toward the abyss on our left. Creeping over the occasional half-buried boulder only served to intensify the experience as it caused our laboring vehicle to drift ever closer toward toppling over the edge. On our right stood a granite wall. The trail was barely wide enough for a VW bug, yet here we were in a full sized, four-wheel drive truck. The mirror on the right side, although folded completely inward, made eerie noises as it scraped along the rock. We continued up this steep trail approaching the end of the rock wall on our right. Then, as we neared a tight hairpin turn to progress ever upward, Rob leaned toward me and confessed that this was the most dangerous part.

Halfway through the hairpin curve, I came to recognize why Rob had made his dire proclamation. Our crew-cabbed vehicle had a much longer wheelbase than a normal truck, thereby requiring a much greater turning radius. Phil abruptly brought us to a complete stop on the steepest section. As we began to drift backwards, he cranked hard on the steering wheel. My heart jumped into my throat. We were edging ever closer to the top of the cliff behind us and at such an incline I felt as though we would actually flip over backwards and be sent hurtling down into the canyon below. I was just about to shout a warning at Phil to let him know how close he was getting to the edge when he let off the brake, causing our speed to increase dramatically. I braced myself for what, I was certain, was the inevitable—the four of us, still inside our truck, toppling over the cliff to our deaths. However, within a split second Phil popped the clutch and gunned the big V-8 engine, spinning the tires forward on the loose soil and stones. Once again, the truck lunged up the steep trail in the high-torque, Granny Low gear.

Throughout the entire thirty second ordeal, the taut atmosphere in the cab was utterly silent. After we had safely negotiated the crux of the route up Ranker's Ridge, the four of us seemed to breathe a corporate sigh of relief. Within seconds, Steven spoke up.

"Nice job, Phil. That's always a bit tricky."

"Yeah, well, I would much rather be the guy driving than riding," chuckled Phil.

"Oh, it's not so bad," shrugged Steven.

"Oh, yeah?" retorted Rob. "You ought to try it back here next time. Nick's as white as one of my wife's freshly bleached sheets."

"I am not. I admit, I thought it was a little tense at times, but I've been through much worse . . . I just can't remember when that's all."

"Well," laughed Phil. "It's a lot scarier going down. Maybe that'll jog your memory"

The air was a touch chilly on top of Ranker's Ridge, but the sun's rays were warm, making for an idyllic day on the Watershed. We got right to work repairing the fifty feet of barbed wire fence destroyed by the massive, uprooted portion of the felled tree. Finishing just before lunch, we decided to assess how to handle the limbs hanging out over the top of the cliff before settling down to eat. While sitting in the truck playing Bones and eating my peanut butter and jelly sandwich, my eyes kept drifting to the beauty of the scenery surrounding us. I decided right then and there that this was my favorite spot in the entire Watershed. I must have continued musing too long because Rob nudged me to signify that it was my turn. After placing a bone on the board, I gazed back out the window.

"Man, when I'm on patrol, if you can't find me, I'll be up here. I love this place."

"On patrol you'd never come up here," professed Phil.

"What? Why not?"

"When you're on patrol," explained Steven, "you have to hit the troubled spots. It's your job to handle problems. There aren't any problems way up here. Well, not since I've been a Ranger anyway. Besides, it's very important that you stay close to the main roads, so you can handle the emergencies that arise during the course of the day."

"So when I'm on patrol I can't drive around where I want to?"

"No, not really," replied Phil. "The only time we actually get out on these fire roads is when someone reports they've seen poachers, a pack of wild dogs, a fire, or something like that. You know, some situation requiring a law enforcement officer. Look, I'm not sure what your perception of this job was, but we don't spend our days smelling flowers, petting bunnies, and hugging trees. We are the only law on the Watershed. We are the only fire fighters out here, and if someone gets hurt or careens their car off the side of a road, we're it. And soon, you'll be it too."

"Come on, Phil," haggled Steven. "The guy's a rookie. Give him a break, okay?"

"Yeah, sure."

"Nick, it's like this," stated Steven plainly, "every one of us out here is similar to a lone ranger. You have to do your job, protect yourself, and others. Don't get in situations you can't handle. Because we all know that we are lone rangers, we drop everything and come running when another Ranger needs help. Just don't be the boy who cries wolf, okay? By the way, it's your turn to lay a bone."

Glancing down at the bones I had left to play, I had difficulty choosing my next move. Randomly selecting one, I hurriedly placed it on the board. Once more I took in the sights and wondered how such a peaceful place could be filled with so much anxiety. I admired the beauty surrounding me: the grassy slopes dotted with the oak and pine trees, which seem to meander in and out of the ravines as they sought water for their growth; a golden eagle with its massive wingspan fully spread, floating effortlessly on the warm air currents from the valleys below; and the white granite cliffs reaching upward to the top of Ranker's Ridge creating a knife's edge against the brilliant blue sky. It was all spectacularly gorgeous. I was beginning to both love and dread this job.

After lunch, with the fence repaired, we set about removing the three large limbs that extended far beyond the edge of the cliff. From the conversation before lunch, I had determined that I had much more experience with climbing equipment than all three of my fellow employees combined. With that in mind, I volunteered to be the human lizard; the one who would crawl out on the protruding boughs. To my surprise, they all agreed. So I assumed the lead in this precarious undertaking.

"First," I requested, "I need someone to take a chain and the come-a-long and attach it to that tree in front of the truck. Then, fasten the other end to the front axle. Next, we'll set a belay using our vehicle as the anchor. Now, who wants to belay me?"

"Be what you?" chuckled Steven.

"Belay," I repeated, finally feeling like there was a subject I knew more about than my fellow Rangers.

"I'll do it," asserted Phil. "I have some training from my days in the Marines."

"Okay. Rob, if you'll make sure the chain saw is ready; I'll carry a machete and take a foray out there on the lowest limb as soon as Phil's ready to belay me."

"I'm ready when you are, Nick," replied Phil with a tone that exuded confidence.

Just then, Steven walked around the side of the truck stating that he had connected the come-a-long to the tree, using the larger of the two chains we had brought with us. Nodding in his direction, I then stared at Phil waiting for his acknowledgement that he had me on belay. After tying his final knot, he raised one thumb in the air.

"Okay," I declared. "I'm on belay. Rob, hand me those six webbing loops and a half a dozen carabiners. That's those little metal ovals with a hinged gate on one side."

"I know what a carabiner is," snickered Rob as he shook his head.

I walked a few steps over to the top of the cliff. While steadying myself on the lowest limb, I peered over the edge. There it was, the beautifully smooth, vertical, granite wall devoid of any visible cracks and nearly four hundred feet of unending air, free of obstructions all the way down to the narrow fire road we had just traversed. Below that, it was another eighty feet to the valley floor below. Wrapping a loop of webbing around a stout branch of about three inches in diameter, I clipped a carabiner into it, then my rope into the same carabiner. I now had my first piece of fall protection in place. Feeling comfortable, I gently stretched my leg out to step onto the overhanging limb. Holding onto another branch above my head, I glanced down to the ground far below. The sensation was quite airy, and with the breeze blowing the exposure was palpable.

Cautiously, I took two more steps and fastened another webbing loop on a branch close to my waist. With four more strategically placed stretches amongst the many branches, I was over twenty feet out on the limb with nothing below me but airy, open space. Taking another loop of webbing, I meticulously wrapped it around the branch above my head and clipped my rope through its carabiner. Sliding my machete out of its sheath, I painstakingly trimmed enough of the lesser branches to clear a small space where I could use a chain saw to lop off the initial section of this overhanging bough. My plan was to let it plummet to the valley below. Then, I would back up about ten feet or so toward the granite cliff and sever another section. My final tactic was to cut the remaining segment while standing on solid ground, releasing it to free-fall to the canyon far below. I figured I could do the same for each of the three huge, projecting culprits.

Feeling comfortable I had cleared enough room to operate a chainsaw safely, I holstered my machete, glanced back at my three land-loving helpers, and gave them a casual thumbs-up as I began to head back toward solid terrain to obtain the chainsaw. Confident I was safe and in no immediate danger, I unclipped the carabiner from the loop of webbing above me.

Unfortunately, with my second step back toward earth I heard a deafening "CRACK!" The limb I was standing on pitched several inches downward. My heart leapt and my pulse quickened. My grip tightened on the branch directly above me as I waited for the moment when I would be suspended four hundred feet in the air with nothing to stand on. My eyes, wide open, darted to Phil to assure myself that he had a firm grip on the other end of my rope while my mouth instinctively shouted the inevitable.

"Falling!"

SIX

There are folks who have experienced near death situations before. They report that in the moments just before someone passes away, most of their life plays before their eyes like a movie. Teetering on this limb, I wasn't seeing a ticker tape of life-long scenes. So, I reasoned, it must not be my time to die. I confess a thought of Kristina did flash through my mind. But thankfully, other thoughts did as well, and I quickly acted upon them. Realizing what any experienced climber would instinctively do when he thinks something is about to go wrong—I checked my anchors, those points of connection I was relying on to hold me securely to something solid, something that couldn't be moved. Although I didn't recognize it until years later, I believe the Lord was giving me a wonderfully vivid illustration of how to solve my growing moral dilemma at my new job as a Ranger. It was a concept. No, it was a principle: a principle of anchors. We all have anchors in our lives, but do we recognize them? I've deeply regretted not having perceived my life's anchors—the people and the valued relationships that hold me steady when the winds of adversity blow upon me. In this tense, exposed situation out on this overhanging limb, I believe God was revealing to me a powerfully pertinent parable.

Emotions are peculiar elements, don't you think? At times they can immediately send us into the highest of pleasurable, personal experiences. In other moments, they can cripple and confuse, if not altogether paralyze us. Through my years of training, both in first-aid and rock climbing, I have come to recognize much of what is developed in the rigors of discipline—an ability to control one's emotions, at least to some degree. Fear is among the strongest of all human emotions, and one we must learn to conquer in each of its myriad of forms. Hanging four hundred feet up in the sky with nothing but air between me and the ground below, I needed to overcome at once. This was not the place for fear to rule. Having glanced at each of my anchors, a steadiness, a composed confidence became my mindset as each decision and action calmed my feelings and strengthened my resolve.

By pulling myself up and transferring my weight onto the limb above, I simultaneously moved most of my weight off the dangerously compromised lower branch. Then, very gingerly I stepped over the large, cracked section of the weakened limb and moved ever so carefully toward the edge of the cliff and onto safe solid ground. Breathing a sigh of relief, I turned to Phil and thanked him for belaying me.

"No problem," replied Phil. "That was a close one."

"Yeah, how'd that feel out there?" chuckled a curiously delighted Rob.

"A bit nerve wracking," I conceded. "The problem is that now I have to go back out there and cut off that limb."

"I'd be careful, Nick," advised Steven. "I think you should cut it off on this side of that crack. I wouldn't walk out there past that."

"I agree. But if I cut it off on this side that will be one huge branch that falls to the ground."

"That's fine. It's more important to remain safe, Nick, than to risk slipping, uh . . . or worse. If you catch my drift?"

"Okay," I agreed. "Hand me the chainsaw, Rob, and let's see how this goes."

Before heading back out on the ominously impaired limb, which had felt more like a spacewalk than a tree trimming expedition, I clipped the eight foot length of webbing that was tied to the saw onto the carabiner attached to my safety harness. If I dropped the saw, at least it wouldn't fall several hundred feet to the ground. Now came the hard part—walking back out there. It took longer this time. Climbing through the branches while toting a chainsaw, I soon found out was no easy task. Not to mention battling the sensation that at any moment the limb I was walking on, with great trepidation, could without warning completely snap off.

Within a few minutes, I was just a foot or so away from the spot where the limb had fractured. I deftly made a loop in the saw's webbing and connected it to another loop I had tied to the branch above my head. This effectively suspended the saw as well as anchored it. Now I could go about the more important task of safely anchoring myself.

Soon, I was securely tethered to the tree. Suspended in my harness, from the branch above, I tentatively rested my feet on the limb below. I was ready to begin the job at hand—lopping off this tree limb, which measured the length of a moving van.

Starting the saw with a yank of the cord, I laid the rapidly spinning chain to the bark. I glanced back at Phil, who was still belaying me from the truck anchor. He nodded. Grasping the saw with both hands, I leaned further back and fully into the harness, tightening the webbing straps that held me fast to the tree. The extremely sharp teeth made short work of the sixteen inch diameter limb. As it neared three-quarters of the way through, I could hear, above the whine of the saw, a cracking sound below my feet. I noticed the initial crack was now extending past my stance toward the edge of the cliff. The huge limb was beginning to pivot below me. It was going to break off leaving me dangling in mid-air. I hastened my cut by placing more weight on the saw. Just as the cut was nearly accomplished, the massive bough released its grip and began the long, rapid descent to the valley floor far below. The limb upon which I had stood, now free of the enormous weight of the branch, sprung upward two feet or more before resting back on the top of the cliff. If not for my anchors, the unexpected jolt upward surely would have launched me into space.

I gazed down as the air borne branch plummeted to the ground, marveling at the lengthy amount of time it took to slam into the earth. I stood on the remaining section of the limb as a cold realization darted through my keenly alert mind. If I were to have a similar fate as the limb now lying on the valley floor, the fall would provide me with much more time to consider my outcome than I would ever want.

"That worked pretty well," shouted a smiling Rob from the safety of solid ground.

I gave him a thumbs up. Then I began cutting a wedge on the underside of the limb above. This would enable me to cut straight down from above without the danger of the branch splitting like the one I had just cut. Next, I moved over to the top of the cliff and sawed off the rest of the lowest bough. I accomplished the same process with the final of the three overhanging members as well. Back on solid ground with the job completed, I handed the chainsaw to Rob. My shirt was drenched with sweat even though the weather was cool. It had been strenuous, unnerving work, but the job was finished. As a result, hikers would have a new place to sit and safely enjoy the view to the west, which is precisely what I planned to do while the others loaded up our truck.

"Nice job, Nick," proclaimed Steven, thrusting his hand in my direction.

"Thanks. It was a little dicey at times, but we got it done."

"Where did you learn how to do all that?" asked Rob as he coiled up one of the two ropes we were using.

"Mostly North Carolina, at a little crag near my home we locals called Leonard's Thumb. There's a much larger rock face called Laurel Knob a few miles outside a small town named Cashiers. The cliffs are pretty high. We climbed there a lot too. Some of my friends and I used to go up to Seneca in the mountains of West Virginia as well.

Those are the places I frequented in high school and college. When I moved out here, I started climbing in Yosemite, mainly in The Valley. However, lately I've been enjoying the high country around Tuolumne Meadows and Tenaya Lake. There's some fabulous climbing up there."

After they wrapped up all the tools, harnesses, and safety gear and packed it in the truck, they joined me on the enormous oak log where we gazed out across the horizon. The sun was getting rather low and the air was beginning to feel chilly. We chitchatted for another fifteen minutes about how the tree trimming job had gone. Everyone felt a sense of accomplishment, which is always a great way to end a day. I was just finishing up a red delicious apple when Phil spoke up.

"We better get a move on. I don't want to be negotiating those fire roads in the dark."

"Good point," agreed Steven. "Let's get going, you guys."

That evening, poor Kristina could hardly interject a word into our conversation. I was quite the chatterbox relaying my day of high adventure on Ranker's Ridge. When she was finally able to wedge in a few words, her question took me by surprise.

"So you're feeling better about your job then?"

"What's that supposed to mean?"

"It means, the last time we talked about your job you had some major concerns."

"Yeah, kind of. But I don't know what I can do about them, so I'm determined to just let things be. You know, easy come, easy go."

"Now what's that supposed to mean, Nicky?"

"Well, uh . . ."

"Look, we're going out with Pastor Charles this Friday night. Why don't you talk to him about it?"

"Just Charles?"

"No, Carolyn will be there too."

"I would hope so . . ."

"Look, Nicky, you should tell Pastor Charles about all this," Kristina insisted with a finger pointing right at me.

"Oh, I don't know about that, honey." I replied. "Besides, there's nothing I can do. This is the job God has for me, and we need the money. So I can't quit or anything."

"Who's talking about you quitting your job? All I'm suggesting is that since you find yourself in a quandary as to what you should do, talk it over with our pastor. That's what he's there for."

"No. I really don't think that's a good idea. Moreover, I already know what he'll tell me."

"Moreover? When did you start talking like that? Learn that from your Ranger buddies? And listen, Nick, you don't know what Pastor Charles would say."

"Whatever."

"Yeah, whatever is right," she replied with more than a twinge of disgust.

The rift between us continued for the rest of that week, right up to and through the dinner we had with Pastor Charles and Carolyn.

Pastor Charles is an incredibly pleasant man when he isn't bloviating about his latest teaching. His wife Carolyn is a year his younger and usually appears a bit haggard. She takes care of their four rambunctious boys; all are under the age of ten. Charles had been the youth pastor for our church until our senior pastor moved on to another church about two years ago. Charles was then hired as our new senior pastor. His counsel is usually sound when discussing topics of doctrine, marriage, or raising children. However, he really considers himself more of a Pauline scholar than a counselor. Implying, he studied those epistles more than any other books in the Scriptures and therefore believes himself to be an expert. If I wanted to change any subject while talking with him, all I had to do was ask a question regarding the Apostle Paul or his letters. He is extremely knowledgeable and always willing to engage in a discussion. I respect and appreciate Pastor Charles, but with matters involving the work environment, he literally has no experience outside of being a pastor. Therefore, I was entirely disinterested in discussing my work situation with him. Especially not over dinner with Kristina and his wife present.

Because I arrived home late that Friday, Kristina called Pastor Charles to inform him we would meet them at the restaurant instead of their home. When we finally showed up, Charles and Carolyn had been waiting nearly thirty minutes and had already finished their appetizers. I felt awful. My father was right; it's never a good thing to be late. It places the tardy one at a terrible disadvantage. No sooner had we ordered our meals, than I remembered these sage words of advice while instantaneously experiencing the consequences.

"So, Nick," began Charles with an understanding face that seemed to be painted on. "Kristina mentioned you've been having some problems at your new job?"

"Really?" I asked tersely as I glared at Kristina. My face may have been smiling, but my eyes were shooting daggers. "What problems are you referring to, sweetheart?"

"You know, those moral issues you were telling me about," she replied with a knowing smile.

"I don't understand, honeybunch," I replied through tight lips and with an undeniably sarcastic tone. "The only real problem I have with work is if I ever have to clean the outhouses along the paths around the recreation areas. But I won't have to do that revolting job unless I get assigned to it. Besides, sweetkins, I doubt Charles and Carolyn want to discuss raw sewage while we're eating our meal in this fine restaurant. Now do you, Chuck?"

"Uh, no . . . I would rather leave that topic for another time."

"You know something, Chucky? Me too," I replied with a smug grin. Then, turning to Kristina I scrunched my face and derided in a mocking, sugary, sweet tone, "Cutesee wutesee, they really don't want to discuss it either, so why don't we just let Charles and I look into it at a later time. Okay, with you, sugar buns?"

"Sure. Whatever, Nick," Kristina retorted with a tone of disgust. "I was just trying to help."

"I know you were, sweetie pie. And thank you for that," I replied with an equally derisive tone while patting her hand gently. "Now, Charles, tell me exactly what you think the Apostle Paul meant by 'a thorn in the flesh?'

Where is that again, the book of Ephesians or is it in Second Corinthians?"

On the drive home the atmosphere was frigidly cold inside our car. Conversely, the temperature outside was unusually warm and pleasant, so I rolled my window down. Noticing other couples sitting comfortably and at ease in their cars at a traffic light, I wondered how Kristina and I had gotten to this place in our marriage. The couple to my left was talkative and laughing. I marveled at how light the atmosphere seemed in their car compared to the heaviness in ours. To the right of us was a similar scene, a couple enjoying one another's company. Glancing in the rear view mirror, I watched a different couple who seemed to be the spitting image of us. I don't mean because of their physical features, but rather by the emotions clearly displayed in their expressions. They seemed so distant, so unhappy. I continued to study them as we sat waiting for the light to turn green. They were a classic picture of pain. What had occurred between them? Had one stepped across an invisible line? Had he been harsh? Had she reacted wrongly? Whatever had transpired, they were obviously miserable.

The light changed to green, and we moved on down the road. My eyes darted back and forth from the unhappy couple behind me to the road in front of me. Several blocks later, the light turned yellow and then red. Stopping, my vision was transfixed on the same couple, still behind us. Who would be the first to take the needed step? Or would they continue in their sad state of affairs and eventually dissolve into a dysfunctional, disloyal couple, whose marriage eventually culminated in divorce?

Just then, I observed the tiniest glimmer of hope. She had turned toward him and said something. What, I couldn't decipher. He shook his head. Now he was talking. He didn't appear angry, but perhaps annoyed. Both were talking. It didn't seem friendly. Nonetheless, they were speaking to each other. The light turned green. I slowly pressed the accelerator moving our car forward. It looked like five or six more blocks before the next traffic light, which was currently green. As we approached the light, it turned yellow. Hoping to see the outcome of the couple behind us, I slammed on the brakes. We came to an abrupt stop. I stared at the car coming into view in my mirror.

"Nicolas, for crying out loud, what on earth is the matter with you?" barked an irritated Kristina with her hands on the dashboard.

"Do you mean now or in the restaurant?"

"Cut it out, Nick. I really don't like it when you play your stupid games."

My eyes were glued to my mirror as I watched the car behind us slow to a stop. I could see the couple was still talking. He leaned toward the woman and, reading his lips, I'm fairly confident he expressed "I'm sorry." Next, it appeared she asked a few questions, which evoked nods and grins from him. Then she reached her arms up and around his neck and kissed him.

The light turned green. This time we had to veer onto the freeway entrance ramp. I never saw the couple again. But they had a profound effect on me. It's strange how we can have an impact on others, yet so many times we're not even aware of it. I resolved at that very moment, if

Kristina didn't take the first step toward healing our relationship by the time we arrived home, I would.

"Nick, I really can't stand it when we're like this." Kristina remarked, making the initial move toward reconciliation as we pulled into our neighborhood.

"What do you mean?" I asked in a calm tone.

"Stop it!" she bellowed. "I am so sick of you always avoiding the issue."

"Which issue are you talking about? I can think of several."

"Oh, really?!" she huffed. "Well, that's just great. Here I was attempting to open up a conversation that hopefully would lead to healing and us being in love again, and you're exploding it into several more problems."

"You're not in love with me?"

"I didn't say that. I didn't mean it that way. I'm just really frustrated with our marriage right now. Lately, you seem to be so distant and have such a cold demeanor most of the time. I want the old, loving, fun, and warm Nick back. The Nick I love. The Nick I knew before the Ranger job."

"I was miserable back then. I hated my job. It was absolutely humiliating."

"Then I want the miserable, humiliated Nick. I was so much happier with him."

Kristina made this last statement just as I stopped the car in our garage. She hastily jumped out, slammed the door, and hurried inside through the kitchen door, which she banged forcefully shut behind her. I sat perfectly still behind the steering wheel while her words, her tone, and her anger kept ringing in my ears. This was a devastating revelation. Kristina had just told me, in so many words, that she was much happier with me and with our marriage when I was miserable at work. And now that I was somewhat happy in my job, she was miserable in our marriage.

"Good grief," I breathed as I climbed out of our car and headed inside. "How could any man ever want more than one woman? I have more than enough trouble keeping just one happy."

I found her locked in our bathroom filling the tub with water. Sometimes Kristina will retreat to a hot, bubble bath when trying to cope with a stressful situation.

"Kristie, what are you doing?"

"Bath."

"Yeah, duh. Well, if you don't want to talk."

"Ha. Yeah, like it's really me that doesn't want to work this out."

"See, there you go again."

"What?"

"Acting like we are on the precipice of divorce or something. Look, I don't know how you did things in your family, but in mine we didn't throw something away just because it was broken or not working properly. We fussed and fought and worked through to a solution. It may not have been pretty while the fighting was going on, but the resolution was much more lasting and rewarding."

"We didn't fight. We talked," she retorted snidely.

"Great. Turn off the water, open the door, and let's talk."

After a few seconds, long enough to send me the wordless message that she was being inconvenienced, I heard the knobs on the faucet slowly being turned off, and soon the water stopped. The bathroom became silent. Then, the lock on the door clicked. Slowly opening the door, I saw her still dressed, sitting on the edge of the tub. I leaned my shoulder against the door jamb.

"I don't know what to say," she shrugged.

"Okay, fair enough. Look, I'll say that I agree, or at least acknowledge, that I may have been easier to live with while I was selling first-aid supplies. But I was really depressed working there. My self-respect hit the skids. I was really hurting. And frankly, you were a lot more understanding back then. Now, here I am with what is looking to be my dream job, and you say you're miserable."

"Wait a second, Nick. It's important for you to know something about me you may not understand even though we've been married for several years."

"What's that?"

"I cannot stress how essential it is for me to feel like I can trust you. I can't give you my heart if I can't trust you. Do you comprehend what I'm trying to say?"

"Yeah, I think so. Well . . . kind of."

"If I can't trust you, I can't give you my heart. And if I can't give you my heart, I can't be satisfied in our relationship. For me, it's unconditionally essential to a happy marriage."

"Okay. I really appreciate you sharing that with me. Seriously, it means a lot. But, honey, you can trust me. I'm still the same Nick. The only thing that has changed is my new job. Now I'm a Ranger and not a first-aid salesman."

"Well, not really, Nicky."

"What do you mean by that, Kristie?"

"I mean, there is something else that has changed—something much deeper. And when this occurred, a tiny seed of distrust was planted in my heart."

"When what occurred?"

"When you chose your job over your faith."

SEVEN

Winter was generally rainy, windy, and cold that year. Regardless, I had determined to spend more time with Kristina, especially doing some of the outside activities we have always enjoyed together. Neither of us wanted a divorce nor to be separated for even a short time. It is true what the Scriptures declare about marriage—it is the most important relationship on earth. In fact, it is the only visible example of the invisible relationship between Jesus Christ and His bride, the church. Don't get me wrong. I realize no marriage is perfect, but our marriage could be perfect for us. Therefore, unwilling to give up on our relationship, I was determined to make every effort to win back her heart.

Hearts are not easy entities to acquire. And one that has been broken or hurt because of a lack of trust is even more difficult to obtain. The more I pondered what the primary issue was between us, the more everything kept pointing back to the Ranger job. Although, as soon as my thoughts drifted in that direction I shut them off as unfounded and absurd. I was not going to give up this dream job—moral dilemma or not. Besides, I had pretty much convinced myself that the whole moral dilemma matter was mostly imagined anyway. Now, all I needed to do was persuade Kristina. I was sure I could accomplish this by showing her, on a regular basis, how much I truly loved her.

Spring was right around the corner and with it my enrollment in the Police Academy. Having passed my Watershed test with flying colors, Henry signed me up for the next available term at the college in the valley. The week before I left for the Academy, Henry sat me down in his office and supplied me with several items, not the least of which was the key to a District car. I would be able to use this vehicle to drive to and from the campus, a distance of more than seventy miles from my home. The ITSMUD sedan reminded me of a used cop car except it was painted pale green instead of the standard black and white. When I punched the accelerator, the sound was every bit the same as a standard police vehicle. I liked it. It felt and sounded like power.

The last Friday at WHQ before leaving for the Police Academy, I was assigned several District Ranger shirts, pants, a gold star, a gun belt with mace, handcuffs, speed loaders, and several other related items. Then, Henry handed me a cardboard box. Inside were twenty-four cases of bullets and a Smith and Wesson .357 Magnum revolver. My eyes widened when I viewed the contents. I'm not at all squeamish when it comes to guns and ammunition. In fact as a youth, my brothers and I went hunting often. But seeing my service revolver for the first time made the certainty of my situation all the more real. A slight chill shot down my spine at the thought that one day I might have to use it, not on a deer or wild hog but on a human.

"These are wad cutters," he announced, pointing to a case of bullets.

"Wad what?" I curiously inquired as I held the shiny revolver with the beautiful, knurled oak grips.

"Wad cutters, and both of these," he emphasized, "that gun and these bullets need to be under your control at all times. You are signing here that you have received them, and you will give an account for them whenever I ask for it, understand?"

"Yes, sir." I leaned forward to sign the document that Henry had just slid across his desk."

"Now, a wad cutter is a type of bullet used mainly for target practice," explained Henry. "They're specifically expended on paper targets. These are .357 Magnum loads because the law requires you to qualify with the largest load your service weapon can handle. We actually use a .38 Special bullet on a daily basis, but our weapons are .357 Magnums, so that's what you have to take with you to the Police Academy."

"What's the difference?"

"Here." Henry opened up a case of my bullets then slid open his desk drawer. Pulling a bullet from each cavity, he handed them both to me.

"Wow, that's a huge difference."

"Yeah, it's about a quarter of an inch heavier load in the .357 Magnum. And you'll feel it when you pull the trigger."

"Really?"

"Oh, yeah, it packs a strong kick. Now, look, you go on and take the rest of the day off, so you can get ready for Monday. The first day always has a lot going on. And I understand you'll be in there with a wide assortment."

"What do you mean by that?"

"Your Academy class includes some State Police recruits, a few cadets from several cities, and a hand full of Fish and Game wardens as well as deputy sheriffs from three different counties. Should be a nice mix of other agencies for you to train with."

"Great!"

"Yeah, it's good to have friends in other places. You never know when they may come in handy. Especially those Fish and Game folks."

"Yeah, I can see how relationships are very important."

"Okay, well, have a nice afternoon. And hey, Nick, don't forget to check in every so often."

"Yes, sir."

"And, one more thing, make us proud, okay?" he asked with a smile. "Some of those other agencies think the Watershed Rangers aren't really cops. Show them we're much more than cops."

"Yes, sir, Captain Cross, sir. I'll do my best," I smiled, snapped to attention, and saluted.

"Alright, enough of that. Now, get out of here," he commanded with a chuckle and a wink.

Kristina had arrived home earlier and was sitting on the sofa reading a book when I walked in the door. Her countenance conveyed an expression of perplexity mixed with a twist of worry. Immediately, she wanted to know what was wrong, and why I was home so early. Next, she questioned if I was sick. Before I could answer any of her previous questions, she fired another inquiry, begging me to tell her if I had been fired. Having dropped my arm load of Ranger paraphernalia on the dining room table, I swung around to face her with my arms stretched out to each side.

"Hang on a second, honey," I pleaded, hoping to put a stop to the interrogation.

"Nick, just tell me. Why are you home?"

"I'm trying to tell you, but you keep asking questions. Now look, it's no big deal. Henry assigned all this stuff to me for the Police Academy. After giving me a few final instructions, he told me to take the rest of the afternoon off, so I would have some time to prepare for Monday."

"Really? Are you sure?"

"Yes, I am, dear," I assured her as I took a seat on the sofa by her bare feet.

"So everything is okay at work?"

"Yes, all is well, at least . . . for now."

"What's that supposed to mean?"

"Nothing. I'm just kidding. Although, if I fail a single class at the Academy, I'm out. I have to pass every single section. So I'm a bit nervous about that."

"Don't worry about it, Nicky. You'll do fine. And I can help you with anything you have trouble with," she affirmed with a nod.

"Oh, really? And what do you think a third grade teacher knows about law?" I baited playfully.

"Well, uh . . . not a whole lot. But I do have a master's degree in education, so I can help you with study habits, memorization, and stuff like that."

"I think all that sheepskin reveals is that you're really good at taking tests," I teased.

"Okay, then I can help you prepare for the tests. We can do it together."

"Now that sounds good, honey, I appreciate that. Thank you. But I'm home early today, and I think we need to use the time to work through some things in our marriage. Now, come Monday, I'm going to be away from home for long hours every day for four months. There could be a lot of room for misunderstandings during those weeks. I know I don't want that . . . and, well, I'm hoping you don't either."

"Of course, I don't, Nicky. However, I have to say again that I think this job is coming between you and your faith in God, and now I think it's becoming a wedge between us as well. Can you even recognize this?"

"Well, maybe to some degree. But I don't think it's a big deal like you're making it out to be. I can quit any time I want."

"Can you, Nicky? Do you think you could really quit?"

"Sure. Why not?"

"Then do it, honey, before you start that Police Academy. I'm really afraid if you begin classes it will change you into someone you never wanted to be. Someone I . . ."

Kristina paused, took a deep breath, sighed, and then sat staring out our living room window. Her face had a faraway look upon it. There seemed to be a sadness that darkened the brightness of her facial features. She sat perfectly quiet and still.

"Someone you what?" I asked with a hint of frustration in my tone.

She didn't answer. I could see tears welling up in her eyes.

"I'm not a mind reader, Kristie. If you don't talk to me, I don't know what you're thinking. Come on. 'Someone you what?'"

A stream of tears trickled down one cheek as she turned toward me. She wiped both eyes, and then setting her book down on the coffee table, she let out another big sigh.

"Nicky, I recognize the last couple of years have been hard on you. I appreciate how much pride you took in being a craftsman, and you were so good at it. I know it was your dream to build beautiful homes and fill them with exquisite pieces of furniture you created yourself. I know that, okay? I also know that your dream to own a shop where that would be possible died when you closed your carpentry business. I've been with you the entire time— through your frustrations, through your questions, through your doubts. I've cried with you, prayed with you, and hurt with you. I understand what you are going through. I could see how humiliating it was to don that first-aid uniform every day. We never even went to lunch together while you worked there. But I came to realize it was because you were embarrassed, so I never pressed you. As difficult as all those months were for you, it was difficult for me too. But at least we were together. We hurt together, we suffered through it together, in all of it we were together!"

"I need this job. It's a very good job and we need the money."

Kristina paused and looked directly into my eyes. "I know you need a job, Nicky. But this isn't it. It's changing you, honey. Slowly but surely, it's transforming you into someone you will regret you ever became."

Forcing myself to look away from her, I sensed somewhere deep down inside my heart that Kristina was right. But what could I possibly do about it now? In three days, I would be starting a criminal justice curriculum that would last for the next four months. Besides, I wasn't a quitter, and I was going to see this job through to the end. Therefore, not wanting to continue what I considered a fruitless discussion, I stood up and announced to Kristina that I was going to change my clothes and take her out to dinner. Turning toward the bedroom, I cocked my head to one side, indicating to her I was frustrated by her comments.

"Nicky?"

"Look, let's get ready to go. We'll drive to that hamburger and milkshake joint up on the mountain, the one with the view of the sunset. I know it's early, but by the time we get there it will be after five o'clock, okay? Maybe we can watch the sun as it sets over the water."

"Nicky?"

"I just need time to process what you ranted about, okay? Let me have a little breathing room, Kristina. Geeez, can't you just give me a . . ." My voice trailed off as I stormed away to change my shirt.

We might as well have stayed home that evening because the tension between us was as thick as curing concrete. To some degree, if I were being honest, my conscience was bothering me slightly. But every time I heard it, it sounded like Kristina's voice. The effect this had on my heart was identical to an alloy on iron—it hardened me even more. I knew I loved her. She was the love of my life. But she was changing . . . or was I changing? Regardless, we were changing, and I didn't like the direction we were heading, not one bit. I was never one to back away from conflict, especially if I believed I was in the right. So I wasn't about to avoid the required conversation with her. We would deal with this before the weekend was over. I had determined it would not be wise to launch into the heavy course load on Monday with a huge disagreement between us weighing me down.

After dinner, it was obvious that both of us were emotionally drained. So when we arrived home, we went straight to bed. Saturday was quiet and, frankly, offered a much needed respite from the taut marital atmosphere. I mowed the grass. She did the laundry. I fixed a broken door knob. She cleaned the bathrooms. In the afternoon we both took a nap; she slept on the living room sofa, and I napped on the recliner in our study. Later we readied ourselves to go to dinner at our friend's home.

Nearly ten years our senior, Arthur and Regina Rathbone are one of the friendliest couples we have ever known. We first met at church. Within six months, we began leading a Bible study on Wednesday evenings where Art and I took turns teaching the well-attended gathering.

We had scheduled this time with them today knowing that my studies during the months at the Academy would have to take priority over teaching the Bible study. Art and I would need to arrange our responsibilities accordingly. He was a dear friend, and one I knew would be more than willing to help.

Regina, or as we called her, Gina, and Kristina were the closest of friends. Some folks thought they were sisters. In many ways they were. They both had a kind yet direct way of communicating as well as a sincerity that put most folks at ease when they were around them. They were even similar in appearance. Needless to say, Kristina and I loved being around Art and Gina and would take the opportunity to spend time together whenever it presented itself. We considered them more than friends. They were family.

However, knowing Art and Gina and how well they knew us, I strongly suspected the tension between Kristina and I would soon be a topic of discussion at their dinner table. Shortly after Gina handed me the bowl of mashed potatoes, my suspicion was confirmed.

"So what's up with you two, Nick?" Gina asked in her direct manner, concern creasing her forehead.

"Nothing," I shrugged.

"Are you sure? I sense some friction or something between you guys. Everything, okay?" she inquired, glancing first at Kristina then back at me.

"Yeah, sure. How about you guys?" I asked just before shoving in a bite of mashed potatoes.

"It's his job," announced Kristina plainly.

"Oh, good grief," I muttered under my breath, with a mouth half full of the starchy mush. Shaking my head, I complained, "Really, Kristie?"

"Oh, come on, Nick," protested Kristina. "They know us like we are family. Gina could sense something was wrong."

"Actually, I could too, Nick, from the moment you guys walked through the door," added Art apologetically.

"I believe his new Ranger job is driving a wedge between us," Kristina stated adamantly. "He doesn't think so. But I see some rather disturbing changes in him."

"And I in you . . . sweetie pie," I sarcastically volleyed back.

"Do you guys see what I mean?" reacted Kristina. "He always throws it back in my face. Like it's all my fault or something."

"Well, you seem to be the one who has the problem with it," I remarked as I stuffed a fork full of meatloaf in my mouth.

"Look you two, if I may?" Art asked gently. "Gina and I have had more than our share of arguments . . ."

"Oh, this is more than an argument, Art!" exclaimed Kristina. "It's more like a crisis."

"What?! Really, Kristina? You are blowing this thing way out of proportion," I declared in a louder-than-polite volume.

"Nick?" Art quietly asked. "Kristina, you too, listen to what I have to say. And if you don't like it, that's okay. It's a free country. But if you would allow us, I think Gina and I could help you guys, okay? I mean, we've been around the block a few more times than you two."

"What block?" asked Kristina.

"The marriage block, dear," I explained with impatience. "Art's using a metaphor, Kristie."

"Come on you guys, calm down," pleaded Art. "Are you interested in what we have to say or not?"

Kristina and I slowly nodded while exchanging wary glances across the table.

"Good," smiled Art as he placed his hands gently upon the table. "First thing you need to know is this—you have an invisible enemy who is trying to destroy your marriage, and he will use whatever means necessary to do so, even a new job. He's the devil, and he hates marriage. I mean, he despises it with a passion and will do whatever it takes to destroy each and every marriage he can get his grubby paws on. He wants to annihilate as many marriages as possible."

"Why would he want to do that, Art?" I asked with a teaspoon of skepticism stirred in my cup of otherwise sincere inquiry.

"Because he knows marriage is the most important relationship on earth. That's why. There is no other relationship that has such far reaching effects. I'm not just referring to the union of husband and wife, but the impact that relationship has for many generations to come. Studies have shown that a marriage based on love and respect that lasts throughout the lifetimes of its partners tends to produce grown children who have relationships that endure as well. However, the marriages that have destructive tendencies or end in divorce, more than likely produce a similar result in their offspring. Look, the backbone of any nation is strong families. The anchor of the family is a healthy marriage. Our enemy knows this and therefore hates a good marriage. He understands this anchor has an overwhelming influence on many generations yet to come."

"We have a good marriage," I stated emphatically.

"I'm not saying you don't, Nick. I'm telling you, although you have an enemy, it is not one another. You two are on one side of the battle field, and he is on the other. He's so sly that he has you thinking that you're fighting each other. When actually, he's the wretched culprit. By the way, did you know this is how you develop a strong marriage?"

"How?" asked Kristina leaning forward.

"By passing through hard times together," replied Art with a smile. "You know, working through the labyrinth of all the various problems that arise in marriage. It's these very issues that make you stronger, less susceptible to our enemy's tricks. So don't get frustrated, Nick, with having to work through issues in your marriage. It's kind of like a complex math problem. There's a solution. It just takes time to discover and work through it. And Kristina, don't be afraid to give Nick a little room as he tries to figure out what God's saying to him. Remember, a watched pot never boils."

"I don't know, Art," confessed a doubtful Kristina. "How can you be so sure?"

Art nodded and stretched out his arm in his wife's direction. "Gina can answer that question better than me."

"If you love each other," ventured Gina, "you can make it through anything. Art and I have been married for over fifteen years, and we have seen some of the most difficult times a couple could ever see. We've experienced poverty and the heartache of losing a loved one. Art has lost his job twice, and I was critically ill for nearly a year. Early on, we even had a landlord kick us out on the street because of a misunderstanding. It hasn't been easy, and we have had our doubts, but we have never been hopeless. I mean, come on, Kristie. Could you see me married to anyone else but Art?"

The four of us erupted into laughter, which helped to break the ice that had permeated the dining room since we had arrived. As we quieted down, I turned to Art and asked a pointed question.

"Why do you think the devil hates marriage so much?"

"Because, Nick, it is the only visible example of the invisible marriage between our Lord Jesus Christ and His church. The enemy detests it. In reality, if you could see it, you guys aren't fighting against each other; you're actually battling the one who is absolutely determined to destroy your marriage. Look at this problem from that perspective, and I think you'll find yourselves on the path to your solution and the fog beginning to lift."

The very next morning at church, our pastor spoke about faith, using the eleventh chapter of Hebrews as his text. He explained how every one of the individuals in the chapter experienced physical hardships before their faith became evident to others. He also said that as long as times are easy, with no real problems or frustrations, it is difficult for anyone to tell if they are living by faith. "Only through hardship," he declared, "will your faith grow."

Kristina and I had agreed to head straight home after the church service. Once we had finished lunch, I sat down to watch some football on the television. Before long, she walked into the living room and sat down next to me.

"Nicky, I want you to know that I love and respect you no matter what you do for work. Well . . . almost anything. However, I really don't want this Ranger job to come between us anymore. I've prayed, and I am releasing it into our Father's hands. He knows way better than I do what you should do. All I ask is one thing."

"What's that, honey?" I asked turning to face her.

"That you promise you'll do your best to stay true to our God."

"My sweet Kristie, I promise I will do my best."

EIGHT

Thankfully, the first day at the Police Academy was primarily filled with registering for the appropriate courses, listening as the various instructors were introduced, and receiving all of the required equipment. Before releasing us to go home, nearly an hour early, our platoon sergeant, a tall, well-dressed man in his early forties with a neatly trimmed salt and pepper haircut and mustache to match, gave us strict instructions for everything that was required each and every day. He assured there would be no guess work as to the time of arrival, manner of dress, how we were to address him as well as minimum passing scores for each section of study, including physical fitness, driving skills, firearms, and personal survival skills. He introduced himself as Sergeant Strictman. He started his instruction like this:

"My name is Sergeant Strictman, and I will not tolerate any smart aleck antics in my academy. Do you understand?" This command, followed by the question became known as his mantra throughout our four months together as he made it a point to remind us of it several times each week.

"Just like you won't be given a second chance when you encounter a gunman," he admonished, "there are no second chances here either. If you receive a failing grade for any of the twenty-two sections, pick up your things and march yourself out the back door. Don't come crying to me to change your score—that will never happen. Any questions?"

Sitting in the second row from the back of this amphitheater, which served as our main classroom, I glanced around at my fellow cadets. There were nearly fifty of us, mostly men. I counted nine women, who all seemed very attentive to our sergeant's direction. Taking my que from them, I too focused on Sergeant Strictman's very straightforward monologue.

"Look, you're all rookies. Actually, you're less than rookies, so your opinion doesn't matter one iota. Therefore, keep it to yourself. I don't want to hear it. I've been a cop nearly twenty years. Over a dozen of those years, I patrolled in South Chicago before taking a position here in the valley. I attended this California Police Academy more than seven years ago. I've been shot twice, been in more fights than I can remember, and was almost run over by a tractor trailer, which destroyed my squad car. The last four years I was undercover in a motorcycle gang until I took this assignment as your Academy Platoon Sergeant. I haven't seen it all, but I've seen a lot more than you have. So shut up, study hard, and wait until after graduation before getting drunk. Now, get out of here. I'll see you tomorrow morning, eight o'clock sharp."

Gathering up my books, I stuffed them into my knapsack and headed for the bookstore on campus. I hadn't yet purchased the two final books for the academy: Vehicle and Traffic Laws and Black's Law Dictionary. The latter is a monstrous volume originally published in the 1890s. We were informed that its definitions would be absolutely essential in passing a number of sections involving law.

Walking out of the bookstore as I was admiring my new, albeit very expensive purchase, I was approached by a slender man of medium height. He was dressed in the police uniform of the city in which I lived. He told me he too was a cadet in the same class and was wondering if I would be agreeable to carpooling together. After determining we lived less than a mile apart, I concurred with his proposal. He then introduced me to the woman standing next to him.

"This is Sasha Verbinski. She and I were hired at the same time. She lives around the corner from me. We could all take turns driving if that's okay with you."

"What's your name?" I asked.

"Oh, sorry about that. I'm William Yamamoto."

"Okay, William. Uh, does everyone call you Bill?"

"No, everyone calls me William. I was raised in a strict home. We didn't use nicknames. My parents migrated to the States from Japan when they were young and insisted we maintain our culture at home."

"Why did they name you William then?"

"Because when I'm not home, they wanted me to blend into the American culture."

"Makes sense to me. Okay, well, Sasha and William, I have been assigned a District vehicle by ITSMUD for the purpose of driving to and from the Academy. I'm sure it would be fine if you guys rode with me since I'm traveling to and from the Academy anyway."

"I'd be happy to pay for my share of the gas," urged Sasha with a smile.

"Me too," agreed William.

"That won't be necessary. They gave me a credit card for filling up the tank. So let me have your addresses, and I'll pick you up in the morning. I'll leave my house at six-fifteen, so you guys be waiting outside, okay?"

"I think maybe you should leave your house at six," advised William. "That would give us plenty of time to be on the freeway by six-fifteen. I don't ever want to be even one second late."

"Okay," I nodded. "That's fine. I'll be at your house first, William. Then, Sasha, we'll swing by your place on our way to the freeway on-ramp."

The first week of the Academy was incredibly hectic. I left our home at six o'clock every morning. After picking up my couple of carpool compadres, we drove the hour and a half to the campus. Inspection and then an hour of drills started at eight o'clock sharp. One minute late and the cadet received a demerit. Three demerits and that person would be kicked out of this Academy class. Brutal, but just. Each cadet was dressed in his or her full uniform with gun belt and all appropriate equipment including their service weapon, minus the bullets. Bullets were sternly forbidden in all activities except when practicing shooting at the range.

Our sergeant took the time to look each of us over very carefully every morning. All leather had to be black, polished, and free of smudges. All brass had to be shiny without the tiniest hint of dullness. The uniform had to be clean, pressed, creased, and without any loose threads. Hair, including facial hair, was to be neatly trimmed and combed. No exceptions. If Sergeant Strictman found something that wasn't up to standard, the cadet was firmly admonished. If he couldn't rectify the deficient item promptly, he was given a written warning. Everyone was allowed only two warnings. The third warning was actually a demerit. I made it my habit to always carry a tiny folded rag in one pocket with a minute amount of shoe polish on it. In another pocket I stowed a rag with a tiny smear of brass polish. And I was never without my Swiss Army knife, the one with the little scissors.

Once he finished inspections, then came the marching—the endless marching under the hot, summer sun. Some days it felt like we marched until noon. In reality, it was usually for no more than an hour or so.

The remainder of the morning was spent in the amphitheater classroom studying various topics like the Penal Code, Search and Seizure, Vehicle Traffic Code, and Officer Survival. Each subject was taught by a different instructor. After a quick lunch, we headed over to the gymnasium for practical instruction in hand to hand combat and how to use grappling techniques as well as the baton. This was the first time I had ever used handcuffs. We practiced all of these things daily. Our fellow cadets played the roles of the bad guys. At times, I got to be a bad guy too.

It was actually rather fun because I knew the guns weren't loaded. Besides, who doesn't like to be mischievous on occasion, especially for a good cause?

Late Friday afternoon, Sergeant Strictman commanded everyone to return to the classroom for a few special announcements before dismissal for the weekend. Being anxious to head home, we all hurried to the amphitheater. Shortly after everyone was settled in their seats, he spoke up.

"Ladies and gentlemen, it's my duty to inform you that we have had our first expulsion. Cadet Frederick McGallen walked into our hand to hand combat practice with his service weapon loaded . . . with real bullets. That's right; he had live ammunition in his gun. This is an inexcusable violation, and he was instantaneously removed from the Academy. Folks, do not, and I repeat, do not ever put live rounds in your weapons except at the range and always under the supervision of the weapons instructors. Do I make myself clear enough?!"

"Yes, sir!" shouted the entire class.

"I can't hear you!"

"Yes, sir!" we bellowed even louder.

"Good. I'm glad we understand each other. Let's have Frederick be the only loss from this class." Sergeant Strictman paused and made eye contact with each of us before continuing.

"Now, one more very important matter before you leave for the weekend. Monday you will need to elect the officers for your academy class. This weekend give some thought to who you think would make a good president, secretary, and treasurer. At lunch on Monday, I will accept nominations. Later that day, you will elect your officers. Any questions?"

A cadet in the front row raised his hand. The sergeant pointed at him and nodded.

"Uh, Sergeant Strictman, sir, you didn't mention a Vice-President."

"Yes, how very observant of you, Cadet Wilson. If only you were as attentive to the appearance of your uniform each morning," the sergeant mocked with a grin. "That's because the candidate for President who receives the second highest number of votes will be the Vice-President. Any further questions? No? Good. We'll see everybody Monday morning."

The sergeant looked around at our attentive faces as he paused for a couple of seconds. Then he barked in a loud voice, "Now get out of here!"

The drive home was unusually quiet. Sasha was sprawled out on the back seat asleep. I knew she was sleeping because I could hear her snoring. William sat up front and had books spread across his lap, trying hard to review what our instructors had taught us today. It seemed to me that he loved to study. Don't get me wrong, I enjoyed learning new things too. But for me it was a means to an end. For William, studying was the goal. He gave the impression he was happiest when he had his nose buried in a textbook. In contrast, I mostly enjoyed learning by doing.

Today, however, I sat quietly behind the steering wheel, pondering my chaotic life. Keeping my eyes on the road, I couldn't stop thinking about Kristina, who was the main topic in my musings. I had been leaving each morning before she had awakened and arrived home each evening late for dinner. Every night the hours after I had eaten had been consumed by my studies until nearly midnight. I commandeered the study. Kristina silently sat in our dining room correcting papers from her third graders. Then she headed for the bathtub just before retiring, usually around ten o'clock. Our marriage, our lives, seemed adrift and unfortunately not in the same direction. In earlier years, when we had argued about our disagreements, we would spend whatever time necessary to find a mutual resolution. Now, we didn't even talk. It was more than uncomfortable. It was disheartening.

"What're you worried about, Nick?" asked a cheerful voice from the backseat.

"I thought you were sleeping," I smiled, peeking at Sasha in the rearview mirror.

"I was. Glad I did too. Man, this week has taken it out of me. Hey, you guys hungry?"

"Sure. What did you have in mind?" I asked as I turned to see Sasha leaning on the back of the front seat.

"Mexican."

"Works for me. How about you, William?"

"What?"

"We're going to stop for a quick bite at a Mexican place. You in, buddy?" I questioned as I gently slapped him on the shoulder.

"No," retorted William. "I've got way too much studying to do. I really need to get on home."

"Ah, come on, Willie," chided Sasha playfully. "You really don't have time for a taco? Really?"

"No thanks."

"Sorry, Sasha," I shrugged. "How about a raincheck?"

"Sure. Or . . . how about the drive through at Taco Bell?" she chirped from the back seat.

"Where?" I laughed.

"Right over there," she cheered, leaning over the front seat pointing to my left.

"Perfect!" I sang out, swinging my head around to see her face to face.

"Ah, come on you guys. I've got a lot of studying tonight," complained William.

"Only take a second, Cadet Yamamoto," I chuckled. "We'll be noshing tacos before you have a chance to finish that next chapter."

The remainder of the drive home was filled with the sounds of munching and crunching as Sasha and I enjoyed our impromptu pre-dinner. Feeling like most of my life was overly scheduled and regimented, I welcomed this spontaneous moment and the relief it brought from the dreary thoughts that were bombarding my mind—Kristina and the sad state of our declining marriage.

"So, Nick," quizzed a smiling Sasha from behind me. "You never told me what you're so worried about?"

"Who says I'm worried about something?"

"Nobody. But you were rubbing your forehead. You always do that when you worry. I've seen you do it half a dozen times in the last week."

"Yeah, right."

"No. You do," she replied, once again leaning forward. "I know because right after you do that you usually say what's bothering you. You've done it the same way every time. You always use your left hand. Your thumb rests against your temple and your fingers rub back and forth across your head just above your eyebrows."

"Oh, really?"

"Yeah. Like yesterday on the way home, you were rubbing your forehead. Then you blurted out that you couldn't remember the Miranda Rights? That's when William here, Dr. Brainiac, started quoting, 'You have the right to remain silent . . .' Remember?"

"Hmmm . . ."

"So what are you worried about?"

"Oh, just thinking about life I guess."

"Do you want to talk about it?"

"Nah, not really."

"Okay. Well, if you ever want to talk about it, I'm all ears."

"Thanks, Sasha. I appreciate that."

"Sure. Anytime, Nick."

With both hands on the steering wheel and my eyes focused straight ahead, my left hand had even more of a sense of urgency to rub my brow. I didn't dare glance in the rear view mirror. It felt like all the air had been sucked out of the car, so I rolled down my window far enough to allow some fresh oxygen to waft in. The silence in the car only emphasized the last words spoken. I wanted to say something, anything, but couldn't find a topic. Hoping William would break the awkward intermission, I, not so subtlety, knocked one of his books on the floor. He picked it up without even an acknowledgement that I had done so. Just then, the feminine voice from the backseat spoke up.

"Hey, William, get your face out of that book. I have a great idea."

"Huh?" queried a weary eyed William from behind his round framed glasses.

"I think we should nominate Nick for our Academy President. Don't you think that's a great idea?"

"Actually, Sasha, now that you mention it, I think that's a really great idea. Nick, you would make an excellent President. In fact, with your permission, Sasha, I mean, since it was your idea, I would be happy and honored to nominate him on Monday. What do you guys think?"

"Wow, I'm not sure," I responded, feeling a mixture of honor and apprehension.

"You'd be perfect for it, Nick," voiced a smiling Sasha, once again leaning on the front seat. "Say you'll do it, Nick. Come on, what do you think?"

"Well, I'm not closed to the idea. But I'm not sure I'm open to it either," I stated while rubbing my forehead. "Give me the weekend to think it over, okay? I'll let you know Monday morning. How's that sound?"

"Works for me," agreed Sasha while William, whose nose was back in his book, nodded his agreement.

With the exciting proposition of being elected President and the ever growing, distant silence between Kristina and me, I hardly got any studying done the entire weekend. Every time I began to make some progress my mind would wander. At one point, I found myself composing an acceptance speech. Finally, late Sunday afternoon, I asked Kristina if she would like to go for a walk. We strolled for almost an hour, meandering through the neighborhood park. As we approached a bench where we've sat and talked many times before, I reached across and gently grasped her hand, urging her to sit down. We chitchatted for twenty minutes about all the peripheral subjects, but hadn't yet broached the elephant in the park—our relationship. After a pause of more than a minute, I turned toward her and began chipping away at the ice.

"Kristina, you are the love of my life. You are more than what I ever imagined a wife, a life partner, could be. I thank you from the bottom of my heart for these years you have been my precious wife . . ."

"Please don't," she interrupted.

"Please don't what?" I asked softly.

"Please don't say what you were going to say."

"Kristie?"

"Nick, stop it. Okay, just stop it. I can't do this anymore."

"What are you saying?"

"I'm saying . . . or, at least I'm trying to say that I can't live like this."

"Like what?"

"Oh, stop it, Nick. I want . . ."

Her pause was unbearable. So I coaxed, "Kristina, what are you saying?"

"I want . . . no, I need the old Nick back. The Nick I married. I don't want to separate. I don't want a divorce. I want my Nicky back."

"And I want my Kristie back," I pleaded with as gentle a voice as I have ever mustered.

Evidently, those were the wrong words to use at that moment because she fiercely glared at me as if I had said I hated her mother. Then she jumped up without saying a word and stomped away toward home. I know that's where she went because I followed her from a distance. Once home, she headed to our bathroom. I heard the tub water running. That evening, I slept on the recliner. Monday morning couldn't arrive soon enough.

Leaving the house early, I dropped by the doughnut shop for breakfast before picking up first William and then Sasha. Before we had even made it onto the freeway, they were both peppering me with questions regarding my willingness to be the president of our class. I told them if they thought I would make a good president, I would be happy to run for the position. They both seemed very pleased with my choice and started planning their strategy immediately.

After lunch, Sergeant Strictman took his place behind the podium in our classroom. First, he announced the rules of the election. Then, he clearly delineated the responsibilities of each office. Finally, he opened the floor for nominations. Seven hands went up including William's and Sasha's. I sat quietly as Sergeant Strictman pointed to each, one by one, writing down the names of the nominees for president. All totaled there were four names put forth; mine was one of them. He did the same process for the other offices as well. He handed the list of names to an assistant, who left the classroom right away. During her absence, short speeches were given by each candidate. Returning twenty minutes later, the assistant had ballots prepared and ready for the election. It was time to vote.

The ballots were passed out and collected. Then Sergeant Strictman dismissed us for our next class, Officer Survival Skills. If we had been tested on what we had learned that day, I would have failed miserably because all I could think about was the outcome of the election. Promptly following class, we made our way, donned in running attire, out to the track to be timed in the one and a half mile run. Our Physical Training instructor introduced himself as Sergeant Jack Conrad, PT Coach. If he was as intense as he sounded, we were going to have an entire summer of demanding physical training. Sergeant Conrad was short and stocky with a flattop haircut that was high and tight. Not only did he look and sound like a Marine Corps Drill Instructor, but later we learned he had indeed served as one. He was living proof of the old adage "Once a Marine, always a Marine.'

This first mile and a half run would establish our base time. At the end of the academy, we would be timed again. That time would be used as our final grade for the run. A recording over eleven minutes meant the cadet had failed and would not graduate. I knew then and there what I would be doing during my free time on the weekends—running. Studying and running, that was my life. It had to be. It was imperative, or I would fail and lose my Ranger job. There was not one thing we cadets did in the academy that was not tested, timed, or judged, and then either recorded as a passing or failing grade. To me, failure was not an option. The pressure was extreme and ever present.

After finishing our timed run, we were given ten minutes to recover. Then we were herded to the obstacle course. Viewing it from the starting line, I thought it looked moderately intimidating.

"Eighteen separate obstacles," shouted Sergeant Conrad. "You will be timed each and every week just like the mile and a half run. Except with the obstacle course, you only have three minutes. Any time above three minutes is considered a failing time. By the way, for you more athletic types, the course record is one minute forty-four and three tenths seconds. Any takers?"

Leaning over toward William I whispered, "Man, I would love to break that record."

"For those of you interested," continued Sergeant Conrad, "I will post the ten fastest times in both events at the end of class each week. But for today, those cadets with last names beginning with the letter A and continuing through the letter K line up here. Everyone else, head to the weight room for strength training."

After class William and I, as well as several others, checked the PT bulletin board for our standings. I was gratified to be among the top ten in the run and top five in the obstacle course, yet disappointed that I was not first in either. "More things to work on," I mumbled under my breath. "Where will I find the time?"

We were instructed to wait on the bleachers in the gymnasium once we had showered and changed. It was nearing five o'clock, and I was tired, sore, and anxious to be heading home. After the last cadet hustled in and took his seat, the door across the shiny, hardwood floor swung wide open, and in strode Sergeant Strictman holding a single sheet of paper.

"Here we go," whispered William. "Good luck."

Up to that moment, the election had slipped my mind in the midst of all the strenuous physical activity. Once again, it was quickly brought to the front and center of my attention. My heart was pounding too. I wasn't sure if it was because of all the running or this pending announcement. I decided both were probably having their effect on me.

In his typically direct style, Sergeant Strictman stopped abruptly and announced, "Ladies and gentlemen, I have here the results of today's election for this academy's officers. Treasurer, will be, Lisa Johnson. Secretary, Bart Wendell. Vice-President, Wayne Whitson. And you're new President is . . ."

Glancing down at the floor, I closed my eyes, reluctant to hear the results. Sergeant Strictman's pause lasted entirely too long. After a few seconds, I looked up to find him gazing at me just as he declared the new President's name.

"Ranger Nicolas Roberts."

NINE

Williiam slapped me on the back as many of the cadets stretched out their hands in my direction to congratulate me. Frankly, the announcement had come as such a surprise that I was at a loss for words other than to acknowledge my gratitude. Several cadets called for me to give a speech. The whole scene appeared to be getting a bit out of control when Sergeant Strictman brought us back to reality.

"There will be no speeches. You are dismissed for the day. Newly elected officers, meet me in my office in five minutes."

Four minutes later, Lisa, Bart, Wayne, and I were standing by the door to his office. Each of us wore a nervous smile as our eyes darted from one face to another. Within a minute, Sergeant Strictman marched down the corridor, unlocked the door to his office, and invited us inside. The room was fairly close to how I had imagined it, stark and very simple. His moderate sized desk sat with the chair facing the door. A bookcase and a window donned one wall while two chairs, above which hung a chalk board, occupied the space on the opposite side. Asking Bart to bring two chairs from the neighboring office, Sergeant Strictman ordered us to sit down.

"Alright, you four, you're the officers, the leaders, and I expect you to act like leaders. You're not cruise directors. You are officers of a para-military academy. No shenanigans will be tolerated whatsoever on my watch. You're cowboys herding cattle, understand? Like the cops that police the cops. That's you four. Any questions?"

The room was silent except for the sound of Wayne clearing his throat.

"Question, Cadet Whitson?" asked the sergeant in his direct manner.

"Uh, um . . . uh, no, sir."

"Good. I'm glad we understand one another," stated the sergeant with a grin. "Now," he continued as he sat on the corner of his desk, arms folded across his chest, "there are some responsibilities you need to know about."

The four of us simultaneously pulled out paper and pen to jot down what the sergeant would say next. He spoke deliberately and succinctly for the next ten minutes. As abruptly as our meeting had started, in the same manner it wrapped up. After dinner, I broke the news to Kristina while we were sitting in our living room.

"Guess what?"

"What?"

"I was elected President of the Police Academy today."

"That's nice, Nick."

"Yeah, Sergeant Strictman told me I garnered more than sixty percent of the votes."

"Good for you, Nick. You must be very proud."

"Well, I don't know about proud, but I am very pleased. I mean, think about it, me a president. Who would have ever thought, right? All I ever really wanted to do was be the best carpenter I could possibly be. Now, here I am the leader of a group of police officers."

"I've always told you, Nick, you never give yourself enough credit. I think you could do anything you put your mind toward trying to do. I'm happy for you."

"Thanks, Kristie. That means a lot to me."

It appeared to me from that evening forward, Kristina and I started to get along a little better. We didn't argue at all, and she never mentioned the whole faith versus job topic. It seemed to me we were getting to a place of understanding in our marriage. But I would come to find out later, she thought we were drifting apart. It's such a curious thing, isn't it? How one member of the same relationship can think all is well while at the exact same moment the other member is miserable. How can these things be?

About two months later on a Saturday morning, I sat down with Art at a local coffee shop. We laughed and joked about life as our conversation floated from one topic to another. It took a more serious turn, however, after he mentioned he hadn't seen me in church for several weeks. He also expressed concern over when I would return to teaching the Bible study. Instead of trying to defend myself, I was surprised to find my mind occupied with how my life was just a series of never ending problems.

My first major crisis had been the lack of work as a carpenter. It was more than being unemployed. It was an identity crisis, not to mention the bills that had been piling up. I fixed the unemployment issue and the money portions of the problem, but the identity part only grew worse when I began selling first aid products. Fortunately, the identity crisis was resolved with my new Ranger job, but then came the problem between Kristina and me. As soon as that appeared to be solved, Art brought up the topic of the lack of my attendance at our church and Bible study. All the while, I've had the daily pressure of knowing if I were to flunk one class at the Academy, I would not only be kicked out, but also be fired from my Ranger position, which would create a whole new set of problems in my life. Shuddering to think where my reputation would be if I were expelled as the President of the Academy, I slowly shook my head as I stared at the coffee shop floor. A grimace must have washed across my face because Art tapped me on the shoulder, interrupting my nightmarish daydream and brought me back to the current problem at hand.

"Nick, you still with me, brother?"

"What? Yeah, why?"

"I was asking when you thought you'd be back to church and the Bible study. You never answered me. You kind of zoned out or something."

"Yeah, I was just thinking."

"About what?"

"Just stuff. You know, my studies and junk like that."

"Have a lot on your mind, eh, Nick?"

"You have no idea, Art. I'm so busy I can't see straight."

"Talk to me, my brother."

"Oh, it's not like that. It's more of what is filling up my mind than what is actually happening in my life. It used to be so much simpler. I went to work, built things, and came home. Kristina and I would have dinner together and sit and talk for hours. It was perfect, at least for us anyway. Then I'd get up the next morning and repeat the whole process again. I know it may sound boring, but it wasn't because it was a simple structure that gave us plenty of time to ponder the really important things in life. Now, it's like, ponder schmonder, what's that? I couldn't tell you the last time she and I had a deep conversation, other than arguing about something, and in my opinion that's not conversing. You know what I mean?"

"I know precisely where you are, Nick."

"You do?"

"Yeah. A number of years ago, Gina and I passed through a similar season. I was working for a big company trying to climb the corporate ladder. Man, I tell you what, brother, I was giving it my all—late nights, special projects, taking extra assignments, and trying to jump over others to obtain the next position higher. I ate, drank, and dreamed about my job. I wanted the money, the prestige, and the stuff it would get me. We had a nice house, nice car, nice clothes, and we went to nice places to eat, to travel, and to party."

"Wow, I didn't know that about you, Art. I thought you had always been an electrician."

145

"I wish I had. But late one evening on our way home from a corporate dinner party, I glanced over at Gina, who was asleep in the passenger seat of our luxury sports car. Something at that very moment hit me like a one ton granite block."

"What was it?" I was leaning forward because this was sounding so astonishingly similar to my own situation.

"I realized the beautiful, sweet, precious woman I had married was sitting right there next to me, but I didn't even know her anymore. She looked the same on the outside, but we had drifted apart on the inside. I remember thinking, 'How in the world did this ever happen?' I mean, Nick, I really had enjoyed being with her. I loved her personality. I loved her mannerisms and her goofiness. I even loved her serious side too. I had loved her enough to marry her—to commit my entire life to her . . . 'in the presence of God and many witnesses.' Then there we were, just a few years later, and I felt like we were more distant than when we had first met. I couldn't understand how this could have happened."

"Wow, Art, I think you just described Kristie and me."

"Really?"

"Yeah, sadly it's true."

"Do you want to know what I did to solve our problem?"

"Yeah. Absolutely."

"I quit my job, Nick."

"Whaaat?!"

"Yes, as strange as it sounds, that's what I did. It was the best decision I have ever made."

"How can you say that?"

"Priorities, my brother. Priorities."

"What's that supposed to mean?"

"Nick, listen to me very carefully. God designed us humans to function under a set of guidelines. Don't get me wrong. We're not like members of the animal kingdom. They are ruled by instincts. We have a free will to choose what we will and will not do. However, seeing that He created us, He has certain, shall we say, recommendations if we want to live in harmony with His plan for our lives. And an essential, elementary ingredient to that plan is having the right priorities. You can ignore them if you choose. I mean, you are free to do as you please, but if you ignore them, you will suffer some consequences."

"Like what?"

"Well, look at the stress you're under and the distance between you and Kristina or folks at church for that matter. You're starting to lose touch with people who really care for you. Perhaps you don't think that's a big deal now. But give it a year or two, and you'll be miserable. We need fellowship. It's in our human makeup to love others and to be loved by them. Our Father in Heaven created us that way on purpose. No man is a lone tree standing out in the storm of life."

"So what are these priorities?"

"That's easy. God is first and foremost. Second is family, and the top priority within the family is the marriage. Marriage is the anchor of the family. Third, and it's a distant third, is your job. Everything else, like hobbies, sports, vacations, entertainment, and other activities follow behind.

Get these lined up right, Nick, and you will see an immediate and vast improvement in your life. Especially up there between your ears."

"I can't quit my job."

"I didn't mention a word about you quitting your job. That's between you and God . . . and Kristina, of course. Perhaps you need to discern if it's the job that's causing you problems. Maybe it's something else altogether. Pray about it. God will make it clear to you. And if you don't understand, ask Him again. He'll help you comprehend. But here's a hint: check the level of unity in your marriage."

"What do you mean by that?"

"I mean, if you are experiencing disharmony in your marriage, you most likely have something out of alignment with your relationship with our Lord. It's like that time you injured your back playing football at the church retreat. You discovered it was some kind of misalignment in your spine, remember? You could hardly walk. Well, it's kind of like that. Your back being misaligned had created some difficulty in your ability to function in other areas too."

"Yeah, I can see that."

"And I'll mention one more clue. If you notice you're having an increased number of opportunities to make wrong choices, it's highly probable that at some point you reached a fork in your road and took the wrong path. My advice, my dear brother, is to backtrack to the fork and make a course correction. However, if you're not completely convinced, sit down in a quiet place, and ask God to show you. He loves you, Nick, and He's always more than happy to help."

Taking Art's advice to heart, I stopped at an overlook on the way home from the coffee shop to think and pray. It's one of my favorite spots to sit and ponder life. It's just off a quiet road, a sort of long-cut route back home. I hopped out of my car and stood with one foot on the guardrail. The view to the north was spectacular. The lake, more than a hundred yards below, reflected the mountains on the other side, including one higher peak that remains snowcapped most of the year. After settling my heart, I prayed. I didn't feel anything. It felt as though the heavens were made of brass, and my feeble flicker of a prayer was barely warming the surface.

A bit frustrated, I headed down the trail to the lake's edge. Having hiked this path many times before, I felt free to let my mind roam because my feet knew just where to step along the twists and turns. The trail, slightly under a mile long, ended at the base of two massive boulders, half submerged and adjacent to the shoreline. The challenge of scrambling to the top was way less hazardous than the feat of getting down would be. Knowing the tricky moves by heart, I ascended the granite ball with ease and took my seat atop its airy summit. Again, I tried to pray. Fumbling through a few half-hearted phrases, I wasn't getting anywhere, so I decided to give up. I wasn't really sure I wanted to know what God thought about my situation anyway. Besides, it was delightfully peaceful on my stony perch. Why should I ruin the quiet with wrestling through a prayer?

Leaning back on my hands with my face turned fully toward the hospitality of the beguiling sun, I closed my eyes and let my body give in to gravity. Laid out, basking in the entire experience, I could feel myself drifting off to sleep. The extent of tranquility I sensed at that moment was so captivating that I determined to make this part of my weekend ritual for years to come. Cool air coupled with warm sunshine has always been my favorite weather. The musk of the dry summer grasses mixed with the sweet perfume of the pine trees wafted upon me as a soothing aromatic balm. The many and varied sounds of the song birds in the trees were most pleasing to my ears. Their melodies were broken only by the occasional distant call of the Mallards, gliding gracefully in the middle of the lake. I was in heaven.

Just at the point of being not quite asleep yet no longer wide awake, I heard a car door slam shut close to where I had parked my car. Then I heard another door shut, and another, and another. Soon my sanctuary of peace and rest was inundated by a tsunami of teenage voices moving along the path through the forest and toward my two boulders. As the voices got closer to my haven, they got louder. Before I knew it, there were more than a dozen bathing-suit-clad high schoolers scrambling up both rocks and jumping off the front side into the deeper water below. A distance, I determined, of about twenty-five to thirty feet. I further surmised it was because of this height that each and every one of the plummeting aquanauts either yelled or screamed, depending on their gender, for the less than two seconds it took gravity to deliver them to their all-too-short-lived, watery necropolis. No sooner did they resurrect with a shout from the depths of their plunge, than they would individually swim over to the beach, climb the boulder, and repeat the whole sequence over again. This was all done to the delight of their noisily cheering friends. I'm sure to them it was good, clean fun. But to me, in my interrupted state of tranquility, it was extremely annoying.

After being dripped upon several times, I decided it was time to leave my once quiet retreat and head home. Gingerly climbing down the back of the larger of the two boulders, I slipped on the now wet surface and completed an awkward back-flip with a one and a half twist, finishing with a belly flop. I must have landed it perfectly because the fans, all of which were youth, roared with a cheer and applauded their hearty appreciation. Hastily struggling to my feet in the chest deep water, I took several bows acknowledging the sarcastic adoration. While I checked myself to assure nothing was damaged, one of the young rascals, who obviously had been stationed as a watchman, shouted that the cops were approaching by boat. As quickly as the group had arrived, they disappeared. Other than being soaking wet, my serene sanctuary had suddenly reappeared.

Isn't it interesting how your inner disposition can make all the difference at moments like these? A few minutes ago, I felt as if I were in heaven. Now, I was aggravated and just wanted to leave. Truthfully, the source of my irritation had departed, but the internal noise was still present. I really dislike that, don't you? I mean, why can't I change as fast on the inside as the circumstances can change on the outside?

Regardless, I was frustrated, wet, embarrassed, and ready to go home. Being a mere twenty yards from the beach,

I started slowly wading toward it. I snatched my old Atlanta Braves baseball cap out of the lake and slapped it onto my soaked head. As I snugged it down, more water came draining down around my shoulders and chest from its circumference. Just then, I heard the loud speaker from the patrol boat that had been racing in my direction pursuing those juvenile swimming criminals.

"Stop right where you are!" emanated the command from approximately one hundred yards away. "Put your hands in the air and keep them where I can see them."

"Oh good grief," I muttered. "I can see the headline in tomorrow's paper. 'President of Police Academy Arrested in Aquatic Crime Spree.'"

The boat slowed as it approached me from behind. I was gazing into the sky in hopes that this was all simply a bad dream, and I would soon awaken still laying in the sunshine on the crest of my boulder sanctuary. Shaking my head in disgust and unbelief, I heard the boat's motor shut off. Next, an unamplified voice I was sure I recognized, chuckled at my plight. Glancing over my shoulder, I viewed a neatly pressed ITSMUD Ranger uniform. The Ranger had a huge smile upon his face.

"Nick, what on earth are you doing here, man? Don't you know it's a crime to swim in a drinking water reservoir in the state of California?" he chided with a sarcastic tone to his gleeful voice.

"Phil, I was minding my own business lying in the sun when this group of kids showed up. They started climbing up my boulder and jumping off into the water."

"Yeah, I know," chuckled Phil. "I was just giving you a hard time. Stephen and Rob are at the overlook writing them all warnings. How'd you end up in the lake?"

"Oh, you're not going to believe this," I complained as I turned for the beach.

"Let me guess," interrupted Phil. "You slipped on the wet rock while you were climbing down."

"Yeah, how'd you know?"

"I've done it a couple times myself . . . once in uniform," he laughed. "Yeah, it took a while to live that one down at WHQ. Hey, pull me in."

Phil threw me his bowline, and I drew his boat to the shore. Reaching over, he dropped the anchor on the sandy beach and jumped out of the speedboat. Then he called into WHQ using his walkie-talkie and some ten code numbers that I wasn't yet familiar with. After gazing up at the overlook, he glanced back at me.

"So how's it going in the Academy? I heard you were elected President."

"Yeah, it was kind of a shock."

"Well you're doing us proud. Keep up the good work, Nick. We Rangers are looked at as the misfits of the law enforcement community. Any good PR can really help our image."

"Thanks. I'm doing my best, but sometimes it's really tough. You know what I mean?"

"Yeah, believe it or not, I actually found it more difficult than my boot camp in the Marines. Way too much studying. The memorization stuff about killed me. But I think a lot can depend on your Academy Platoon Sergeant too. Who'd you get?"

"His name is Strictman. He was an undercover guy from over in the valley."

"Shelly Strictman?"

"I don't know his first name. He tells us to call him Sergeant Strictman or Sir."

"Yeah, that sounds like Shelly. I wouldn't call him that though. He's kind of sensitive. Or, at least he used to be. You see, his real name is Shelby Strictman. He was in the same Academy class with me back when I first got out of the Marines and went to work for the State Police. One day our Academy Platoon Sergeant was doing roll-call, and he accidentally mispronounced Shelby. It sounded like he said Shelly. From that day forward, we called him Shelly. He hated it, which gave us all the more reason to use it."

"Well, I won't be calling him that."

"No, I wouldn't advise it. That is, if you want to graduate."

Phil and I talked for almost an hour. It was really good to see him and a reminder of where all of this training was eventually leading. After shaking hands and shoving off his patrol boat, I turned and started up the path toward the overlook. My clothes felt nearly dry by the time I arrived at my car. The group of would be thrill seekers were long gone as well as Stephen and Rob. I stood quietly with one foot once again resting on the guard rail as I gazed across the lake below. The sun was much nearer the horizon than when I had first begun my Saturday futile foray for tranquility. I had all but forgotten my feelings of annoyance on the boulder as well as the angst of my earlier conversation with Art.

That is until I arrived home.

TEN

No sooner had our kitchen door shut behind me, than Kristina entered from the living room. Her arms were folded across her chest, and though many would not have considered her expression a frown, I knew better. Her face definitely revealed the anger percolating somewhere on the inside. She wouldn't admit it was anger; no, she would say she was merely frustrated. However, she would expect me to recognize that she was fit to be tied. My second sign that trouble was brewing was that her hair was pulled up as if she was readying herself to go out on the town. The final clue was that she was wearing a full length slip, the kind she puts on under her best dresses. When my mind began putting all the pieces together, I figured I had goofed up big time. Preparing myself for the unavoidable interrogation, I smiled sheepishly.

"Where on earth have you been all day?" was the first in what I was sure was going to be a long line of questions. "Do you have any idea what time it is?"

"Well, I, uh . . ."

"Art told me you guys left the coffee shop at eleven thirty."

"That sounds about right. Wait a second. You called Art?"

"I was worried."

"Really," I stated plainly, realizing her phone call was indicative of more than just concern for my well-being.

"Yes. Well, Nick?" With arms still crossed, her fingers on one hand were rattling off a rhythm on the opposite elbow. I knew if I didn't present a legitimate excuse soon her opposing foot would start tapping out a similar beat.

"Uh, honey . . ."

"Nick. Listen to me. You left here at nine-thirty this morning. It is now quarter after four. Where have you been the entire day?"

"It's a long story."

"Are you still taking me out to dinner tonight? Or did you forget we have reservations at six?"

"That's tonight? I mean, of course I am. I have over an hour before we are supposed to leave. Right? I'll be ready on time."

Her foot was tapping now. "Nick, we have dinner reservations in the city at six o'clock. We need to leave here in an hour at the latest. I know you can get ready that quick. What I need to know is—where have you been all day!?"

"I was at the lake."

"What? Why? Nicolas Harrison Roberts, you tell me the truth. Are you messing around with someone?"

"What? Are you crazy? I have a hard enough time keeping one woman happy. I'm sure not foolish enough to try two. That's ridiculous. Put that thought completely out of your mind."

"Nick!?" she stomped her foot.

I cautiously walked across the patterned linoleum floor of our kitchen and stood close to Kristina, so I could reach out and gently hold her hands. Looking into her worried eyes, I slowly shook my head.

"Honey, look . . ."

"What's that smell?" She interrupted. "Nick, you stink to high heaven."

"Well, I fell in the lake."

"What? How did you do that?"

"There was this gang of kids. No, I mean, I was lying on this boulder . . ."

"Is this going to be a long story?"

"Yeah, kind of. I mean, it did take from eleven-thirty to quarter after four."

"Well then, you can tell me while we're getting ready."

"So you believe me, Kristie?"

"Well, I haven't heard the whole story yet. But from what I've heard . . . and smelled so far, and knowing you the way I do, I think it may be plausible."

The rest of the evening we enjoyed sincere conversation mixed with tender affection and humor. Kristina and I used words and did things that we hadn't said or done in weeks. As I was drifting off to sleep with her in my arms, a quiet thought floated across my mind. My eyes flashed wide open as a smile gradually broke across my face.

"Maybe God heard my prayer at the lake after all," I whispered. "Thank you, dear Father."

The final five to six weeks of the Academy were brutal. The hours were long, the studies increasingly more difficult, and the pressure to succeed was intense. As commencement day approached, a curious evolution was taking place within our platoon. Not only were we feeling more confident in ourselves individually, but we were becoming extremely competitive with one another as well. No longer were there wholehearted cheers for a fellow cadet as he or she struggled to complete a necessary task. Now, the primary focus was who would be the strongest, the fastest, the best marksman, the best driver. Our test scores made each of us keenly aware of where we fell among the class ranking. No one wanted to be number forty-seven out of forty-seven. My personal goal was to graduate in the top half of my class. I decided if my name was called with the number twenty-three or better beside it, I would have respectfully represented the office of President.

It's a curious thing when you think of how one starts an undertaking like this. The first day is confusing and can even be quite discouraging. Then there are times along the way when you are absolutely convinced you're never going to make it to the end. And if you do, you assure yourself it will be only by the skin of your teeth. I determined early on if I was going to be successful, I was going to have to learn to ignore the ups and downs. If I made it to the next day without being expelled, that was enough to get me out of bed and to be able to fight through another day. It's really a wonderful analogy to life here on this earth. Don't you think?

Commencement day finally came. And yet still more pressure—my closing speech as president. That morning the final scores were posted along with our graduation ranking. I waited to look until everyone else had moved away from the bulletin board in the corridor outside of Sergeant Strictman's office. Thankfully, I had passing scores on every section. I received extra points for holding the office of president and for breaking the obstacle course record. Others received extra points for top marksman, top student, top driver, and first place in the physical training tests, among other things. My eyes followed my finger as it scrolled across the sheet to the class ranking column. My number was fifteen.

"Whew," I heaved a loud sigh of relief.

"How'd you do, honey?" whispered a familiar feminine voice from behind me.

"Great!" I quipped as I swung around to embrace Kristina in a celebratory hug.

"Surprise!" shouted Kristina and most of my family, who had traveled from the East Coast to attend my graduation. I was pleasantly taken aback and started making the rounds giving each one including my parents and my sweet grandmother plenty of hugs and kisses. After a final pinch of my cheek, Grandma teased, "Well, are you at least going to tell me the answer to Kristina's question?"

"I finished number fifteen out of forty-seven, Grandma, the top one-third of my class. I'm really happy

160

with that result. And between you and me, I'm very glad to have this whole thing over with."

"Wow, number fifteen, son. You've done the Roberts family proud."

"Thanks, Dad. I tried to do right by you and Mom."

"You did wonderfully well, Nicky," smiled my mother.

"Who finished first?" inquired Kristina. "Your friend William?"

"Yep. William did it."

"Who's William?" asked my mother.

"William Yamamoto. He's an officer who carpooled with me to and from classes. The guy is brilliant. He helped me more than once with my studies. I wasn't at all surprised that he was ranked number one. By the way, he's going to be a police officer in our own town."

"That's nice, Nicky," replied my mother with a nod.

Just then Sergeant Strictman poked his head around the corner. "There you are. You're needed on the platform immediately President Roberts."

"Yes, sir," I responded, snapping to attention. Then, as I started down the hall, I glanced back at Kristina and my family. "Sorry, you guys," I shouted, "I've got to go. But we'll all have dinner after the ceremony, okay?"

The entire event lasted an hour and twenty minutes. My speech was short and to the point. I highlighted some of our difficulties at the Academy as well as some of our challenges ahead. Lastly, I summarized with a heartfelt, "Keep your head down out there, and may God be with you all."

Following the closing prayer by the Academy chaplain, I stepped down the stairs, off the platform, and right into a group of people that included Chief Bruckman, Captain Cross, and several of the Watershed Rangers. My hand was becoming weary of all the many vigorous shakes, although my ego was thoroughly enjoying all of the attention. Seeing my family waiting toward the back of the auditorium, I hurriedly moved through the crowd, shaking hands and offering my congratulations to the many cadets I had become close with over these last four months. Many of us don't care to admit it, but difficulties really do bring people closer together more than any other circumstances I can imagine.

It was really great being at WHQ again and back to my Ranger responsibilities. ITSMUD has a rather strange policy of requiring a Ranger, who has recently graduated from the Police Academy, to return to the laborious duties on the work crew for at least thirty days before being assigned to patrol. Henry expressed the reasoning for the rule this way:

"It makes dadgum sure we get that hyped up, gung-ho, cop stuff out of your head before releasing you out on the Watershed by your dadgum self."

Later that evening, when I told Kristina what he had said she laughed out loud. "Then why on earth do they spend all that money to have you trained a certain way if they don't want you to act that way?"

I wasn't at all sure how to answer her, so I simply shrugged. However, I did agree with her assessment.

The weeks on work crew passed quickly. Before I knew it, I was on patrol, fully decked out in my neatly pressed and polished Ranger duds. My tan shirt and forest green pants looked sharp with my gold star, polished black gun belt, and the dark wood grips of my .357 Magnum revolver. I had even polished my black fire boots, which doubled as the final piece of the Watershed Ranger patrol uniform. I did a triple take in the mirror on my way out of the patrol room. This was my first day on the Watershed, and I was proud of what I had accomplished, and who I had become.

Having been assigned to the early morning shift, I joined my Field Training Officer, which we called an FTO, at WHQ at five o'clock in the morning on the first Saturday of October. Normally, Saturday would have been my first day off. But because I was on patrol, it turned out to be the first day of my work week. For the next ninety days, Thursday and Friday became my weekends and six a.m. until two p.m. my shift. Any other time, getting off at two in the afternoon would have meshed perfectly with Kristina's schedule as a school teacher, but not at this time of year because October in California is the height of wildland fire season. As it happened, more than once a week I had to work well into the evenings fighting fires. I'm not complaining. I really enjoyed firefighting, much more than police work, but the long hours began to take its toll on our marriage. Many mornings I had gotten up and left before Kristina had even awakened. And many nights I arrived home long after she had fallen asleep.

On my first day of patrol, I met my FTO, Johnson MacEntyre. Our first order of business was to thoroughly check every detail of our patrol truck, a four-wheel drive, pickup truck with a hundred gallon water tank along with a number of assorted firefighting tools. The light-bar was mounted above the cab and housed both red and blue spinning lights as well as non-flashing ones to the front and rear. I then checked both spot lights. The siren, which I tested next, worked perfectly.

"Hey, Nick, on the early morning shifts we don't test the siren until we get out in the country a few miles, okay?"

"Sure, sorry about that."

"It's no big deal. It's just that Fred lives in the Ranger House behind the WHQ building and gets a little fussy if we wake him up every morning at five thirty."

"Yikes, I had no idea."

"Yeah, don't worry about it. He's probably still sleeping. But if he isn't, you'll definitely hear about it."

"Well, I'll tell him it was my fault, and I'll apologize."

"Oh, you won't hear from him."

"What do you mean?"

"He's old school, close to retirement, a bit of a curmudgeon. He'll fuss at Henry. And then guess what?"

"Henry will fuss at me."

"Yup. So it's better if we remember to blow that siren out in the country somewhere, okay?"

"Gotcha. And thanks, John."

"You bet. Now let's get going."

John was one of the most straightforward men I had ever known, and a real pleasure to have as my FTO. Possessing a naturally gruff voice, one would think him harsh. But nearly six inches shorter than me with red hair and beard, he resembled a leprechaun in appearance and height. These features gave him a less intimidating bearing. He was strict, to be sure, but reasonable when I made mistakes. For example, one Wednesday afternoon, which was like our Friday, there was a call on the radio from a Ranger at one of the Recreation Areas. He needed a Code Three response. We were approximately ten miles away, but John determined we were the closest backup and needed to respond.

Making a quick U-turn, I flipped the lights and siren on then keyed the microphone, giving the Ranger needing assistance our ETA. Using the stick shift, I jumped up through the gears, slamming my foot down hard on the gas pedal. By the time I was shifting into fourth gear, John told me to slow down a little because we needed to make a right hand turn about a half a mile ahead. I glanced down at the speedometer and discovered, to my surprise, that we were flying down this country road in excess of ninety-five miles per hour. Seeing our turn just up the road, I immediately started braking with all the strength I could muster. Unbeknownst to me, a truck with the additional weight of a full hundred gallon water tank was difficult to slow down once it had a full head of steam on it. Even though I was applying more and more pressure on the brake pedal, we weren't slowing nearly enough to negotiate the upcoming right hand turn, now just one hundred yards away. To

165

R.J. Graves, Jr.

exacerbate the situation, a shiny Cadillac sedan of some sort had pulled up to the stop sign where I was supposed to turn.

Downshifting, I jammed a lower gear forcefully while I continued to stand upon the brake pedal. John's feet were now on the dashboard, bracing for the crash. Lights swirling, siren screaming, John barking, and the elderly couple, in their luxury Coupe de Ville, obviously panicking, all while I was desperately trying to make the right hand turn. With less than thirty yards to impact, and still traveling in excess of forty-five miles an hour, I yanked the steering wheel to the left and avoided certain disaster. We continued to slow down over the next quarter of a mile. Just then the radio crackled, "Cancel Code Three. I've got the situation at the Recreation Area under control." John instructed me to pull the truck over. Then he advised me to turn off the lights and siren. The silence of the cab was in stark contrast to the chaos of the previous few minutes.

John picked up the microphone, "Ten-four. Cancel Code Three."

At this point, the older couple in their Sedan de Ville drove by, blaring their horn and shaking their fists. I waved politely, trying to mouth the words "I'm sorry". They didn't seem to appreciate my apologetic gesture. Bringing my attention back to John, I didn't dare speak first. After what seemed like several minutes, John, in his typically gruff tone, broke the hush in the cab.

"Well, Nick, that was rather exciting. Don't you think?"

"Yeah, sorry about that, John."

"This is a classic example of why Henry wants us to get that gung-ho Academy stuff out of our system. Because if we don't, we end up doing something stupid like you just did. These trucks are actually fire trucks that we use as police vehicles. They're not agile, nor are they quick to pick up a chase. And as you undoubtedly understand now, it takes a much longer distance to bring them to a stop."

"I'm really sorry, John."

"Look, Nick. You did everything wrong. Everything! Right up to the point where you veered left and avoided a collision with that Cadillac. That was brilliant. Now, don't get me wrong. I'm writing you up for your actions today, and it's not going to be good. But I can tell you it would have been a lot worse if you had hit that Caddy."

"How much worse?" I asked, not sure I really wanted to know the truth.

"Well, that would be for Henry and Chief Bruckman to decide. But we don't have to worry about that because you avoided the crash. So let's head on back to WHQ."

The cab was very quiet as we made our way back—at a much slower speed. I was feeling very insecure and unsure as to what I could say or do to appease the verdict I knew I deserved. We pulled into the parking lot and around to the gasoline pump to top off the tank before signing off for the day. When I slammed the hood closed, after checking the oil, John suddenly appeared by the driver's door.

"Hey, Nick, so here's the deal for today. You have passing scores on every aspect of your training with one exception—an incident of reckless, high speed driving.

Look, it's not the end of the world because it's your first failing score."

"But it's only been a couple of weeks," I acknowledged.

"True. But it's only one failing score, so don't worry about it. Go home, take the wife out to dinner, tell her all about it, and then forget it. I know I will. See you Saturday, bright and early."

"Thanks, for your help, John."

"No problem. Remember, we're all in this together."

"Hey, John, one last question."

"Yeah?"

"If I had hit that car, I mean, instead of veering off like I did . . ."

"What?"

"You know, what would happen . . ."

"What would happen to you if you hadn't avoided that collision?"

"Yeah."

"Today would have been your last day as a Ranger."

ELEVEN

After last week's bungling blunder behind the wheel, I had become much more sensitive to the extremely tentative nature of my employment. Until I could pass my ninety day Field Training Probation period, I had become convinced I would constantly be on the edge. Approaching my one year anniversary, I felt as though my entire time spent as a Ranger had been an audition, and that my job could be terminated at the drop of a hat. The first ninety days of my employment had been probationary, pending my passing score on the Watershed Knowledge Test. Four months of Police Academy followed, where one failing grade would have resulted in immediate dismissal and, consequently, termination of my Ranger position. Now, I was under three months of law enforcement probation while being graded each and every day by my FTO. The pressure was relentless, and at times I thought I was going to crack.

Halfway through this final probationary period I started my stint on the late shift. In practical terms this meant, arriving home well after midnight and sometimes not until dawn the following morning. Also, my days off switched from Thursday and Friday to Monday and Tuesday. I hated it. And more importantly, I had a new FTO. His name was Drake Remington. He was extremely well suited for cop work, like a cheetah was specifically tailored to run. I'm not just stating opinion; he repeatedly declared this to me and anyone else who would listen. Drake and cop, two names with practically matching definitions. However, in the same breath, he also proclaimed there was only one thing he loved more than being a cop, and that was being a wildland firefighter. Drake was a typical Type-A personality, who kept the volume of the scanner turned all the way up, so he wouldn't miss a single opportunity to show up at the scene of a fire, crime, traffic accident, or any other action in our neighboring jurisdictions. He couldn't remember the last time he was on work crew because he always volunteered for patrol. Unfortunately, Drake and I were polar opposites.

Knowing that my new FTO was the last obstacle standing between me and the end of my long probationary process, my objective was to be as gung-ho cop as I could possibly tolerate. To be sure, it wasn't going to be an easy few weeks. But I kept my mind on the goal, the finish line, the time when I could finally be on my own roaming the Watershed. For my encouragement, I kept a calendar hanging on the wall of our kitchen. Each night upon arriving home, the first thing I did was walk over to that hopeful symbol and cross off another day. Kristina thought it strange that I wanted to count down the days of something she believed I absolutely enjoyed.

Her comments were my only indication that something deep within me was changing. Little did I recognize or even consider the possibility that I was morphing into someone I would never, in my saner moments, want to be. However, she could clearly see the gradual transformation and had become acutely aware of the disturbing metamorphosis. All I knew was I had a target, a goal in mind, and I was determined to obtain it. So I figured the end justified the means, right? Drake gave me passing scores each day as long as I demonstrated an aggressive demeanor. Therefore, I became more forceful in my actions and more hardline in my opinions. In spite of this, Kristina saw the deeper issues. She discerned the intangibles. Her concern was that her sensitive, loving husband was evolving into a prideful, intolerant, pushy man, who could legally carry a loaded firearm whenever and wherever he wanted. I had even purchased an off duty weapon to wear incognito under my jacket or sweatshirt. This gave me a feeling of security from all of the criminals who I had become convinced were hiding everywhere just looking for an opportunity to kill a cop. Kristina was growing wary. These things completely dumbfounded her and were dreadfully alarming.

No longer viewing myself as the friendly "Ranger Roberts" who helped children understand weather readings and gave directions to lost hikers, I now, according to Drake's definition, represented the only law and order in the vast Watershed. And without the Rangers, all chaos would soon overwhelm the tranquility of the hills and valleys. In the third week of my field training with Drake, we encountered a couple of situations that proved his point.

It was very late on a Thursday night. Well, actually it was early Friday morning. Drake and I had just heard a call on the scanner from a Park Policewoman, who was adjacent to our Watershed lands in her park. She had inadvertently come upon three men she suspected of dealing illegal drugs. Identifying all three by obtaining their driver's licenses, she radioed their information into her dispatcher. We could hear her voice on our scanner as I proceeded down the road toward WHQ to finish our shift.

"That's Officer Sharon Barkley," stated Drake confidently. "She was in my Academy class. Three against one aren't good odds."

Immediately, he directed me to start heading in her direction. We were about three miles away when the dispatcher advised Officer Barkley that one of the suspects had multiple warrants. Quickly Drake keyed our microphone, which he always seemed to have in his hand, and notified our dispatcher that we were three minutes away from stopping in the park to provide mutual aid to a Park Policewoman. Then he glanced at me.

"Turn on your cop lights."

"No siren?"

"No. Whip in there to the right; she should be toward the back of that parking lot. I'm sure she has her scanner on, so she would have heard we're close by. There's nothing more comforting than to know you have backup only minutes away—especially at this hour."

I could see the flashing lights of her Park Police vehicle and pulled up to the left of and just behind it. Drake and I shined our truck's spotlights on the suspects then hopped out. We both left the doors to our truck open. Drake spoke quietly with Officer Barkley, who was standing behind her open car door.

"Whatcha got, Sharon?"

"That guy in the middle has about a dozen warrants from all over. He's a bad apple. I've got to haul him in. He's a must-take."

"Okay, well, Nick and I will cover you. Have you patted them down yet?"

"No, the whole thing just kind of happened. I pulled in here, just routine, and next thing I knew I've got these three in my face. Besides, I didn't want to try and frisk one with the other two close by."

"Sharon, this is dangerous. Look, do either of the other two have warrants?"

"No, just that guy in the middle. His name is Bernard Lowensen."

"Okay, let's go get him."

Drake glanced in my direction and flicked his chin. I knew precisely what to do.

Seeing Drake and Officer Barkley move toward the suspects, I did the same thing. Remembering Sergeant Strictman's words "Hands are what will kill you," I watched their hands intently for any movement whatsoever. Instinctively placing myself in a position of triangulation, I moved my left foot slightly forward and placed my right hand on my gun belt close to my .357 Magnum. Briefly eyeing Officer Barkley, Drake, and then the suspects, I was ready. At that moment, a thought flashed through my mind. She was either incredibly brave or extremely stupid. Taking on three men in the middle of the night in a remote location was practically suicide for any cop, but much more so for a woman with her petite frame. In a situation like this, the rule of the jungle takes over. She may be as feisty as a jaguar, but these three rhinos could stomp her to death.

Truthfully, I was a bit on edge too and felt quite apprehensive about this whole situation. If it hadn't been for the impressive presence of Drake, I was sure this was a scenario I would not have volunteered for. I mean, I'm not a man of small stature, but the silhouette of Drake's six foot four inch height with his physique that looked more like that of a body builder than a park ranger cast an intimidating shadow on this cold, dark night. He stood about eight feet to Sharon's right. I was about the same distance to her left. She boldly approached the man she intended to arrest. He twisted back and forth, resisting her efforts to place him under arrest. She tried to pat him down for weapons but he continued to repel her. This lasted for nearly a minute. Then, thankfully, Drake stepped in.

"Hey, you two," Drake bellowed forcefully. "Where did you park your car?"

"In the other lot," replied the man on the left.

"Great. Look, we need to speak with your buddy here for a few minutes. Go get your car, and by the time you get back we should be about done."

No sooner had the two men walked out of sight, than Drake slipped his leather blackjack out of his back pocket and clocked the suspect on the side of his head. He staggered a few steps until Drake grabbed his left wrist with one hand and his upper arm with the other and slammed him face first to the ground. He then placed his large fire boot on the side of the suspect's neck while directing Officer Barkley to handcuff him. It all happened so fast I didn't have time to recognize what was going on until together they helped the handcuffed suspect to a standing position. Officer Barkley frisked him, read him his rights, and then put him in the backseat of her patrol car. After shutting the door, she turned to us.

"Man, oh, man, Drake Remington, was I glad to hear your voice come across my scanner."

"Yeah, that could've rapidly turned into an ugly situation. What were you thinking, Sharon?" inquired Drake as he placed a hand on her shoulder.

"I wasn't. I was just reacting," she acknowledged as she shrugged and shook her head.

The two continued their get-reacquainted-visit as I listened for any lessons I could glean from this late night encounter. It was nearly one a.m. when we hopped back into our truck and started for WHQ. As I drove, I asked Drake about his blackjack. He pulled it out of his back pocket, so I could get a view of it. Made of thick leather, it was maybe six or seven inches long and about an inch and a half wide. At one end, sewn inside, was a hard ball of some sort.

"What's that?" I asked.

"Lead. When you buy it, it's a round lead ball. I hammered on it, so it's more of an oval now."

"Why did you do that?"

"It's easier to keep in my back pocket, especially when I'm sitting. Besides, if it was round, it would leave a significant knot, you know, a bruise."

"Does the District provide that? I'd like to get one."

"No, they don't. And between you and me, I'm not supposed to have one out here. But as you witnessed tonight, I've found it to be very effective, so I carry one anyway. Look, that could have been a real fight with one of us or the suspect getting hurt. He was a felon with outstanding warrants, and as you observed he was resisting arrest. But with a little subtle persuasion, one moderate knock on the head, the job got done quicker, cleaner, and safer."

"Yeah, that was awesome. But I didn't know you carried a blackjack. How come it doesn't stick out of your back pocket?"

"Because I had my tailor sew a special pocket in all my uniform pants. It works great and none of the sergeants know I'm carrying it."

"Yeah, but since you're not supposed to carry it, why don't you just use Mace or your baton?"

"Like I said, this is much more effective. Those don't work as well. And . . . they're not discreet."

While Drake continued singing the high praises of his blackjack, I turned onto the road that ran parallel to the stream that fed the reservoir behind WHQ. About halfway to our entrance gate, we spotted a car parked in a turnout on the right side. Drake directed me to stop behind the car and turn off my lights.

"Poachers. We need to sneak in on them," he instructed in a low tone. "If they hear us coming, they'll throw their equipment in the stream. We need the fish they caught for evidence and their equipment to prove intent. Be careful, some of these guys carry guns."

Glancing at my watch, I mentally recorded the time. It was twenty-seven minutes after one. I called in our location to dispatch. My palms were sweaty, my heart pounding. If Drake was indicating this was a dangerous situation, then it must *really* be a dangerous situation.

"Take your flashlight, and when you close your door just let it click shut. We need to be quiet as mice if we're going to catch these guys," Drake confided. "Poachers are more slippery than any other criminals we deal with on the Watershed. And they almost always work very late at night."

Nodding my response, I quietly stepped out of the truck, closed the door, and walked over to the darkened car in front of us. Neither Drake nor I used our flashlights. I could barely see him in the cloud filtered moonlight. He held one finger to his lips indicating silence. Then, with both of us on either side of the rear of the car, he held up one finger, then two, then three. Simultaneously, two brilliant beams blasted the interior of the car with light from our flashlights. It was empty. I walked to the front and placed the back of my hand upon the hood, which was still warm. Drake silently acknowledged and then motioned for me to follow him. Turning off our flashlights, we waited at the entrance to a trail until our eyes adjusted to the darkness again. Drake led the way down the nearly pitch black trail. From twenty feet back, I followed cautiously. After about half of a mile, I could hear the babbling of the stream and knew that we were most likely getting close to the poachers.

Although the trail twisted and turned, I knew it well. Before leaving for the Police Academy, I had helped design and build the footbridge that crossed this stream. The same bridge we now gingerly tiptoed across to prevent our heavy fire boots from giving away our location. Just as we approached mid-span, we heard a distant laugh. Stopping dead in my tracks, I glanced downstream as Drake peered upstream. Several hundred feet away in the streambed, I detected the faint glow of a lantern. I stepped forward and tapped Drake on the shoulder, motioning for him to look downstream. He nodded his head, and we silently moved across the bridge, then continued stealthily into the dark woods. We crept ever closer, trying to avoid cracking a twig or rustling the leaves. As we slowly advanced, the voices grew louder. Soon, we were crouching in the bushes, atop the streambank, peering down at four men who were fishing in a spawning area. They were using a light to draw the fish closer and throwing chum into the water. Two were wearing a holstered firearm. All of these actions were crimes in the state of California.

Sensing Drake's eyes were on me, I glanced over at the position he had taken behind a large pine tree, about twenty feet to my left. Having instinctively stopped behind another pine adjacent to the edge of the streambank, I gave him a thumbs-up, indicating I was ready. Drake held up four fingers. I nodded. He quietly unholstered his revolver and pointed it along with his darkened flashlight in the direction of the poachers. I followed his actions precisely. Then he nodded once, twice, and on the third nod both of our flashlights lit up the area, like a bright flash of lightening streaming through a window in a dark room. At that precise moment we shouted,

"Rangers! Freeze and keep your hands where we can see them!"

Two of the suspects were so shocked they threw their fishing rods straight up into the air. Another culprit jumped face first into the water. But the fourth one, a much calmer, steely eyed character with a demeanor that appeared to be looking for trouble, began to slowly reach for his pistol. Drake abruptly shouted,

"You want to die tonight, scumbag? Pull that weapon, and you're a dead man. Go ahead, I'm waiting on you."

From my position, I yelled for the other three men to lay face down on the beach with their hands spread out to their sides. The fourth man slowly did the same. I hastily jumped down off the bank, put my knee in between his shoulder blades, pulled his gun from his holster, and tossed it in Drake's direction. I handcuffed him and told him not to move. As soon as I had neutralized him, I moved to the other suspect with a visible gun, and progressed through the same process. Moving quickly to the third suspect, I heard Drake's handcuffs hit the sand close by, so I picked them up and cuffed this one too. Finally, with Drake still covering me, I secured the last offender. Then, one by one, I frisked each suspect, reading them their rights. With them seated by their lantern, which I had turned to the brightest setting, I totaled their violations—poaching, trespassing with the intent to poach, trespassing with a firearm, poaching in a designated spawning area, chumming, and several other misdemeanors and infractions. These four men were going to jail tonight.

"So gentlemen," started Drake in a sarcastically friendly tone as he holstered his revolver. "What on earth are you doing out here at this hour?"

"Fishing," replied the youngest of the four.

"With all these weapons?" questioned Drake, waving his hand over the arsenal, which included four hunting knives, three handguns, a shotgun, and something that resembled a flare gun.

"Well, sir, you never know what you're going to run into out here late at night," confessed the youngest.

"Shut up, Jimmy," barked the eldest of this foursome. He was the steely eyed criminal who had been the least compliant when we had first approached them.

"Uh, Jimmy?" asked Drake in a less intimidating tone. "What's this thing used for?" Drake was holding up the homemade looking flare gun.

"It shoots a small explosive, like a cherry bomb or M-80."

"And that's why you have that pile of fish over there?" Drake asked with a sly smile.

"Yes, sir."

"Okay, let's go, boys," commanded Drake. "Ranger Roberts, I'll take these three and head for the truck. You take the cuffs off Jimmy, so he can help carry the fishing equipment and ice chest. Unload those weapons, gather them up, and we'll see you in a few minutes."

By the time Jimmy and I made our way to the truck, the Sheriff's Deputy was there with his transport wagon for the county jail. After loading up the four criminals, we headed for WHQ. No sooner were we seated in our truck, than Drake began his lesson-of-the-day lecture.

"Two excellent hauls today, kid. The first, a dirt bag from out of state who was fleeing warrants. Plus, we got to help a fellow officer. That's important, Nick. It shows neighboring agencies we have worth, we have value in being close by. The second haul brought in four unlawful citizens poaching in a spawning area. If we weren't here to stop that kind of activity, soon our lakes would be depleted of fish. These aren't the only four who have tried their hands at poaching. You'll come to find poaching is the most active violation on the Watershed. And I don't mean just fishing either. There's quite a bit of hunting too. In fact Phil, on his early morning shift last week, found evidence that someone was out there using traps. Now, that's a felony."

Back in the patrol room, I changed clothes and filed my reports. Turning to leave, I told Drake I'd see him tomorrow afternoon.

"Hey, you want to grab a beer?" he coaxed.

"It's three-thirty, Drake."

"Yeah, I know. What's your point?"

"I don't really feel comfortable going into a bar, especially at this hour."

"No, Nick, we have a ton of confiscated beer in the Patrol Room refrigerator. They won't miss a few of those."

"What?"

"Yeah, don't worry about it. Take a seat in the conference room. I'll be back in a minute."

Several minutes later, the door to the conference room swung open, and in marched Drake with a six pack.

"So, where you from, Nick?" he asked as he opened the first bottle.

"North Carolina. You?"

"I'm from Indiana originally. I've been in California for nearly twenty years though."

"Wow. Why did you move here?"

"Oh, I was fresh out of high school. I applied to several universities around the country including Pepperdine. When I got accepted there, I was sure that was the place for me. I don't miss the Hoosier state."

"What's a Hoosier anyway?"

"Uh . . . I don't know. I think it has something to do with a local yokel, redneck, or something like that. You married, Nick?"

"Yeah, my wife's name is Kristina. She's a really sweet gal, an elementary school teacher. We've been married a little over four years. How about you?"

"Nah. I was for about seven years. But she didn't like my work schedule. I mean, it's true; we hardly ever saw each other so why be married, right?"

"Oh, I don't know. I like being married."

"Well, it's hard to maintain a marriage with this job, buddy boy. But that's okay. Since my divorce, I've had more women than you can imagine. You know Sharon Barkley, the officer we helped earlier tonight?"

"Yeah."

"She and I shacked up for a year. Yeah, she's nice. Maybe I'll give her a call."

"Really?"

"Yeah. Do you want me to see if she's got a friend?"

"What? No, I'm married, Drake. I'm not interested in that sort of thing."

"Not yet you ain't. This job and marriage just don't get along. You'll see."

He grabbed the remote control and turned on the television mounted in the corner. After opening another bottle, he leaned back, resting his large fire booted feet upon the conference table. As I sat across from him, my mind started to wander, flipping from topic to topic like the television screen in the corner. This was the first time, in my remembrance, that I seriously questioned whether the Ranger job was really for me. I mean, here I was at nearly four a.m., drinking beer with a cynical man, who had given his entire life to law enforcement. What was I thinking? Why wasn't I home, under the blankets, sleeping next to the love of my life? Was this really my dream job? Would I choose this life for myself? For my marriage?

Unable to face the sobering reality of these thoughts, I justified my position in my divided mind. I had no choice. For now, this was the job I had, and I certainly didn't want to go back to selling first-aid supplies. That was demoralizing. But . . . was it worse than this? I never had to be out all night hunting down armed criminals in the woods. Yeah, it spiked an adrenaline rush, you know, it was exciting, but for how long? At what point does this kind of activity cease to be exciting and become what it really is—insanely dangerous. But, I reasoned, I needed this job, and I needed the money it provided. Plus, I liked the pride it fueled in me and the respect I received from others. Soon I'd be out on my own. Then things would be different. I wouldn't have to do crazy stuff like we did tonight, not unless I wanted to. I could be more selective, a bit more cautious.

As my mind faded back into reality, I concluded that I could handle any situation that came up. And if anything ever presented itself that I couldn't handle, I'd just avoid it. Secretly, I didn't like these thoughts, but it was how I dealt with the possibilities that I knew could happen on any given day. I had convinced myself I could shoot to kill any man who required that kind of force. But suppose it wasn't a man. I could never gun down a woman. That would be absolutely horrible. But could I kill a man? Would I actually pull the trigger when the situation presented itself? In that moment, in the heat of it, would all of my police training take over, or would I resort back to waffling and questioning my motives, or the suspect's intent? Was he really enough of a threat to justify killing? Would I have to shoot him, or could I reason with him? Are words strong enough? At what point are bullets a substitute for words? What would I actually do if I ever found myself in a situation where words were not enough? I hoped and prayed I would never have to find out.

TWELVE

What I had believed was an intimate conversation I was having with myself within the deepest chamber of my mind, apparently had given some visible evidence to a longstanding, skilled Ranger like Drake. After taking a long swig of his adult beverage, Drake broke the silence that had fallen on the conference room several minutes ago.

"So you're having some doubts about a career in law enforcement?"

Stunned by his keen insight into my non-verbal argument, I was at a loss for words when he opened the discussion with this probing question.

"What? Why do you say that?" I asked with a blank expression, trying to hide my astonishment.

"It's kind of obvious."

"What? Uh . . . what do you mean?"

"Look, Nick, I graduated from Pepperdine with a degree in Biology. Yeah, great, so what was I thinking, right? But a friend of mine from Northern California asked me if I wanted to move up there to work in his family's business. Do you know what that family did for work?"

"No."

"Guess."

"Uh . . . they owned a chain of hardware stores," I sighed, somewhat annoyed with where I thought this conversation was headed.

"Stucco."

"What do you mean stucco?"

"The entire family was in the stucco contracting business. I had a degree in Biology from a major university, and I was a hod carrier for plasterers."

"I'm not sure I'm following you, Drake."

"My point, Nick, is sometimes you find out the job you're in isn't a good fit for you."

Silence again reigned for a few minutes while I pondered what Drake had candidly stated. Not knowing how to respond, I stared at the television. A *Leave it to Beaver* rerun was playing. Thankfully, a few minutes later, headlights from a car pulling into the parking lot flashed across the windows, bringing the awkward lull to an end. Drake glanced at his watch as he pointed the remote control toward the television and clicked it off.

"Looks like Phil is here to start his early shift," Drake acknowledged with a flip of his chin toward the parking lot. "Man, for a second I thought it might be Henry."

"I've got to get home, Drake. My wife is going to be getting up about the time I arrive. If I'm not there she'll be worried sick."

"Alright, man. See you back here in eleven hours," chuckled Drake.

"Busy night, you guys?" questioned Phil as he stepped into the room.

"Yeah," nodded Drake. "The rookie did himself right. We arrested several scum bags including one with more than a few warrants out of Louisiana and Texas."

"Man, I need to get back on the late shift," complained Phil. "Nothing happens on early patrol except some traffic accidents."

"I'll trade with you as soon as I finish my Field Training," I offered with a smile.

"If, you finish your Field Training," laughed Drake.

The fifty-five minute commute home seemed particularly isolated. The skies were clouded over with a heavy morning fog, and the highways were practically empty. I felt so all alone. A dark, dreary haze had fallen over my otherwise happily numb disposition. Speeding down the freeway at more than twenty miles an hour over the posted limit, I felt an unexplainable urgency to arrive home before Kristina awoke. I whipped the car into the driveway, jumped out, and jogged to the front door. Quietly stepping inside, I noticed the kitchen light was on and the aroma of fresh brewed coffee was in the air. I shut the door softly and placed my gear bag gently on the entry floor. Turning around, I saw Kristina standing in the archway to the kitchen, backlit by its light, her arms akimbo.

"All nighter, eh Nick?"

I walked over to her and threw my arms around her, swaying as I kissed her cheeks. It was one of those perfect moments in life I wished I could somehow save forever. She held onto me tightly as tears filled my eyes. She could sense, as I could, that something was wrong. Something was most definitely wrong, but what was it? Did she know? She had a sense for things like this, a kind of intuition. I remembered the drive home and how I had felt so empty, so lacking. It was like some great void, some cold emptiness had taken root in my heart and was slowly sapping the lifeblood from my inner being. Was it a slow leak that I was just now noticing, or was it a meticulous surgical removal I hadn't detected because the incision had healed so rapidly? Whatever it was, here in Kristina's arms felt extraordinarily perfect and the vacancy imbued to full size, like a balloon being inflated to capacity. As I squeezed her even tighter, I determined I never wanted to lose this wonderful person—ever.

"Uh, Nick . . . could you ease up a bit? You definitely got stronger working out every day in that Police Academy."

"Oh, sure, honey, I'm sorry. I didn't mean to hurt . . ."

"No, no, don't misunderstand. I love it, Nick. I really do. But maybe a little less firmly next time, so I can breathe, okay?"

"Of course, my love."

"My love?" questioned Kristina in an edgy tone as she pushed back about an arm's length. "Nick, are you okay?"

"Yeah, of course. Why?"

"You haven't called me 'my love' for several months now. Nick, tell me what's going on?"

"Oh, I don't know, honey. I've really been missing you, I guess."

"What happened at work? Is everything alright?"

"Yeah, I think so. I don't know. I'm not sure. Well, to be honest, I'm not totally convinced I'm cut out for law enforcement."

"What do you mean, Nicky?" Kristina's voice was more tender and sympathetic now.

"Oh, I don't know. I'm struggling with some things. I'm not really sure I can put it into words. It's like an internal wrestling match I'm having with myself . . . it's almost like I'm having an argument that no one else can hear, just me. Some days it's very quiet with hardly any words or emotions, and other days it's a full blown war raging in my thoughts. Occasionally, I feel so confused, so double minded. Sometimes, I'm happy and content, other times sad and confused. And frankly, honey, I'm beginning to think it all has something to do with this job."

"Oh, I'm not so sure about that, Nicky."

"What do you mean by that?"

"It isn't the job. Uh, unless they're asking you to do something immoral, unethical, or something like that. If that were the case, then I think you could blame it on the job. But if you're sensing some disruption of your peace of mind, some pricking of your conscience, then I would advise looking to the Lord for an answer to your crisis."

"What crisis?"

"Look, Nicky, I can't be late for work. Let's have some breakfast, and we can talk about this more. Better yet, why don't I go take a shower, and you can get breakfast ready for both of us. This will be a treat. Usually you're fast asleep at this hour of the morning."

"Yeah, fine, whatever," I mumbled as Kristina skipped down the hallway and into the bathroom.

A little while later I heard the shower shut off, and within a few minutes her blow dryer turned on. Having poured a cup of coffee and added the amounts of cream and sugar she likes, I walked down the hall and opened the bathroom door. Obviously, she didn't hear me because she continued drying her hair. I really didn't mind because it gave me a chance to gaze upon my pretty wife wearing only a towel. Turning the hair dryer off she picked up her brush and continued her morning regimen. She must have caught a glimpse of me in the mirror because she swung around with a smile, still brushing her hair.

"Aren't you the sweetheart today?" She took a sip of the aromatic beverage. "Mmmm . . . perfect. Thank you, Nicky," she exclaimed as she planted a kiss on my lips.

"Western omelet, okay, Kristie?"

"Sounds yummy. Thanks, honey."

"It'll be ready in ten minutes."

We finished breakfast without ever broaching the subject of my internal wrestling. Kristina seemed preoccupied with something and anxious to get to work. Before I knew it, she gave me a peck on the cheek and shut the door on her way out. The house was silent, yet within my mind blared a deafening noise. I couldn't make it stop. I tried to sleep but to no avail. Knowing I would have to leave for work no later than twenty minutes after two o'clock, I shut all the blinds and doors, put ear plugs in my ears, a mask over my eyes, and lay down on the living room sofa.

Waking at quarter of two that afternoon, I charged around the house and didn't really concern myself with my situation until about halfway to Watershed Headquarters. Every time a doubtful thought tried to bully its way into my thinking, I pushed it out of my mind. Work was actually a welcome relief from the relentless, nagging doubts regarding my capabilities. Fortunately, I only had two more weeks of riding around with Drake. Despite my secret doubts, surely I could last that long.

Surprisingly, even with my internal wrestling, I was gaining confidence that maybe I might just make it as a Watershed and Recreation Ranger II after all. Soon I would be on my own, and that, I was convinced, would make all the difference in this job. Then I could choose what I would and would not respond to. If I determined it was too dicey, I could simply pass it by.

My last day with Drake and my final day of Field Training had finally arrived. Because of a scheduling conflict, we had been assigned to the early shift, and I finished the day with little fanfare. In fact, the only acknowledgment whatsoever came when Henry handed me a brass nametag that indicated "N. H. Roberts Ranger II" along with a handshake and a declaration in his typically dry, sarcastic tone.

"Congratulations on passing your law enforcement field training. Except for a hiccup here and there, you passed with flying colors, Nick. You're now assigned to work crew for the next six weeks."

"What?"

"Work crew on Monday. A command don't get much simpler than that, Nick."

"Okay, thanks, Henry. I guess that will give me a chance to get to know my wife again," I smiled.

"I figured things at home might be getting a little uncomfortable, Nick. You deserve a few weeks of eight to four-thirty with weekends off. See you Monday."

"But, Henry, I'm supposed to work patrol tomorrow and Sunday."

"Did you hear what I said? Now, get on home and hug that wife of yours. We'll see you Monday morning. By the way, Nick . . . don't be late," chuckled Henry with a wink.

On the way home, a wonderful idea flooded my mind. The more I thought about it, the grander it grew. I knew Kristina had a PTA meeting for another two hours, so I was sure I had time to set my plan in motion. After changing my clothes, I telephoned the hotel out on the coast. I was able to reserve the same room where we had spent the first night of our honeymoon years ago. I also made us reservations at the restaurant in the hotel that overlooked the ocean. I accomplished all of this on the sly and actually was hanging up the phone when I saw Kristina's car pull into our driveway.

"What are you doing here?" she asked with a smile.

"Henry sent me home. He also gave me this," I proclaimed as I pointed to my new official Ranger nameplate.

"Wow, you did it, Nicky! You are now an official Ranger. Congratulations, honey. I'm so proud of you!"

"Thanks, Kristie. He also gave me the weekend off."

"Really?"

"Yeah, on Monday I start back on work crew for the next six weeks."

"That's too funny. They spend all that money to get you fully trained, legal, and official, and then they send you out to fix barbed wire fences. I just don't understand those guys."

"I don't either, but I'm kind of glad. I'm sick of this shift work. It will be nice to work a regular schedule for a while."

"I agree. It hasn't been easy, Nicky."

"I know, honey. So let's go get a pizza. I thought Francellio's sounded good. Do you want to go?"

"Yeah, sure that sounds fine. I didn't have any lunch, and just realized I'm starving."

The following morning after breakfast, I proposed we take a drive out to the coast and get an early dinner so we could make it back before it got dark. Kristina really doesn't like driving on those windy, narrow roads after sunset. She initially replied that she had too many papers to correct. However, after a little subtle persuasion from me, as well as a suggestion that she could correct the majority of them as I drove. She finally agreed to our impromptu adventure. While she showered, I stealthily, yet hastily, packed a small suitcase with most of her essentials including two changes of clothes. I did the same for me. Dashing out to the car, I literally threw them into the trunk and ran back indoors, launching myself onto the sofa just seconds before she walked out of the bathroom.

"What are you doing, Nicky?" she asked as she peeked into the living room.

"Oh, nothing. Just waiting on you, my love."

"Okay, I'll be out in a few minutes."

"Oh, no hurry, take your time."

A few minutes later, out walked a magnificently gorgeous woman dressed in a beautifully vibrant, floral print sundress with matching sandals. My mouth dropped wide open as she pranced around the living room and then sat down on my lap, sliding her arms around my shoulders. She kissed me so sweetly and tenderly that I knew today was going to be a perfect day.

"Looks like it may be foggy out on the coast, honey," I advised as we headed west on the highway. "See the fingers drifting over the coastal range?"

"Yeah, I hope it's not too bad though," she replied, looking up from her student's papers, which were lying in her lap. "I have my bathing suit on under this dress. I was hoping to lie out in the sun for a while."

Regrettably, when we arrived the entire area was completely fogged in, and the temperature was at least fifteen degrees colder than when we'd left home. With the breeze and the lack of sunshine, it felt downright chilly. Therefore, we opted for an afternoon of indoor shopping before heading toward the coastal highway around four o'clock. After cruising around for about forty-five minutes, I headed in the general direction of the restaurant and hotel where I had made reservations for us to stay the night. As discreetly as possible, I turned one direction and then the next, inching us ever closer to our secret destination. Finally, I turned onto the road that led right past the entrance to the hotel. Once we had passed it on our left, Kristina cranked her head around.

"Hey, Nicky, stop!"

"What? Why?"

"Isn't that where we ate our first meal as a newly married couple? Yeah, it is. And that's where we spent our first night together as husband and wife. Hey, honey, please turn around. Let's eat dinner there tonight. What do you say? Wouldn't that be so nice?"

"Oh, I doubt we could get reservations this late in the day for some place that fancy. I mean, I'm sure they book up weeks in advance. With that view of the ocean, they may be booked for months, honey."

"Oh, come on, Nicky. Let's at least try. Wouldn't it be so romantic? Let's try, okay, Nicky? Please?"

"Well, alright, we can try, but don't get your hopes up. That's a pretty snazzy place, you know."

After making a U-turn, we started back toward the hotel's restaurant; Kristina wore a hopeful expression, while a tiny grin crept across my face. Pulling into the parking lot, we walked through the lobby door and then across the marble floor to the restaurant's entrance. It was every bit as beautiful as it had been when we were first married. The maître de walked us to a table adjacent to the windows overlooking the magnificent Pacific Ocean. It was just like we both had remembered. After a few minutes of feasting our eyes on the extensive menu and sampling the warm, sour dough bread, we both decided what we would order for dinner. The waiter approached our table as if on cue.

After introducing himself and tempting us with tonight's specials, our waiter exclaimed in his subtle French accent while donning a smile, "I remember you two. You were here about four or five years ago, right?"

"Almost six," I replied. "You have an amazing memory."

"Wow, has it been that long? What struck me the most about you two was how you both seemed to be so very happy. Tell me, are you still happy?"

I glanced over at Kristina, who was beaming from ear to ear as she answered the waiter, "Absolutely."

"Oh, that is wonderful to hear. So many couples don't seem to stay happy. I'm very glad that you are, my friends. Now, what can I get this happy couple for dinner?"

"My lovely wife would like the rib eye prepared medium rare with a fully loaded baked potato and asparagus. I would like the fillet mignon, Oscar it please, and a side order of whipped potatoes."

We thoroughly enjoyed our delicious meal, and as the evening wore on the most delightful thing happened— our conversation transformed into heartfelt, intimate communication. The love for one another that we had known so well seemed to be slowly, yet most assuredly, flooding into our hearts. So much so that I couldn't find an appropriate time to excuse myself from the table until we were finishing our desserts. Giving as my reason a need to use the restroom, I jogged out to the front desk and searched for a bellboy. Upon finding the lad, I handed him my car keys and written, detailed instructions regarding our luggage and how to leave our room just the way I wanted, which included candlelight, soft music, and the drapes open to the ocean view. After slipping him a twenty dollar bill, I sprinted back to the entrance of the restaurant. Once in the dining room, I slowed down to a casual walk just before sitting down at our table. Knowing my secret mission had been accomplished, I confidently smiled across at Kristina.

"Where's the restroom?" she asked in a whisper.

"What?"

"The restroom," she repeated with slightly more volume as if I hadn't heard her. I had heard her loud and clear but didn't know the answer to her question. Before I could respond she clarified the urgency of her inquiry.

"I thought I'd better go before we hit the road for home. It's a two hour drive, you know."

"Uh, yeah . . . it's out in the lobby." I shrugged my shoulders and waved my arm in the direction of the lobby hoping to indicate it wasn't difficult to find, though I hadn't a clue myself.

"Where, Nicky? I don't want to be wandering around out there."

"You know, out there, not too far from the front desk."

"Can't you point me in the general direction, Nick?" Kristina's tone gave indication that her level of frustration was beginning to pique.

"Yeah, go out of the restaurant into the lobby, turn toward the front desk, and ask anyone behind it."

"Thanks a lot, Nick," she huffed as she got up from the table, throwing her napkin on the chair.

"Sorry," I replied apologetically.

Having paid our bill before Kristina returned from the restroom, I met her in the lobby. I wrapped my arm around her waist and steered her for a walk around the hotel.

"Where are we going, Nick?"

"Oh, I thought we'd take a short stroll. You know, memories and all."

"That's a nice idea, honey. Why are we getting in the elevator?"

"Let's see if we can find the room where we spent the first night of our honeymoon."

I pushed the button for the top floor. After the door closed, I enveloped her in my arms and gave her a long, deep kiss. She kissed me back. When the door opened, we stepped out of the elevator, and I asked Kristina if anything looked familiar. She shook her head. We walked down the corridor past several rooms until I stopped in front of a door.

"I think this is the one," I whispered.

"Are you sure? I thought it was over on this side?" she whispered as she turned and pointed toward the opposite wall.

"No, honey, our room faced the ocean remember? This side is facing the right direction."

She stood close to me staring at the room number as I slipped the key into the lock. The door swung open and both her hands cupped her mouth as she let out a gasp. It was absolutely perfect. Every detail was just as I had hoped it would be. I scooped up my petite, feminine bride of a half-dozen years and carried her into the room. As the door shut behind us, she wept precious tears of joy on my shoulder.

THIRTEEN

Work crew on Monday morning was a breath of fresh air. None of the pressures of law enforcement were present. Plus, the guys were welcome company. I hadn't had the opportunity to enjoy being around them for a few months. Our first assignment was to clean up all of the fire roads on the south end, a task that would take us at least three weeks. I didn't mind the hard work, just the wretched poison oak. I loved being outside, working with my hands, and doing something productive. It felt good. It felt healthy. It felt invigorating. Phil called it therapeutic. I had to agree with his assessment.

For the first several days back on the crew, I operated the bulldozer, scraping smooth the dirt roads we all used to access the expansive wilderness of the District's Watershed. It was noisy, to be sure, but very satisfying work. We even worked up on Ranker's Ridge for nearly two weeks. This gave me a chance to create a climbing route up its smooth rock face. During lunch each day, I ascended fifty to one hundred feet with the help of the other Rangers, who took turns belaying me. Then, one weekend toward the end of the month, I finally completed my coveted first ascent, which had three long pitches. I named it "In the Nick of Time" because I finished it just before we pulled off Ranker's Ridge to work on the North End of the Watershed.

Glad to be feeling like a married couple again, Kristina and I enjoyed spending time with one another during the nearly eight weeks I was on work crew. However, once I was assigned back on the late shift patrol we slowly began drifting apart again. This vicious cycle continued for the next two years. It had a brutal effect on each of us individually and a devastating impact on our marriage. Something needed to give, and soon, or I feared a separation was looming on the horizon. The "D" word is not easily pronounced among church going folks. When that awful verdict is rendered upon a couple's relationship, most of their former friends become utterly scarce, thereby isolating the struggling couple even further. Divorce brings with it a most unique sense of failure. What seemed final and forever when standing at the wedding altar, has disintegrated into an emotional abyss that few ever completely recover from. In the end, it is at best, a relief to have it over with, which is an incredibly sad commentary. And at worse, divorce is a terrible blow, leaving a jagged psychological scar that can endure for a lifetime.

Regardless of the symptoms, I didn't want our marriage to end. I still loved Kristina. It seemed she still loved me. But everything else was pointing in the direction of irreconcilable differences. It was a dreadful, sinking, almost suffocating feeling, which I knew at some point I would just want to go away. However, at least for now, I was still fighting. No, fighting is too strong of a word. I was hanging on, not quite willing to let go, not yet anyway. But I did believe that all it would take was one more blow to our marriage and it, we, me, would completely unravel. Little did I know what was just around the next corner.

It was a Saturday in mid-December, twelve minutes before midnight. Although a hazy ring circled a brilliantly bright full moon, the sky was clear, the air was moist and chilly. It was the heavy kind of air that when I exhaled a cloud of moisture hung in front of my face before dissipating seconds later. The Watershed was eerily quiet that night. Way too quiet. Having completed my fifth year as a Watershed and Recreation Ranger II the previous week, I was all too familiar with this type of stillness. It made the hair on the back of my neck stand at attention.

With my window partially down, I patrolled the north end, slowly making my way back toward WHQ. Coming around a curve in the canyon road, I noticed a dilapidated, four-door, Lincoln Continental sitting at the far end of one of our reservoir overlooks. This was a particularly remote and lonely stretch of winding road with very little traffic at night except for those who were either looking for trouble or trying to ditch their trouble. Late last month, Stephen had found another dead body in the area. It was the ninth one this year. Evidently, some of the gangs from the city on the other side of the mountain, who were having some kind of turf war, had decided our watershed was a convenient dumping ground for their victims. Weekends were popular for this type of activity, especially Saturday nights.

In my years of law enforcement, I had found that evil was not equally divided among the seven nights of the week. Historically, Saturday has garnered more trouble than all of the other days combined, and if it happened to be a full moon that night, mayhem was nearly guaranteed. This dank, noiseless night furnished both foreboding omens.

Pulling up behind the vehicle, I turned on my flashing lights and directed my spotlights into its windows. I radioed my position as well as the license plate number of the Lincoln. Cautiously approaching the car, I stepped slowly, my every sense taking in volumes of information and quickly processing it. Something about this situation sent chills up my spine. I tried to shake it off, but it was effecting the better part of my reasoning skills. Then, I observed that the car seemed to be leaking something onto the gravel underneath. The vehicle seemed to be leaning back as if some great weight were within the trunk. Only a few feet away from the rear of the car, I shined my flashlight inside the windows. I was startled by what I saw. Garbage was strewn all over the floor and across the back seat. In the midst of this chaos rested a single baseball bat and a large crowbar. Discovering the doors were unlocked, I moved around to the hood and placed the back of my hand upon it. The degree of warmth indicated that whoever the driver was, he hadn't been here long and was probably still close by. Perhaps he was even watching me from the cover of the nearby brush.

I rapidly walked back to my truck, shining my light several times toward the bushes that surrounded this overlook on three sides. Hopping up in the cab, I felt an unusual uneasiness. Something about this situation was unsettling. At that moment, a voice on the radio broke the silence. The dispatcher advised that the owner of the vehicle had warrants for armed robbery and attempted murder. He was to be considered armed and dangerous. No sooner had she finished her transmission than another voice broke the airwaves, "Unit 314, Code Two. ETA seven minutes." It was the gruff, albeit, calming voice of my first FTO, Johnson MacEntyre.

Those were the longest seven minutes of my life. I slid out of my truck but remained behind the safety of my open door. I could hear John's truck racing along the winding canyon road long before I could see it. Finally, he rounded the curve and pulled up next to my truck. John also focused his spotlights on the Lincoln. I met him in between our trucks.

"What's ya got on this cold, damp night, Nick?" His gruff, almost grandfatherly tone instantly put me at ease.

"Well, nothing, except an empty car owned by a wanted felon."

"Yeah, I heard. You searched it yet?"

"Just an exterior look-see. I didn't open it up though."

"Alright. Let's see what we've got."

The two of us, with flashlights in hand, approached the vehicle. As we drew closer, John pointed me toward the trunk and told me he would look inside the rest of the vehicle. I mentioned how I thought the car was leaking some kind of fluid and to be careful. He nodded as he opened the driver's door and leaned inside. I watched him for a few seconds, then crouched down behind the trunk to determine what the mysterious seepage was. On my hands and knees, behind the trunk of the car, I started to reach underneath toward the puddle when I heard John shout.

"Freeze! Keep your hands where I can see them. Get them up now!"

Springing to my feet behind the back of the car, I saw a large man dressed in black sweat pants and a white tank top raise his hands slowly upward. One hand clutched a large knife covered in blood. John held him at gunpoint, and I immediately drew my revolver as well. The man's hands were bloodied, and more stains were visible on his shirt. Every sensory portal I had was now on high alert. My eyes darted around the brush, looking for any movement in the shadows. John commanded the suspect to walk over to the side of the car and then to place the knife in the tray between the hood and the windshield.

"Now, put your hands on the hood of your car."

"That ain't my car," came the snide reply from the beefy, belligerent suspect.

"Do it!" charged John in a louder voice.

The suspect hesitantly complied. John, while I covered him from the side of the car, holstered his weapon and then started to frisk the suspect.

"What's your name?" demanded John.

"Cleaver."

"What's your first name?"

"Vic."

"Victor Cleaver. What are you doing out here at this hour?" pried John.

"Don't call me Victor. And my last name ain't Cleaver. It's Deaver, Vic Deaver, okay? But don't be calling me no Victor."

"Why not, Victor?"

"Call me, The Cleaver. That's what everyone else calls me. Vic 'The Cleaver' Deaver, got it?"

"Well, Victor, if this isn't your car, who's car is it?"

"I said call me, The Cleaver!" bellowed Victor.

"Just answer my question!" John barked back. "Whose car is this?"

"It's mine!" shouted another voice from the edge of the bushes in front of the Lincoln. "And I'm going to blow your stinking head off, pig!"

John raised his hands and turned slowly toward the threatening voice. He was a smaller man than Victor "The Cleaver" Deaver, and he was holding an automatic handgun, pointed directly at John. I couldn't see him from my position behind John and the enormous Victor. Evidently, he couldn't see me either. The man with the gun yelled again at John telling him this was his last night on earth. He then directed Victor, who I was sure must have known I was there, to take John's weapon out of his holster. It was at this very point in time I knew what had to be done. As Victor reached for John's holstered weapon, I darted out from behind the two of them and into full view of the suspect with the gun.

"Freeze! Drop your weapon or I will blow you away!" I commanded in as loud and as forceful of a voice as I had ever mustered.

In less than a split second, the suspect turned his attention and his gun on me. Simultaneously, my mind made the decision to pull the trigger on my revolver. The electrical impulses, in less than a nanosecond, raced through my body at speeds faster than light, and my finger obediently pulled back on the trigger. Instantaneously, a flash and a bang exploded from the muzzle of my .357 Magnum revolver and the semi-jacketed, hollow-point bullet streaked across the forty-three feet of overlook, whizzing past John by less than eighteen inches. It hit its mark, the suspect, squarely in the chest, throwing him to the ground. On his way down, he fired two shots, but thankfully they zinged off above our heads. At that second, John started wrestling with the larger Victor for control of his service revolver. I shuffled forward with my gun pointed at him while yelling,

"Drop it! Drop it! Drop it now, or I'll blow you away too!"

John was yelling as well. Both of us were so completely focused on getting control of this huge man nicknamed The Cleaver that it came as a complete shock when another shot pierced the night air. It was the suspect on the ground, the man I had shot. He wasn't dead, just wounded and was preparing to fire at John and me again. His first shot inadvertently hit his own partner in the back, shattering his shoulder blade. But now he appeared to be taking more careful aim. Upon hearing his first shot, I swiftly swung around to see him lying on his back with his gun pointed right at John. Immediately, I fired two more shots at him as I charged forward. Both hit him in the torso, one was fatal. Then I heard John's stressed voice behind me. He was crouched over the wounded behemoth, Victor, trying to handcuff his enormous wrists.

"Shots fired! Code Three! Shots fired! Shots fired!" John blared into the microphone of his portable radio. "Two suspects down. EMS needed. Code Three!"

The dispatcher responded within seconds confirming our location and that ambulances were rolling. As soon as she completed her response, Drake Remington and Sergeant George Munson called in their ETAs of nine minutes and seventeen minutes respectively. Feeling that all danger was past, I holstered my weapon.

"Don't holster that yet. We don't know if there is anyone else hiding in the bushes. Besides, you need to cover me while I handcuff this guy."

"Yeah, gotcha," It was the first time I noticed the adrenalin coursing through my body and the trembling in my voice.

"You, okay, Nick?" inquired John as he glanced between the suspect and me.

"Nick," stated the suspect coldly. "When I get out, I'm going to do to you what you did to my friend."

"Shut up!" shouted John. "You're never getting out, so just shut up!"

Once John had him handcuffed, seated, and leaning up against the front tire of the Lincoln, I moved slowly over to the other suspect lying lifeless on the gravel. Reaching down with one hand, I picked up his gun with a stick I had found close by. I checked his pulse at his left wrist and then at his neck. I found nothing indicating he was alive. The pool of blood he lay in was enlarging. I patted down his pockets and found a large amount of cash, a small amount of what appeared to be marijuana, and more than two dozen pills in a clear plastic baggy. I also discovered his car keys. Walking past John to the back of the car, I told him I had located the keys and was going to open the trunk. He replied he would be there as soon as he finished administering first aid to Victor. My hands were shaking as I slid the key into the lock. Just as I began to turn it, an unnerving thought flashed through my mind. Quickly, I unholstered my revolver, and as the trunk sprung open I took a step back.

"Oh, dear, Lord Jesus," I gasped.

John jumped up and jogged to the back of the car. "Oh, that is the most gruesome thing I have ever seen," he echoed while holding his hand over his mouth. "What kind of sick people are you?" he shouted at the wounded suspect.

"I told you," Victor replied calmly. "When I get out, you're both dead."

"Shut up!" yelled John. "Just shut up!"

Much to my relief, Drake showed up at that moment. He had a commanding presence that reassured me everything was going to be alright. Within a few more minutes, Sergeant Munson arrived and directed me to sit in my truck. He then assigned John as lead Ranger on the scene. Shortly thereafter, he walked over to my truck and asked me several questions about what had happened and when it had occurred. After he seemed satisfied with my answers, he put his hand on my shoulder.

"How you doing, Nick?"

"Uh, a little shaky. But I'm okay."

"Do you need a paramedic or anything?"

"No thanks."

"How are you feeling about what happened here?"

I just stared at Sergeant Munson and didn't reply. Honestly, I wasn't sure how to answer a question like that.

"John told me you saved his life. Good job, Nick."

"Thanks. At least if I had to kill a man, it was to save another."

"Look, Nick, listen to me. That guy was a dirt bag. He was wanted for armed robbery in several states as well as shooting a cop in Nevada last month. You did society a favor. You saw what was in that trunk. He killed those people. And he would have killed John and you too if you hadn't fired your weapon when you did. I know this is a horrendous thing to deal with, but you made the right choice, okay?"

"Yeah, I'm not sure. I mean, I think I did everything I could have done to avoid what happened; but man, is my mind running wild with all the things that could have happened, uh . . . or that I should have done."

"I understand. That's why I've got John running the scene on this one. Not that you can't do it, Nick. It's just better this way. I mean, in the eyes of the state it's better."

"The state?"

"Yeah, look, CHP is on their way out here. Technically, being as this is a state roadway, it's their jurisdiction. So until they determine that your shoot was justified, they're going to be a little rough to deal with."

"Great."

"Yeah, I know. So here's the deal—I need your gun, your gun belt, your gold star, and your Ranger identification card. Don't adjust anything, don't even reload your gun. Just take it off and hand it all to me, okay?"

"Yeah, sure."

"How many shots did you fire?"

"Three."

"Let me see here. Good, there are only three unused shells in the gun. So far everything you've told me lines up with what John reported. That's good, Nick. Sometimes in these situations things can get somewhat confusing. Just give the CHP the facts as best you can recall them. I'm convinced you're a hero. And hopefully, after their investigation they'll declare you a hero too."

"I don't feel like a hero."

"You are, Nick. I know it's a tough thing to deal with now, but later you'll come to recognize, you did the right thing. Remember, it wasn't your choice."

"Thanks, Sergeant."

"No problem. Hang in there, buddy."

"No, I mean it. Thanks, George."

"You bet. Don't worry, we'll make it through this."

Within minutes of the CHP arriving on the scene, they ushered me back to WHQ where their investigators set up in the conference room. Three of them asked me the same pointed questions several times. They kept telling me I wasn't a suspect, but I sure felt like one. It was shortly after ten a.m. when they finally told me I could go home. Having been up for more than twenty-nine hours, I was an exhausted mess when I walked across the parking lot toward my car. Just then, I heard a voice behind me calling my name. It was Henry.

"Nick, wait just a second."

"Yes, sir."

"Hey, how you doing?"

"Frankly, Henry, I'm so tired both physically and emotionally that I can't tell which side is up."

"I would expect so. Listen, Chief Bruckman and I want you to know that we think what you did was heroic. You saved John's life and took two very dangerous criminals off the streets. You are a hero, Ranger Roberts."

"Thanks, Henry," I muttered.

"And one more thing, Nick. Now, this isn't personal so don't take it that way, okay? But . . . uh, I need to tell you that you are on temporary administrative leave until further notice."

"What's that mean, Henry? I didn't do anything wrong."

"No, it's not like that, Nick. This is standard procedure, although it's one we've never had to use before. But it has no reflection on you whatsoever, okay?"

"Well, what do I have to do?"

"Nothing. You are off duty, with pay, until this investigation clears you of any wrong doing. Don't worry, I'm sure they will determine it was a justified shoot. It just takes time; that's all."

"How much time?"

"Oh, maybe two to four weeks."

"What? Why so long?"

"There is a dead body, Nick. And you had something to do with it. Come on now, just give it a few weeks, and everything will be back to normal."

"Maybe for you it will be, Henry. I don't think I'll ever be normal again. Unfortunately, this is my new normal now."

"Nick, listen to me. Take some time and think this through. The way I see it, you didn't have a choice. Now go on home and enjoy your time off. Stay close though. I'm sure the CHP hasn't finished their questioning yet. I'll call you next week to see how you're doing."

"Thanks, Henry. I appreciate that."

The drive home seemed way too long and yet not long enough. A harsh reality was settling upon my heart. I had killed a person, a human being. I had taken his life. He would never breathe again, laugh again, or . . . hurt someone again. My emotions were as unstable as the Richter scale in an earthquake. They were all over the page. My mind kept accusing, then justifying, and then accusing again. Pulling into the driveway at the same time as Kristina, I slowly moved over to open the car door for her. She gave me her usual polite hug and a peck on the cheek. As we walked into the house, she chitchatted about the church service and our Sunday school class, telling of all the different people who had asked about me and why I wasn't there. While she fixed our afternoon meal, she flitted and floated from one topic to another as if life could go on forever with nary a care. Finally, she turned toward me, having noticed my silence.

"Don't you care anymore, Nick?"

"Care about what?" I whispered, my mind barely able to control my emotions.

"About me, about the things that matter to me. Why are you so distant these days? What is going on with you?"

"Oh, all kinds of things," I mumbled.

"Then, why don't you talk to me?"

"Because you really don't want to hear what I have to say. You're always so caught up in all the things that interest you. Ever think to ask me what I need to talk about?"

"Yeah, like what?"

"Stuff."

"What stuff? That prideful Ranger job you've got? Or how handsome you think you look in that uniform? Or how arrogant you are with your Command Present, or whatever you call it."

"See what I mean?! You don't even know what Command Presence is."

"Oh, yes, I do, Nicolas Harrison Roberts. And I wish you would leave it out on the Watershed where it belongs. It has no place here in this house, and to be perfectly honest with you, I am sick and tired of putting up with it."

"Oh, really?"

"Yes!"

"Well, you poor, little, spoiled wifey you. What ever shall you do?"

"Oh, shut up, Nick, before you make me say something we'll both regret."

"Like what? What could you possibly say that both of us haven't been thinking for years?"

"Nick, stop it! What on earth has gotten into you? Why are you acting so hateful?"

"Oh, I don't know, Kristina. Why are you being so obnoxious?"

"Because I miss us, and it hurts. I guess I'm just really hurting all the time," she confessed with tears welling up in her eyes.

"I'm hurting too, you know."

"Oh, really?

"Yes, really, but you go first. Why are you hurting, Kristina?"

"No, you first, Nick. I insist. Tell me what's wrong. Why are you hurting so badly? Is it something you think I've done?"

"No."

"Then, what is it, Nick? Tell me what's troubling you. There's still a chance for us. We just need to talk it through. So please tell me, why are you hurting?"

"Well, okay. How's this for starters . . . last night I killed a man."

FOURTEEN

Whatever Kristina may have considered as my problem, her face revealed it was nowhere near the magnitude of what I had just confessed. With eyes and mouth agape, initially her expression was a mix of disbelief and annoyance. Then it morphed into one of shock and terror, followed by a dismayed, yet wistful grin, indicating she was hoping my declaration was a horribly sick joke. My continued blank stare confirmed her worst fears as was demonstrated by the wagging of her head from side to side, slowly at first, but as the cadence increased so did the volume of her, "No, No, No!"

Subconsciously, she began slowly creeping backwards almost as if I had told her she was going to be my next victim. Sitting silently at our kitchen table, I watched her shuffle all the way to the door leading to the backyard. She stopped just short of bumping into it. Then, as if by some outside force, the fear washed from her face. She regained her composure and slowly began walking toward me. She gently pulled out the chair opposite from where I was seated and slid down into it with a plop. The entire episode lasted no more than forty-five seconds, but it spoke volumes to me about her devotion to our marriage. It revealed how at times she may be uncertain about us when some unexpected difficulty arises. And yet, once she has gathered herself together and mustered up the courage, she is still wholeheartedly committed to our marriage and to me.

Watching her from across the table, I knew at that moment we were somehow going to make it. Our marriage would survive. Come what may, Kristina and I would most assuredly remain married and not just married, but happily married. It would take some time, perhaps years, even decades. But there was no doubt in my mind, when my precious wife sat down at the kitchen table she was declaring to me, in her unspoken way, that no matter what happened in the past she would always be my life-long partner. We would somehow get through this together. An ever-so-slight smile wrinkled the corners of my mouth as tears flowed down my cheeks..

"What is it, Nicky?" she asked softly with tenderness in her tone. It was a genuine love I hadn't heard or felt from her in a long time.

"I just realized something."

"What? Tell me, Nicky. I know you're hurting. Let me help," she pleaded as she slid her hand across the table and gently grasped mine.

"I have always loved you, Kristina. I could never . . ." I choked on the words as I began to weep. All the emotions that had been building since last night came pouring out. She squeezed my hand firmly to let me know she cared.

"You could never what, Nicky? What were you going to say?"

Through the sobs I mouthed in a whisper, "Loving you. I could never stop loving you."

Kristina immediately sprang up and softly slipped her arms around my neck as she eased down on my lap. We both wept uncontrollably for what seemed like an hour. The dam had finally broken. It was as though an earthquake had jolted our relationship, forever changing the landscape of our marriage. We were broken and joyful all at the same time. It hurt so deep and yet was so splendidly glorious. We closely held each other, neither willing to be the first to loosen our embrace. Our love seemed to, by some mystically marvelous form of osmosis, permeate our hearts with a deep healing balm. There were no words, no coaxing, no explaining, just holding. It was spiritual. It was absolutely precious and overwhelmingly intimate. Up to that moment, I had declared many times that our marriage would need a miracle to be restored to its former intimacy—I never imagined restoration would require such brokenness.

I'm continually astonished at how God can take the most horrid of circumstances and produce something so amazingly beautiful out of them. Prior to this point in time, I was convinced that after killing that suspect, healing would never come to me. I had taken a life and felt sure I would be scarred forever. But now I saw healing blossoming in our marriage, and it gave me hope that one day my heart, too, could be whole again.

As the day wore into evening, I eventually felt ready to share with Kristina some of the details of what happened last night. Although it actually took several weeks before I could release it all from the hidden chamber where traumatic memories like that are secretly stored, it felt good to include her in what I was going through. I'm not so sure that time heals all wounds. But I would agree that healing does take time. Often, in the most unusual ways, healing would occur. For example, one day Kristina and I were sitting on our living room sofa watching a college football game. A commercial came on showing a father playing with his young son in a field. I broke down, disclosing to her what prompted my display of emotion. Another time, I awoke in the middle of the night in a cold sweat, fearful of what I had just dreamt. The scene of that terrible night had played like a horror flick before my eyes. I was still in the movie but the outcome had changed. Directly after both of these episodes, as well as many others, Kristina and I sat and talked, sometimes for hours. We started the conversations by exploring what happened to be troubling me at the moment. Then, as time went on, we touched on so much more while our conversation floated from one topic to the next. We even asked forgiveness of each other for things we had said or hadn't said, done or hadn't done. It's a wonderfully strange phenomenon how the hand of healing has such long fingers, touching that which is hidden deep within us.

During one of these cherished sessions, the telephone rang. Upon answering, I recognized the distinctive voice on the other end as that of Captain Henry Cross. This wasn't something that alarmed me in any way as Henry had been calling me twice a week since that dreadful night. However, today he seemed to have an almost amused tone to his words.

"How you doing today, Nick?"

"I'm doing alright, Henry. Just sitting on the patio, enjoying the afternoon sun with my wife."

"You getting tired of your vacation yet?"

"Oh, you know, Henry, I want to be back on patrol, but this time with Kristina has been something we both really needed."

"Well, you sitting down, Nick?"

"Yes, sir."

"Uh, maybe you should stand up for this."

"Okay."

"Nick . . . I'm kidding you. Earlier this morning we got news regarding your review."

"Yes, sir. What's the status, Henry?"

"You have been cleared of any wrong doing. In fact, they acknowledged that under the circumstances you acted bravely and decisively. The report further states that you are to be commended for your actions, which were done in a professional manner and in accordance with the law. So, like I asked you before, Nick, are you getting tired of being on vacation?"

"Yes, sir! When can I start back?"

"How about you come on in Monday?"

"That's great, Henry. What shift?"

"You'll be on work crew."

"Why?"

"Nick, look, I talked this over with Chief Bruckman, and we both agreed. It would be better for you to be on work crew for a time. You know, just until you get back into the swing of things on the Watershed."

"For how long, Henry?"

"Six months."

"What?! I thought you said I was cleared of any wrong doing?"

"Yes, I did. But this will be a good transition for you. It's not punishment. It's preparation for getting you back in the saddle."

"I've heard the best medicine for someone who falls off a horse is to get right back up in the saddle?"

"Yeah, but this is different, Nick. You know that. Now come on, this will be good. You'll see."

"Henry, to use your metaphor, I think I need to be back in the saddle right now, or, uh, maybe in a couple of weeks but not six months."

"I agree with you, Nick. But remember, you didn't just fall off a horse."

"What's that supposed to mean?"

"It means, what happened was way more serious than a horse bucking you off."

"What are you saying, Henry?"

"You know what I'm saying. I'm sure when you're in a less emotional state you will recognize my meaning exactly."

"Henry, shoot straight with me—will I ever, as an ITSMUD Watershed and Recreation Ranger II, be allowed to wear a gun again?"

Henry's voiced dialed down to a whisper. "It's so much bigger than that. It's so much bigger than you . . . than me, or even Chief Bruckman. There are very powerful forces at work here. I'm talking about powerful people in powerful places in this state. Perhaps the most powerful, if you get my meaning?"

"Henry, what on earth are you talking about?"

"Listen, I can't explain the whole situation to you over the telephone. But I will brief you on everything when you get in on Monday. I know this whole unfortunate situation has been extremely difficult on you. I understand that. But you have got to see, and the sooner the better, that this thing is huge. And, regrettably, you are smack dab, squarely in the middle of it. Until things blow over . . . and hopefully they will, the Chief and I thought it best to keep you as far away from the limelight as possible."

"Henry, what are . . ."

"Look, this is all I can tell you over the phone, okay? There are folks in high places that want to take our guns away. Yes, I know it's hard to believe, but it's absolutely true. The proposals are already in the process of being drawn up. These are tense times for the Rangers, Nick. You understand?"

"Yes, sir. But what's that got to do with me being on work crew for six months?"

"The Chief thinks this whole thing will, one way or another, be resolved within six months. His plan is to keep you on work crew until we find out what has been decided regarding our law enforcement status."

"But again, Henry, what's that got to do with me?"

"Nick, because of what happened that night, you killing that suspect, they are regarding you as the poster child for their campaign against the Watershed Rangers' right to bear firearms."

A shockwave shuddered across my being as Henry's words pierced deep into my mind. I couldn't reply. I was in utter disbelief. How could I be used as an example to take away our guns, when the very same example showed how undeniably imperative the guns were to our safety and existence on the Watershed? It was a most significant and poignant answer to Kristina's question which she had posed years ago, "Why do the Rangers need a gun to keep the peace on the Watershed?" At that point in time, I had just started this job and didn't have the foggiest idea how to answer her. Now I had more than the answer, I had the experience and, lamentably, the internal scars to go along with it.

How could a group of powerful people use me as their example to justify their premise that Rangers should no longer carry guns? Though I tried, I simply couldn't understand how they reached their conclusion. In my feeble attempt to place myself in their shoes, all I could ever conjure up was the unquestionable necessity for guns to remain in the hands of law enforcement. I mean, suppose that night John and I hadn't been wearing sidearms; we both, most assuredly, would be dead. What would be the argument then? Would there be an outcry that the Rangers need weapons to protect themselves and others? It appeared to me that confusion was ruling the day.

It was as though my mind was desperately trying to swim in a vortex of chaos when I suddenly realized I was still on the telephone with Henry. I could hear him calling my name. Before I came completely back to reality, I plainly told him I would see him Monday morning. Then I hung up.

"Have you been cleared, Nicky?" inquired Kristina as she handed me another cool glass of her homemade lemonade. I hadn't even noticed she had headed into the kitchen while I was talking with Henry. The hazy fog hung thick in my mind. I must not have responded to several of her questions because the one inquiry that got my attention brought with it a tone of elevated exasperation.

"Nick!?"

"Uh, yeah, honey . . . I'm sorry. What were you saying?"

"Which time?"

"I'm sorry, Kristie. Henry shared a lot of stuff with me. I'm just trying to process it. That's all. Now, what were you saying, honey?"

"I asked if you had been cleared."

"Oh, yeah, sure. He told me I could go back to work on Monday."

"That's great, Nicky! I'm so glad this whole thing is over."

"Uh . . . I think it is long from over, Kristina. It may just be beginning."

"Why do you say that?"

"Henry wants me to go on work crew for six months."

"Why?"

"I don't know. He thinks it would be better for me to acclimate back into the job slowly. I guess."

"Nicky, I don't think I'll ever understand how things work at ITSMUD. They go to great expense to train you, equip you, and pay you. Then they don't want to use you for what they spent all that money training you to do. And now, after being off for several weeks with pay, they tell you to come back to work but not in the position they trained you for. I'm really confused."

"Yeah, me too."

Monday morning arrived all too soon. After my telephone call from Henry, I was dreading going back to work. It felt like I had a scarlet letter tattooed on my forehead. I had been well trained, but now I was prohibited from using that training. I felt impotent. Before getting out of my car, I determined to have a cheerful disposition irrespective of how I felt. Upon stepping through the door at WHQ at six forty-five, I heard Henry's all too familiar voice.

"Good afternoon, what's your excuse?"

I had to chuckle as we had both enjoyed this kind of animated, lighthearted banter ever since my first day at ITSMUD. He jabbed with a sarcastic remark. I dodged and threw back a quick witted reply. Hearing it, he usually smiled and winked. Regardless of the motive of his teasing remarks, he always had a half-smoked, long-ashed cigarette hanging from the corner of his chapped lips. It had only been a few weeks since I had last seen Henry, but he looked much older. He seemed beyond tired; it was more of a deep seated weariness. I was genuinely concerned for him.

"Good morning, Henry. You feeling okay? You look tired."

"I've done more work asleep than you'll ever do wide awake."

"Somehow I believe you on that one, Henry."

"You better, kiddo. Hey, listen, Nick," he whispered, "I want you to stay around the office here today. After a while, you and I will go out for a drive. I want to brief you on some of the stuff that's going on."

"Okay. I'll help the guys get all their equipment together before they head out. Then I'll get things straightened up in the barn."

"Fine. I'll come find you in a couple of hours."

The clock in the barn had just struck ten when I heard Henry's truck pull around to the big, rollup door. He waved me over, motioning for me to get in. I jumped in the passenger side, and before I could close the door we were off. Once we got away from WHQ, he started right in with why we were having this mobile conference. He explained in detail, while we were driving down the road toward the south end, what he could only tell me in generalities on the telephone. Revealing first what the legislature was intending to do, he then went on to tell me how they proposed to accomplish it. He also wanted me to understand that, at all costs, I must stay out of the spotlight. If I were to have another incident, all would be lost for our cause.

"What cause?" I asked as we stopped at a fire road to open the gate.

"Our goal is to remain law enforcement Rangers. It is imperative in the eyes of all the Rangers that we maintain our law enforcement status. It isn't just about the guns, Nick. There's so much more to it than keeping our weapons—it's about our identity. You understand that, don't you?"

"Yeah, sure, absolutely." My head was nodding, and my mouth had acknowledged, but my thoughts were moving faster than my mind could comprehend. I wasn't sure yet, but I thought what I had just heard Henry say was an enormous clue in finding the answer to my own personal dilemma—my identity. Determining to revisit his words later when I could give them more attention, I asked him a pointed question.

"How did this whole mess get started anyway?"

"Oh, it's a long story, Nick. But the short version is this: There's a park district somewhere up north. They employ about two dozen law enforcement Rangers. About two years ago, one of their Rangers was out on patrol before sunrise. He came upon a lone poacher, who was crouched down cleaning the deer he had just killed. When the Ranger called out for him to freeze and keep his hands up, the poacher threw his hunting knife at the Ranger and then turned to get his rifle. The Ranger fired one shot, hitting the suspect in the abdomen. The bullet lodged in his spine, resulting in permanent paralysis from the waist down."

"Was it a justified shoot?"

"Oh, yeah, absolutely. The suspect was tried, convicted, and sentenced. But his family went after the park district in civil court. They sued for fifty million dollars claiming all kinds of false testimony. Seeing as it had only been the Ranger and the suspect there that morning, their attorney painted an entirely different picture. Essentially, it was the suspect's word against the Ranger's word."

"What happened?"

"The park district settled out of court for seven million dollars."

"What?!"

"Yep. As you know, there's a different standard in civil court than in criminal proceedings. But where it affects us is now the precedent is set. The powers that be were looking for any excuse to remove the law enforcement section from the Ranger job descriptions wherever they could throughout the state. Your unfortunate incident a few weeks back lit up ITSMUD in neon lights."

"Great, now I'm right in the middle of a power struggle, and no matter which way this thing goes, I lose big time. This is unbelievable!"

"Yeah, I have to agree; it really stinks."

"So is there anyone fighting for the Rangers?" I hopefully inquired.

"Oh, yeah."

"Who? The union? Chief Bruckman?"

"Well, no," replied Henry candidly. "The union doesn't see this as an issue where they can win any votes. As they see it, the change would actually be more beneficial to the Ranger's overall well-being. You know, set work schedule, weekends off, nobody shooting at you . . . stuff like that."

"What's the Chief's position?"

"Privately, he is one hundred percent for the Rangers keeping their law enforcement responsibilities. Publicly, however, he needs to appear as neutral as possible. His comments will be scrutinized as a public official. He must be perceived as someone who places the best interest of the Watershed and the citizens that use it above everything else."

"Really?"

"Yes, and he's working hard behind the scenes to help us."

"So who's really fighting for us, Henry? I mean, who is riding point on this, so the worst case scenario doesn't actually become reality?"

"Me."

"You? What? Why?"

"Look, the Chief and I discussed it several times. I'm going to spearhead our defense. We've got it all worked out. The evidence, the testimonies, the attorneys, the whole case is planned out. That's why it is imperative that you lay dadgum low until we get through this. I have also been commanded not to return your service revolver, gold star, or your other law enforcement equipment to you until this whole dadgum brouhaha is over."

"Oh, brother! Why not just fire me?!"

"Nobody wants you fired, Nick. You can't think like that. Look, again, it's not about you personally. All the Rangers think what you did was incredibly brave. Chief Bruckman and I both regard you as a hero."

"Yeah, right," I mumbled under my breath. Then with more volume I confessed, "I wish someone else was the hero."

"I can understand that. But nothing can be done about that now."

"Yeah, I know," I replied with a sense of resignation.

R.J. Graves, Jr.

"Now look, here's something else Chief Bruckman and I discussed. If you're interested, I want you to help me with the research for our case. I think we'd make a good team. I would still be your superior, and you would still have your daily assignments on work crew. But you could help with the interviews, the legal work, and researching for precedents. It will be a lot of extra work with no pay, but it'll be very gratifying if we end up winning this thing. So what do you say, Ranger Roberts, you in?"

FIFTEEN

Weeks seemed to pass like months, months like years, since being sequestered on work crew. I was trying to see the best in it even though my conscience kept scolding me, like the dentist drilling a tooth all the while reminding his patient that he was the cause of his own pain. To the one squirming in the chair, it really doesn't matter whose fault it is. He's still miserable until the drilling stops. I was convinced that until I got off work crew and back on patrol this feeling of dejection would be with me continually.

During that time every day, Monday through Friday, was basically the same routine: work crew with Phil, Stephen, Rob, and some of the other Rangers from eight in the morning until four-thirty in the afternoon. Then after dinner, I did research for the case that Henry would present to the legislature committee at some point in the future. Every few days, Henry and I met to go over the latest discoveries and developments. Chief Bruckman joined us incognito about every third meeting to see how things were progressing. It was exhausting work but gratifying to think I was helping our cause. Late that summer, we finally received word of the date Henry needed to be in Sacramento to share our findings with the committee.

He insisted that I go with him, but I had been subpoenaed to be in court as a witness for the prosecution in the criminal trial of Victor "The Cleaver" Deaver that started this whole fiasco in earnest for the Rangers. Coincidentally, it was the same day Henry needed to be at the state capitol. As a consolation, however, he agreed to allow me to wear my full uniform to the trial, including my gun belt with my service revolver. I remember it was a stiflingly hot day. Having not worn my bullet-proof vest for months, I began sweating profusely within a few minutes of putting it on. This wasn't a good look for a police officer on the witness stand. Therefore on several occasions, as I waited to be called to testify against the defendant, I stole away to the men's restroom to cool and tidy myself, ensuring I was presentable.

Some of my fellow Rangers relished the courtroom setting. I detested it. I felt like I was the one on trial rather than the defendant. What appeared to be cut and dried out on the Watershed became convoluted and twisted in the courtroom. The murder case of Victor "The Cleaver" Deaver followed suit. The defending attorney certainly scrutinized my every move, questioned my every motive, and shined his glaring light on the minutest of details that had occurred that fateful night. It was as if everything I said or did was under intense suspicion. I had learned during my first time in court three very important lessons: answer questions with as brief an answer as possible; refrain from guessing what the defendant may or may not have been thinking; and never presume anything except what I had taken in as evidence through my senses. That's it. That's the law. For a witness, everything else was shaky ground.

Sitting next to Ranger Johnson MacEntyre in the section of the courtroom reserved for law enforcement, I glanced around the room trying to assimilate any information that would assist in calming my emotions. Several people moved quietly in and out of the pews, which were aligned like a theater with the judge on stage, front and center. The jury members had been selected days before and were seated in their orchestra pit, listening intently to the Assistant District Attorney, who appeared to be playing them like the maestro that he was. Except for his composed, even tones there were no other voices audible in this performance. That is until he turned around and called me to the witness stand.

Stepping around John, I leaned down and assured him I felt calm and confident. He smiled and whispered, "Good luck with that." Truth be told, I was apprehensive. But I was equally ready to have this chapter in my life behind me. Having turned to face the gallery, I placed my left hand on a Bible, raised my right hand, and swore to tell the truth, the whole truth, and nothing but the truth. My palm left its moist imprint on the leather cover. I sat down, took a deep breath, and started reading my report aloud.

After finishing my statement of the events of that pivotal night, the Assistant DA asked me a few direct questions. I gave the best version of my much rehearsed answers. Several times the defense attorney objected. Some were overruled, others sustained. My entire time on the witness stand for the prosecution may have lasted ten minutes. However, when the Assistant DA sat down, the long grilling process of cross-examination began with the first probing question of the defendant's lawyer.

"Why is it, Ranger Roberts, that you think my client should be charged with murder?"

"I didn't charge him with the crime, the DA did."

"Just answer my question, officer."

"As I stated in my report, when I opened the trunk to his car, there were two dead bodies, both appeared to have been killed by knife wounds."

"Whose car was it?"

"It was his partner's car, but the knife was his."

"Oh, really, and how do you know that?"

"When Ranger MacEntyre confiscated it, your client, Victor 'The Cleaver' Deaver yelled, 'Give me back my knife, and I'll cut your throat too.'"

"I object, Your Honor, this is hearsay. My client tells me it was his partner's knife. He had nothing to do with it," barked the defense attorney.

"Overruled," declared the judge plainly. "Ranger Roberts heard Mr. Deaver make the statement."

"It wasn't his knife," argued the attorney for Mr. Deaver.

"The defendant held the knife that had blood on it," I volunteered. "The same blood he had on his hands and clothes as well. His partner held a gun. No blood was found on it, his hands, or his clothes."

"Except his own after you killed him!"

"Objection, Your Honor!" shouted the Assistant DA. "Ranger Roberts is considered a hero for his actions that night, Your Honor. He has been cleared by a review board and further, Your Honor, Ranger Roberts is not the one on trial here."

"Sustained," declared the judge. He instructed the attorney for the defense to limit his questions and comments to the trial at hand. Immediately, as if the judge had said nothing, the attorney resumed his relentless grilling of my every thought, motive, and action. This continued for nearly an hour. Obviously, he had decided my testimony was crucial to the jury in determining their verdict, so he did everything he could to discredit me.

The air in the courtroom that day was suffocating. From where I sat on the witness stand, the cloud of cigarette smoke hung a few feet above my head, adding to my increasingly gloomy disposition. Two enormous ceiling fans turned the paddles slowly through the thick air as if complaining of the effort. Glancing out at the faces, all of which were staring back at me, I dispassionately responded to yet another probing question, accusingly posed by the defense attorney. Though I never looked his way, I could sense the piercing glare of the defendant with each of my condemning responses. I'd never been called to testify in a murder trial before. The atmosphere was tense. My brow wet. My throat dry.

Leaning forward toward the microphone to give my answer to his final question, my torso shifted under the bullet-proof vest revealing the extent of sweat that had accumulated within its impenetrable cocoon. Like I mentioned before, I had learned to keep my answers short and to the point when testifying. This, I was certain, I had accomplished in this proceeding as well. Having been dismissed by the judge, I stood, adjusted my neatly pressed uniform, and proudly strode back to my seat in the courtroom, knowing the defendant's eyes would follow me across the room. Although I hated his intimidation, I refused to reveal I felt it. While remaining stone still and staunchly unwavering in my demeanor, my mind, in an effort to defend itself, pondered how I had arrived in this courtroom amidst this distressing situation. It was very apparent to me if The Cleaver was acquitted, the first thing he would be determined to do would be to settle the score, first with me and then with John. Not only did the state want a guilty verdict, but John and I needed it.

My drive back to WHQ was completely silent as I was deep in thought. Where had I gone wrong in life? There must have been a fork in the road I had failed to recognize. All I really wanted to do was build beautiful homes and have a wife and family to love, and to be loved in return. What crazy circumstances had brought me to this insane situation with a malicious felon threatening my life? Would he get an acquittal and be free to roam the streets? Would I run into him again out on patrol? Would he be waiting for me in the darkness of a fog filled forest? Or would he discover where I live and awaken me one night while staring down at me with his malevolent grin? This final thought actually made me shudder as chills shot up my spine.

The parking lot at WHQ was empty with the exception of Jill's car, the cars of the six Rangers on late patrol, and my own. I sat quietly in the Ranger truck for what seemed like nearly thirty minutes before scooting out and walking over to the back door. I was ready to quit, hand in my resignation, and call it a day. The pressure was so intense and my mind so agitated that I really couldn't consider any other option. Having changed my clothes in the locker room, I stopped at the soda machine and bought two Cokes, one for me and the other for Jill. Hers was a thankless job with long hours spent cloistered in a tiny room with very little gratification. Dispatchers are the unsung heroes of law enforcement. Having recognized this from my early days at WHQ, I made an effort to bring a little sunshine into her dreary existence. Besides, helping to brighten another's day always had a positive influence on mine as well.

"Oh, thanks for the Coke, Nick. It's difficult to step away from the radio knowing that the guys out there may need me at any second."

"Yeah, I thought you might need a pick-me-up."

"Absolutely. This time of the day when the work crews have all gone home is always the hardest for me. Sometimes, like today, it can get so incredibly boring."

"I understand. But speaking for all of us Rangers, we're so glad you do what you do. Thanks."

"Oh, you're welcome. I like helping you guys . . . well, most of you anyway," she chuckled.

Not wanting to get into a conversation of who she liked and didn't like and why, I chose to quickly change the subject.

"Hey, Jill, have you heard from Henry yet?"

"No, should I have?"

"Well, yeah, I think he would have left Sacramento by now. Doesn't he always radio in?"

"I think he does most of the time, but lately he hasn't been as consistent. Last week I noticed on two occasions he hadn't signed off before he had arrived home. That's not like Henry."

"I think he's so concerned with the whole situation regarding our law enforcement status that he sometimes forgets the mundane things he's used to doing," I confessed plainly.

"He's got a lot on his mind, Nick. Yesterday, Chief Bruckman and some upper management guys from the home office came out here. They all walked down to the creek, and when they came back Henry looked as if they had really chewed him up."

"Man, I wonder what that was all about?"

"I don't know. But Henry spent the rest of the day in his office with the door shut. When he finally left, he didn't even say good-bye. Strange things are going on around here."

"Yeah, I know what you mean, Jill."

The following morning, I arrived at work extra early, so I could have a chance to speak with Henry before the other Rangers showed up. Pulling into the parking lot, I spotted his captain's truck parked exactly where it was nearly every morning. I jumped out of my vehicle and jogged over to the front entrance. Before I even had an opportunity to shut the door behind me, I heard the sarcastic yet friendly greeting I had come to enjoy.

"Good afternoon, what's your excuse?"

"Hey, Henry, how you doing today?"

"Better than you."

"Why do you say that?"

"Because I'm already working on my second cup," he winked as he held up his steamy cup of Joe. His half-smoked, unfiltered cigarette had an ash nearly two inches long.

"What time do you get up each day, Henry?"

"Earlier than you."

"Yeah, I figured that. But you probably get up at what, four-thirty?"

"Something like that. What's it to you?"

"Oh, nothing. Just wondering. You've been here a long time. Have you always been this ornery in the morning?"

"Oh, no, I've mellowed in my old age, Nick," he smiled with a wink.

"How old are you, Henry?"

"Young enough to work circles around you and old enough to know not to."

"You're really something," I laughed. "But really, how old are you?"

"I'll be sixty-two next month."

"Really? Wow, Henry. You're in great shape for sixty-two."

"I'm not sixty-two just yet, Nick," he chuckled. "Let's give me another month being sixty-one, okay?"

"Sure, I understand. But why didn't you retire when you turned fifty-five? The state has that age fifty-five with

239

twenty-five years of service rule. You could have retired years ago. Why didn't you?"

"Oh, I don't know. I guess so I could keep young Rangers like you in line. Or maybe so I could fight this fight for you guys. As you know, I don't wear a gun and, between you and me, I don't really have a dog in this fight, Nick. Other than for safety reasons, I don't really care if we have weapons or not. But the fact that there are some folks so opposed to us keeping our guns makes me suspicious and all the more willing to fight for us to keep them."

"Yeah, how'd it go yesterday?"

"Oh, hard telling. There are some extremely powerful forces at work in this whole situation. I'm not even sure those senators on the committee have the freedom to vote for us. Sometimes I felt like I was talking to a wall. I presented our entire case. I answered all their questions, and even summarized how taking our guns away would leave a huge void in the law enforcement coverage out on the Watershed. But no sooner had I sat down, than they started discussing how they could patrol the Watershed lands with the local Sheriff's Departments. In other words, they had already formulated a response for each and every one of my points to keep our guns."

"What? How could they know that? Only you and I researched our side of the case. Nobody else knew, right?"

"Well . . . the other day several members of the board came out here. We walked down to the creek and they gnawed on me pretty good. They wanted to know what I was going to tell the committee. I have an awful feeling that someone in that group is a rat—a wretched, worthless, spineless rat."

"Who was there that day, Henry?"

"Chief Bruckman. Boy, do I feel sorry for him with his office in the same building as the rest of those guys. But I'm not worried about him. It's the CEO and three of the board members, along with the guy who drove them out here in the District limo. I'm a bit concerned about the board members, but I really didn't trust the driver. He stood aloof, more like a hitman for the CIA than a driver for a water district board. Even though he was several feet away, I'm sure he could hear everything we were discussing."

"Whoa, Henry, do you think he's like a mole or something?"

"I wouldn't put it past some of those board members. Where they went to school law enforcement wasn't looked upon fondly. I know two of them are as close to being cop haters as you are to hating the outhouse pumper truck."

"Thanks for that, Henry."

"Nick, I don't have a good feeling about any of this. And honestly, I'm concerned for the safety of anyone who may stand in the way of them taking away our guns."

"What are you saying?"

"I'm saying, I thought I was being followed all the way back from Sacramento yesterday."

"Really? Are you sure, Henry?"

"Yes, I am. There may be something more sinister going on here than I ever would have imagined."

Out on work crew that week, I didn't dare bring up the topic of our law enforcement status. Phil, Stephen, and Rob were continually discussing world politics and the economy. For me to add another hot subject to the conversation would have sent them over the top. The weather had been sunny and seemed to have the same effect on our dispositions, so why drift some clouds over the landscape. We were building a foot bridge over a creek in the back country of the Watershed. I was using my carpentry skills, and the others on the work crew appeared to be enjoying the progress we were making. It is interesting to note how progress is a basic need for most folks. It's nearly as necessary as food and water. Everyone seems happiest when things are moving forward. I can't think of anyone who thrives on being stagnant.

Late that week, as we were wrapping up the bridge project, I received a radio call from Henry asking me to drop by his office before leaving for home. After helping with the cleanup and getting ready to head home, I poked my head in his office.

"You wanted to see me, Henry?"

"Come on in, Nick. Close the door and have a seat."

"Uh, oh, does this meeting require a shut door?" I chuckled nervously.

"Yeah, it does. Brace yourself, Nick."

"Yes, sir?"

"That murder case you were working on, uh . . . you know, that Victor Deaver guy."

"The Cleaver? Yes, sir."

"Well, he's been acquitted of murder. The only charge they brought back with a guilty verdict was the felony trespass with a weapon. He got three and a half years. He'll be out on parole in twenty-four months."

"What?"

"Yeah, it's like we can't convict a criminal in this state anymore."

"This is devastating news, Henry. What am I supposed to do? I can't hang around here wondering if that scumbag is stalking me, waiting for the right time to take me out, or worse, trying to mess with my wife, or something."

"I understand how you must feel, Nick. That's why I wanted to tell you myself. I already broke the news to John. He had the same concerns as you. And truthfully, I felt similar when I heard the news too."

"I can't believe this. Seriously, what am I going to do? I can't sit around here waiting for that guy to show up. No way! I mean, he told me flat out that he was going to do to me what I did to his partner. He doesn't see my actions as self-defense. Nor would it matter to him. He's going to be out in two years, and after finding his weapon of choice he's going to be looking for me. Good grief, a criminal with a nickname like The Cleaver free to roam the streets. What was that jury thinking?"

We walked out the front door and across the parking lot to my car. Henry tried to comfort me with reassuring words, but all I could think of was having to face that hateful beast alone on some dark night. He put one hand on my shoulder and told me this wasn't something we could solve today, so for now I should go on home and spend time with my wife.

"I'll see you in the morning, Nick. Try to have a good night."

"Thanks, Henry. You too."

Wrestling with how to break the news to Kristina, I finally pulled the car over on a street just around the corner from our home. My mind was running at a thousand miles per hour. The only way I could find any level of peace was to decide not to tell her the verdict, at least not quite yet anyway. As I pulled the car into our driveway, I determined to call Pastor Charles to see if he would have a few minutes for a cup of coffee this coming weekend. After dinner, that's precisely what I planned to do. However, just as I was about to pick up the telephone to call him, the phone rang.

"Hello?"

"Nick?"

"Speaking."

"Hey, Nick, it's Drake. Brace yourself; I've got some bad news."

"Drake, you're the second person today to tell me to brace myself. And, I doubt what you have to say is going to be half as bad as what I was told the first time. So just tell me, okay?"

"Sure, Nick. Henry's dead."

SIXTEEN

My mouth dropped wide open. I wasn't sure I had actually heard Drake correctly. Fumbling around until I found a chair at the kitchen table, I gradually lowered myself down, covering my eyes with one hand as the other firmly gripped the telephone. My heartbeat was heavy, and my head felt like it was starting to spin. This news was completely unexpected and nearly overwhelming. How could Henry be dead? Just then, I felt Kristina's hand on my shoulder.

"You okay, Nicky?"

I slowly shook my head from side to side but said nothing. Drake continued.

"Evidently, you were the last one to see him alive, Nick. Jill told me you and Henry walked out to your vehicles together."

"Where did he die?" I asked quietly.

"Who died?" gasped Kristina, shaking my shoulder with her hand.

"Well, that's what's kind of strange, Nick," confessed Drake. "His captain's truck was pulled over on the side of the road, not a mile from WHQ. He was slumped over the wheel. His truck was turned off, but the flashers were on. It looks like he may have had a heart attack."

"Oh, no. That's awful. Not Henry."

"Yeah, I know. John and I were heading in to grab a bite at WHQ when we saw his truck. The ambulance took him to the emergency room, but when he left here he didn't have a pulse. We just received a call a few minutes ago. They are considering him DOA. I'm sorry, Nick. I know how fond you were of Henry. Uh . . . look, I've got a lot of calls to make, so I better get going. I'll see you tomorrow, okay?"

"Yeah, Drake, thanks for the call."

Hanging up the telephone, I glanced at Kristina, who appeared every bit as shocked as I was. We talked late into the night, and I shared with her the other bad news of the day. I was surprised to find her reception of the convict's reduced sentence to be calm and measured. Perhaps she hadn't fully grasped the reality of our situation. Regardless, I believe her advice would have been the same whether she had or not.

"You should call Pastor Charles first thing tomorrow morning and discuss this with him."

Taking her counsel to heart, I set up a time with Charles for the following Saturday morning at the local coffee shop on Main Street. Sitting outside at an umbrella table, Charles was his typical cheery self. I maintained a more realistic outlook. After I conveyed all that had been happening over the last several months, he responded with a very annoying quip, intimating these things might not be happening if I had listened to reason years ago. He must have sensed I was ready to leave because within seconds he changed his disposition though not the subject.

"What's Kristina think about all this, Nick?"

"She told me to have a talk with you."

"Wise woman, your wife," chuckled Charles.

"Yeah."

"Look, Nick, all kidding aside, I've never really had a job. I mean, other than ministry, so I'm not sure what to tell you. If you're wondering if God will protect you, I can confidently say that He will. Could it be uncomfortable for a while? Yes, it could. But He will be with you through it."

"Thanks, Charles."

"Sorry, there are no guarantees."

"What's that supposed to mean? I'm out there risking my life to help keep others safe from scumbags like The Cleaver, and all you can say to me is 'Sorry, there are no guarantees?' That really stinks, Charles."

"Now hold on, Nick. I don't mean there are absolutely no guarantees. We have our eternal security, His love, His kindness, His care, you know, those kind of things are guaranteed. It's He . . . Himself, His character that He declares will never change, not our circumstances. You must know, on this planet we will have trouble and difficulties, but He is greater than our troubles. Faith is a powerful force. You just have to tap into it. For a long time, you've been trying to do things yourself. He has to bring you to your knees, so to speak, before you can recognize faith's potential."

"Well, I hear what you're saying, Charles, but it's not at all comforting. I mean, I'm considering having to quit my job and move far, far away from here."

"And therein lies the guarantee you're seeking."

"What?"

"He promises to be with you no matter where you go or what trouble you find yourself in."

Charles had given me some things to consider, but I determined he didn't fully understand my dilemma. So after thanking him for his time, I excused myself and headed home.

The weeks following Henry's death some disturbing rumors began circulating within the ranks of the Rangers. The first story was that the coroner's report showed trace elements of a chemical, with a name longer than the Mississippi River, that brings on cardiac arrest within seconds of it being injected into the body. The second was that the report also found two tiny skin pricks at the back of his neck. Had Henry been assassinated? If so, it appeared to be accomplished by a professional. But who? And more importantly, why?

This tale was linked to another concern. Why wasn't ITSMUD actively pursuing a replacement for our Captain's position left vacant by Henry's death? Drake even called the Human Resources department to inquire about the opening. The reply was simply that the position wasn't being filled at this time. It appeared obvious to the Rangers that these were not just coincidences, but that these latest events were closely tied to the legislature's desire to remove the law enforcement aspect from our job description. One week later, John discovered that the Sheriff's departments, which were looking to benefit from our demise, had been lobbying the committee too—the very committee that Henry had testified before. But they had been arguing against us.

The evidence was mounting. It seemed reasonable to us that as the spokesman of the Watershed Rangers, Henry was the target of an assassination. As several of us continued to investigate the prime suspect, the ITSMUD limousine driver, he disappeared into thin air. When searching the records at the Human Resources Department, no account was found regarding the elusive character. The HR manager advised John that the driver must have been under short term contract, hired directly by the ITSMUD Board. However, when John approached the board member he considered most sympathetic to our plight, he simply stated that the driver was an employee of a service they contract with on a yearly basis. John and I drove together to pay these folks a visit. Upon questioning the agency's owner, it became apparent he'd never employed a driver that matched the description of the ITSMUD limousine driver. All fingers were pointing back at the board—but whom on the board?

Drake and John decided it was time to call a meeting of the Rangers to present our findings to the group as well as determine what could be done to keep our guns. We met at a remote location way out on the Watershed late that Sunday evening. Everyone was in attendance with the exception of our sergeants, the lieutenants, and Chief Bruckman. This was a meeting of the rank and file and the start of a grassroots effort to get at the bottom of what was happening to our jobs. The whole situation had started as nothing more significant than a ripple on an ocean but was now a full blown, tidal tsunami. The mood among us was a mixture of semi-controlled hostility, bewilderment, and more than a boatload of frustration. Before things got entirely out of hand, Drake took his stand on a tree stump and quieted us down.

"Ladies and gentlemen," he boomed in his classic, commanding style. "Let's not lose our cool. At this point, we still have our sidearms. If we don't take the high ground, however, I think we will lose the entire battle without even understanding why. Now come on, let's stay professional here."

A few in the crowd shouted out comments calling for strong action, but when Drake, who has an undeniably intimidating presence, held up his muscularly massive arms everyone quieted back down again.

"Look," he continued, "it's pointless to make ominous threats as though we could actually deliver on them. We are Peace Officers, citizens of the highest calling. We enforce the laws of the land, not usurp them. So just shut your trash-talking, and let's get down to business. Now, John has a strategy to help us get to the bottom of this thing. I don't know about you, but I'm not giving up my gun without a fight."

The whole group cheered then quickly settled down when John climbed up and stood on the stump. The sight of him with his five foot-five inch stature offered an entirely different impression than Drake, who measured in at six foot four. But I recognized immediately the wisdom of the two men. They had been the FTOs for nearly everyone present and had garnered the respect of all. Drake was a fierce combatant and one you always wanted on your team in a fight. Whereas John was smaller, but he was definitely the most intelligent one among us. What he lacked in impressive presence, he more than made up for in scholarly cognition. The pair was a force to be reckoned with, and for the first time since this all began I felt a sense of hope rising inside of me.

"Now, listen up," began John in his typically scratchy, gruff tone. "For us to have a chance of fighting and hopefully winning this thing, each of us has to be willing to take on some individual assignments. It's research and investigation time, people. That's the name of our game right now, and we don't have a whole lot of time to accumulate evidence for our side. So if you accept an assignment, I need you to jump on it and complete it fast, got it?"

Everyone agreed with a nod of their head or with a grunt or two.

"Okay. Where's Nick Roberts?"

I raised my hand but was completely unsure of what John was about to say to me.

"Nick, you did most of the research for Henry, correct?"

"Yeah, I believe he had some information he didn't share with me, but I did the majority of the research. Why?"

"We need you to obtain as much of the information that Henry presented to the committee as you can. Do you think you can find it all?"

"I'll talk with Jill. We'll find it one way or another."

"At this point, everyone," continued John, who almost had to shout to be heard above the chatter. "I believe we have only two options to pursue in the fight to keep our guns. We must argue our case before anyone who will listen including the committee, local city officials, county commissioners, and even your neighbors. Our second option is to prove that Henry's death was an act of foul play and expose those behind it. Nick, you will lead the team that will gather what we need for the first option. I will lead a team to investigate more thoroughly the events surrounding what actually happened to Henry."

"Hey, Leon," bellowed Drake. "Didn't you used to date that gal in the coroner's office?"

"Yes, and no."

"What's that supposed to mean?" asked Drake.

"It means, yes, I did date her and, no, I'm not asking her for a favor."

"Oh, yes you are," boomed Drake. "We all have to make some sacrifices here, Leon, and this is how you can take one for the team. Get us that report on Henry and any other inside information she might know about. They ruled it a heart attack, but we all know Henry was fit as a fiddle."

"He smoked like a factory," retorted Leon.

"Just get the report," Drake replied firmly.

"Where's Brian?" inquired John.

"Yo."

"You still close friends with that board member's son? You know, the one you attended Cal Poly with?"

"I'm already on it."

"Good man," praised John.

"Okay, everybody else, please keep your eyes and ears open. And if Nick or I need help, please be prepared to jump right in. In fact, I think I can speak for Nick; we would be appreciative if you volunteered, so we don't have to collar you. This is our job, our career, people. Let's fight for it with everything we've got, okay?"

"Well, we wouldn't have to fight for it if Nick hadn't killed that guy."

"Who said that?" shouted Drake. "What low-life, dirtbag . . . was that you Leon?"

"Jonesy."

"What?" barked a furious Drake. "Where is he? Did you say that Jonesy?" shouted Drake as he pushed his way through the crowd looking for Ranger Jones.

"Yeah, I did. Everyone's thinking it. I just happened to say it."

"You see that man right there, Jonesy? Huh? Do you see John standing there on that stump? He wouldn't be here today if it hadn't been for Nick shooting that scumbag. Do you hear me, man? Nick saved John's life!"

"But . . ."

"But what?! I was there that night. It was a justifiable shoot. The review board confirmed it as well. They also found two dead bodies in the scumbag's car. He was a bad dude, both willing and able to kill. And John was next on his list. So how, Ranger Jones, do you figure that it is Nick's fault that we are fighting to keep our guns?"

"Especially, Jonesy," added John, "when you consider that the topic of taking our weapons had been on their agenda ever since the incident in that park up north."

"That's what I mean," replied Jonesy. "Because of Nick's actions, they now have a strong argument to remove our law enforcement responsibilities."

"Are you brain-dead, Jones?" shouted Drake as he took another step towards Jonesy. "I just told you he had no choice. It was the suspect or John. Now, which would you have chosen, huh, Ranger?"

"Look, Nick put himself in that position," argued Jonesy.

"What's that supposed to mean?" I contested in a loud voice.

"It means, Nick," continued Jonesy, "that you didn't have to stop that night. You could have driven on by. You know the gangs dump their bodies out there, and I'd dare say that's precisely what was going on in your mind before you stopped. But because you wanted to be some gung-ho, hero Ranger, you placed John in danger, and now all of us are having to fight for something that is legally ours—our guns!"

"Shut up, Jones!" shouted Drake. "That's a steaming pile of absolute garbage. If I ever hear you spout that manure again, prepare your mouth to receive the business end of my fist. I was there. John was there. Sergeant Munson was there. Where were you, Jones? At home, laying in your recliner, watching cop shows on television? You weren't there! So shut up!"

"Fine. I'm just saying what everyone else is thinking."

"Shut up!" shouted Drake as he lunged at Jonesy. "You know nothing of the events of that night. When's the last time you arrested anyone, huh? Tell me, Ranger Jones, what's the last ticket you wrote? A parking violation? Ranger Roberts was doing his job. And, yes, you are correct in one assessment, he is a hero."

When the meeting broke up, many of the Rangers came up to me and offered their support. Many told me I shouldn't pay any attention to what Jonesy was saying. They assured me they still believed I was a hero. Nonetheless, their words offered little comfort or encouragement. The barb had been set, and I was spiraling downward into a dark place. Not wanting to believe a single word of what Jonesy had declared, I fought it off at first. But with every indifferent look or ignored question, I soon became convinced that more of the Rangers than I cared to admit were believing what he had proclaimed was the cause of our problems—my actions that night, or more specifically, me. Although we had never been friendly before, I loathed Ranger Jones for his cutting comments that night.

Nobody likes to be the scapegoat, the fall guy. But human nature seems to require one. If something went wrong, somebody somewhere must be to blame. I remember this happening on my childhood playgrounds, and I see it occurring today. For some strange reason, we can't be satisfied with what my old Gullah friend from the Lowcountry region of South Carolina used to say when something bad happened "It's all good." There's some real wisdom in those three little words. I believe there is some Biblical truth in them as well. However, as with other declarations in the Bible, they're easier to profess than to actually put into practice. So we look for where we can cast our blame. That is, until we ourselves are the scapegoat. Then we come to recognize, in all too vivid relief, our own shortcomings, our own finger pointing, our own judgmental thoughts. We hear them in others' cutting remarks and in their unsympathetic expressions. On the other hand, if we could just remember how we felt when it was our turn on the scapegoat merry-go-round, perhaps we would begin to change our ways and refuse to cast blame on another. Then maybe, just maybe, what we've had to suffer would in the end actually cause us to proclaim 'It's all good' too. Regardless, I was definitely learning not to cast the first stone.

Two weeks flew by and our next clandestine Ranger meeting was upon us. I presented all of the information I had discovered, regarding Henry's case before the committee, to our group, which was about half the size of our first meeting. The decrease in attendance was demoralizing. Leon shared his findings from the coroner's office. There had been suspicious circumstances surrounding Henry's death, but the coroner had ruled it a heart attack. The two pricks on the back of Henry's neck were bee stings. He refused to give Leon any further information because he stated the overwhelming evidence was that Henry died of cardiac arrest. When Leon asked him if he had been influenced or pressured in writing his report, the coroner abruptly walked away shaking his head.

Working to verify the identity of the limo driver, John ran into a dead end. The man no longer drove the ITSMUD limousine, and nobody seemed to know his name, where he was from, or where he could be found. When John approached the county's District Attorney, who had jurisdiction in the city where the ITSMUD home office was located, he refused to take John's findings any further. He claimed John was paranoid and should focus his efforts on maintaining law and order in his own jurisdiction—the Watershed.

Just before the meeting adjourned, John reaffirmed his commitment to present our findings before the committee. It was the one positive takeaway from an otherwise very discouraging meeting. As I was leaving, Drake approached me from behind.

"Hold your head up, Nick. We haven't lost yet."

"Yeah, I know. But it's not looking good."

"Nick, you've done all you can do. Why don't you take some leave time? You know, get away for a week. Go to Hawaii, Colorado, or someplace."

"Oh, I don't know. I think I'd feel like I was letting you guys down."

"Man, you're not letting us down. There's really nothing more you can do."

"Well . . ."

"You need to lay low for a while, Nick. I'm telling you straight. Stay out of the limelight. Don't give any one reason to blame you for what's happening."

"What? Who's accusing me? I mean, other than Jonesy. Who said something?"

"Oh, it's nothing. Don't worry about it. Just take some time off, enjoy that wife of yours, and keep out of this fussing for a few weeks. I think it would do you some good, that's all."

"Really? So you believe them too?"

"No, I didn't say that, Nick. Look, when I was your FTO, you told me one day that you really hadn't figured on being in law enforcement. Remember how I responded?"

"Yeah, I do."

"Okay, then, why let yourself get so tied up in knots? This whole awful situation happened that night because you were doing your job. Others don't see it that way. But I know better. I see what they don't."

"What's that?"

"That it took everything in you, all the courage you could muster, to pull over and stop that night. You didn't want to, but you did because you are a good cop, a responsible guy, who knew it was his job to investigate the situation. You didn't ignore it. You headed toward it. You're a hero in the truest sense of the word, Nick. You, a man who doesn't like danger and confrontation, headed straight into it because it was the right thing to do."

"Thanks, Drake. It has been a struggle. "

"Now, here's the really amazing part of this whole story," continued Drake in his candid style. "This occurred at precisely the same point in time when our guns are up for grabs. And you, the only Ranger among us who really didn't want to be a cop, are thrust smack dab in the middle of the whole situation. I'm sure this has got to be gut wrenching for you. I mean, you're probably wondering what you did to deserve this, right? So Nick, listen to me and take a few days off until this whole nasty business calms down a bit, okay?"

"What are you really saying, Drake?"

"Nothing, man."

"Are you suggesting I quit?"

"Whoa, hold on there, Nick. That's not what I said, nor is that a decision that I have any say in. That's strictly between you, and, uh . . . your wife."

"But you're not saying I shouldn't resign, are you, Drake?"

"Again, Nick, take my advice and use some of your leave. Go away for a few days. Get some perspective. You're obviously stressed out."

"I don't know. I feel like I can't leave."

"That's probably the best time to go on a vacation."

"I know what some of the Rangers are thinking, Drake. I see the looks. But I can't quit. Not now."

"Okay, I understand. And I'm not telling you to turn in your resignation. However, I can see you struggling. You're taking this situation way too personal. It's wearing you out."

"What's that supposed to mean?"

"Well, let me ask you this?"

"Yeah, what?"

"Nick, be honest with me. Are you happy being a Watershed Ranger?"

SEVENTEEN

Drake's question rang in my ears louder than the time when I had forgotten my hearing protection at the shooting range. More confused than convinced, I knew the only thing I was sure of was that I was very unhappy in my job. What had started as a dream career nearly six years ago, had evolved into a nightmarish existence. How do these things happen? Where had I gone wrong? At what point had I taken the wrong fork in the road? It reminded me of what an old carpenter had said to me years ago when I was pondering what career to choose.

"Most of the choices you will have to make over the course of your life are not clear cut intersections with a right or left turn. They are but vague forks in the road where you will have to veer slightly to the right or to the left. But these seemingly insignificant decisions are, in reality, extremely important; for they will determine your future."

Deciding to heed Drake's advice, I took a week off. Kristina and I vacationed in the gorgeous Lake Tahoe area. The air was crisp and clear, and the scenery was breathtaking. The longer we stayed, the more I felt the fog in my head lifting. There was a poignant awareness of the rapidly approaching fork on my life's path, but I desperately needed clarity to make the critical decision. Time alone with Kristina was a healing balm to my raw nerves and seemed to be just what the doctor prescribed. As we hiked to the top of a mountain early one morning, with the snow crunching under our boots, there was a nearness in my heart I hadn't sensed in years. I wasn't sure then, but now I think it was God. We sat down on a huge boulder just a few feet below the breezy summit with the entire Tahoe area laid out before us. The temperature must have been hovering around freezing causing Kristina to snuggle cozily into me. Just then, a soothing wave of emotion washed over me, and tears started rolling down my cheeks.

"What's wrong, Nicky?"

"I, uh . . . don't know. It's just so peaceful or something."

"Yes, it is, honey. And I love being here with you. I wouldn't want it any other way."

"Really, Kristie? Are you sure?"

"Absolutely. I love you and I will love you forever."

"Why? How could you possibly love a wretched mess like me?"

"Because, it's what I love to do, and it's what God wants me to do. I know it pleases Him. So I decided long ago if this is my calling, then why not enjoy it."

"What?"

"I had to make a choice, Nicky."

"There's that word 'choice' again," I mumbled.

"What did you say?"

"Nothing, honey, please continue."

"I chose you, Nicky, for better or for worse, for richer or for poorer, in sickness and in health, as long as we both shall live. I determined if that was the choice I made, why not make the most out of it. Don't you think it is so beautiful up here?"

"Yes, you are."

"Ha . . . thanks, honey."

"Kristina, I think I made a huge mistake."

"Really?"

"Yeah, I do. The problem is, now I don't know how to escape from it. I mean, I'm in it up to my eyeballs, but I just don't know what to do to get out of it."

"Get out of what?"

"My Ranger job."

"Nicky, are you serious? Is that what's been bothering you this week? You're thinking of quitting your job?"

"Yeah, as much as I hate to admit it, I don't think it's a job I can live with any longer. I can't even live with myself anymore. In case you haven't noticed, I'm really miserable."

"Well, you haven't been real open with me lately. But I will confess, I knew something was wrong. I just didn't know what. To be honest, I'm relieved it's only your job."

"What?!"

"I mean, I'm glad it's not our marriage or something really serious like that."

"What's that supposed to mean?"

"It means, Nicky, you can get another job, and I dare say something you'll be much happier doing. But you can't get another liver, or lung, or someone like me," she chuckled. "Jobs are temporary vehicles to provide resources for the things we like to do and have. However, a job isn't who you are. It's not your identity. That's precisely where I think a lot of folks miss the mark. Look, I teach school. I like it. I enjoy the kids. I love seeing their eyes light up when they finally get a concept or solve a problem. But as much as I appreciate teaching, and will miss it when I retire, it's not me. It's only a part of me."

"Yeah, I think I get what you're saying."

"Nicky, ever since I first met you, you have always had to have something to identify with, you know, some job, some sport, some hobby. Why not just be who you are and rest in that? Maybe then, what you do for a job wouldn't matter to you as much as it does now."

"Okay, fine. Who am I?"

"Who do you say that you are?"

"Cut it out, Kristina. Help me out here. Who am I?"

"Okay. Well . . . first and foremost, you are a Christian. Now, I know that doesn't mean as much to us living in Western societies as it does in Eastern cultures. Nevertheless, it is, in a very real sense, who you are . . . not just now but for the rest of your life and throughout all eternity."

"Hmmm, but . . ."

"Wait a second, Nicky, there's more. So whether you're a carpenter, a first-aid salesman, a Ranger, or anything else, you are a Christian. Next, you're a husband,

and for as long as I live you are precisely that—my husband. Now, that doesn't mean as long as you're a Ranger or something. It means for as long as we live. It's the same with being a father. These are lifelong responsibilities and roles that have much broader and longer lasting ramifications, depending on whether someone has been a good one or a bad one. These three roles influence others for generations to come, not just for the length of your employment. Why not focus your efforts on these things . . . the things that really matter for a lifetime, and for even longer—throughout eternity?"

"Wow, Kristie, I never knew you felt that way."

"I'm not sure I've ever voiced those feelings before. But I do believe them. And I'm saying them to myself too, not just to you."

"Thanks, sweetheart, you've given me a lot to consider. I believe you have some very valid points. I just need to figure out how to apply them in a practical sense."

"Okay. While you're contemplating these matters, could we head down to the cabin? I'm freezing up here."

During our hike down the mountainous trail, the snow under our boots turned from crunchy, to slushy, to muddy the further we traveled. The adventure had taken us nearly three hours to reach the summit, but only ninety minutes to descend. We stopped at a slope-side café for a bite of lunch before arriving back at our accommodations with plenty of time for a much needed afternoon nap. Kristina fell asleep immediately, but I tossed and turned for more than twenty minutes.

Finally, I gave up trying to sleep, got up, and started pacing the floors. After the seventh or eighth lap around the interior of our two bedroom cabin, barefoot and wearing my old alma mater's sweat suit, I dropped to my knees in front of the sofa. I felt such a strong compulsion to pray that I didn't dare miss the opportunity. Before I knew what was happening, I began confessing every sin I had ever committed and some I wasn't sure whether I had or not. I wanted . . . no, I needed a clean slate with God. I was absolutely exhausted from trying to work things out on my own. I just couldn't do it any longer. It had become heartrendingly clear that I had turned my back on my faith in order to get what I wanted, the Ranger job. However, I was now ready to make things right no matter what the cost.

Praying and praising, praising and praying, I continued for what must have been hours. The time didn't matter. What was imperative to me was to have this matter of my faith settled once and for all. After humbly asking for God's forgiveness, I thanked Him for all He had done in my life. Then, in this pivotal expression of faith, I worked through every heart issue that came to mind. Deciding from that moment on, I would follow His leading, His guidance, His Word, His Spirit. I tried to leave no stone unturned. This was excruciatingly painful, but I didn't want to have to do it again anytime soon. In His fathomless love, He opened the door to the deepest chamber of my heart, and all of this disgustingly filthy mess came cascading out. I couldn't bear to perceive it, until He began to wash its feet of wretchedness, like Jesus did for His disciples. He was, because He loved wicked, sinful me, cleansing me through and through. I was broken to my core. But I saw it in a new light—the piercing light of His perspective. Above all, true brokenness is most exceedingly beautiful.

The joy that filled my heart was completely inexpressible. All at once, I knew I was healed and exactly what I had to do. It was crystal clear that I needed to resign my position as a Ranger. Instantly, an inexplicable peace flooded my soul. For the first time in many years, I was at rest. However, just at that very moment I felt a tremor, an ever so gentle flutter across my awakened spirit.

"What is it, Lord?" I asked in a whisper.

The only thought I had was, "Wait."

Two times I asked if I had heard correctly. Each answer was the same—I was to wait. I inquired as to how long I would have to wait and also asked for a simple sign, so I would be assured it was time to leave my position. There was no other reply, real or imagined, other than "Wait." It was a difficult concept to bear. Once a matter had been decided, I had always been ready to move forward. But I was beginning to understand this was part of the problem that had gotten me into this situation in the first place. Surmising the thought to wait was from the Lord, I determined it was better not to move forward until I heard from Him again. But for how long? How would I know? Would He give me some sort of sign, some message? Within minutes I concluded He was more than able to make it clear. So my posture for the time being would be to wait on Him for clarity.

"It's dinner time. Are you getting hungry, Nicky?" asked Kristina in a groggy whisper as she poked her head around the corner.

"Uh . . . sure. What time is it?"

"Ten after six. How about we try that Hibachi restaurant?"

That evening I shared with Kristina how God had touched my heart, and how I felt confident I should resign from my Ranger job. She was very supportive and thought it was the right decision for me, for our marriage, and for our friendships, which had been very difficult to maintain while on shift work. I also expressed I had felt a nudging to wait until God made it clear it was time to leave. Her only question was how would I know when it was time. I had the very same concern. Would God send me a sign or something? Would I get fired? What would be the indication my time at ITSMUD was over?

Almost all vacations are too short, and this one was no exception. At least that's how I felt driving back to WHQ the following Monday morning. Uncertain how I would handle the pressures I had been free from while on vacation, I pulled into the parking lot early, shortly after seven o'clock. Walking through the back door and into the work area, I had the unique sense that my days as a Ranger were over. I was done, and it was time to move on. Now all I needed was some sort of signal from God, clearing me for take-off.

The work area was abuzz with a story about a man found murdered on the far side of one of our reservoirs, opposite a recreation area. Apparently, Tuesday afternoon, a couple of hikers had discovered the body with multiple stab wounds to the chest and shoulder region. There were no suspects, and the investigating Ranger was anticipating the coroner's report any day. Everyone was hopeful that as a result of this tragic circumstance the case to keep our guns would be strengthened or at least reconsidered. This was the first confirmed homicide that could be proven to have been committed on Watershed lands. Surely this would clearly demonstrate the need for the Rangers to keep their firearms.

The following week, the coroner's report was released. The victim had died of a cardiac arrest and not as a result of the stab wounds. A curious discovery had been made: tiny shards of bone were found embedded in two of the thirteen wounds. The coroner deduced that a sharpened animal bone of some sort had been used as the weapon. The wounds weren't deep enough to cause mortal damage but were considered a contributor to the death of the victim.

Phil and John, both long time Rangers, weren't convinced. So while on work crew, they drove out together to the scene of the crime and had an encounter that solved the mystery. The victim had evidently strayed too close to a Golden Eagle's nest. The mother, trying to protect her eaglets, must have attacked the man, slamming repeatedly into his chest, talons first. The proposition attained convincing proof when the same eagle swooped down, missing Phil by less than a few feet. The case was solved, but the proponents for the removal of our guns used the incident to mock us, implying that we needed guns to hunt down winged mothers, who were only trying to protect their young. Incredibly, the incident actually weakened our case rather than strengthened it. The air had been knocked out of our fight to keep our weapons. It had been completely pounded out of me as well. The following Monday provided a pertinent example of my sentiments in a most, shall we say, explosively convincing way.

Shortly after eight o'clock, Sergeant Munson assigned me one of the oddest jobs I had ever done as a Ranger. The day before, a group of mushroom pickers had stumbled upon an old cache of explosives in a metal, military ammunition box. The Ranger on patrol who had responded thought they were harmless. But he took the precautionary measure of scheduling the bomb squad, from the university on the other side of the mountain, to come dispose of it. Normally a very dangerous task, they asked for a Watershed Ranger to be present to direct traffic and keep onlookers a safe distance away. I was the Ranger.

The squad consisted of two men, a somewhat short, thin, middle-aged fellow named Stanley, and his younger assistant, a quiet man of sturdy stock, who appeared to be in his late twenties. Stanley, with his south Jersey accent, called his assistant Jackson. I wasn't sure if that was his first or last name. They arrived at the location soon after I had. I walked with them several hundred yards up a heavily forested, narrow canyon with a tiny stream bubbling below. We located the container of explosives. It was no bigger than a large box of laundry detergent. Then, they suited up for the removal. While Jackson dug up a substantial amount of earth around the container so as not to disturb it, Stanley advised me that sometimes these old stashes were booby-trapped. After laying the entire root ball on a large piece of burlap, they picked up opposite ends and cautiously carried it to the road where their transport vehicle waited. Keeping a safe distance myself, I arrived at the roadway about a minute before the suited pair and abruptly stopped the few vehicles traveling on this backcountry road.

Their transport vehicle was a large, pickup truck with a trailer, which had a concrete ball permanently attached to its metal frame. This ball appeared to have been sliced in half horizontally. Within its hollow cavity lay a large amount of sand. Jackson placed the cargo in this sand, securing it with mounts pressing in on every side. Stanley waved his arm at me, indicating it was time to go. I followed at a distance with my police lights flashing. To my surprise, they drove to the farthest point east on the Watershed and then turned off onto a little known fire road. After locking the gate behind me, I caught up with them about a mile later. We stopped at a rustic shack in a pristine, little valley surrounded by steep-walled mountains. The grass was green and lush for this time of year, and the trees overhead gave the place a beautiful park-like setting with the exception of a large pit on the far side of the field.

Hopping out of my truck, I watched the two bomb squad guys scurry across the field carrying the suspect package still in its root ball. They disappeared into the crater. A few minutes later, Stanley emerged with a roll of wire, which he had anchored to the military canister. Jackson walked out with the burlap used to carry the explosives. I strolled over to their truck and intently watched their fluid and precisely choreographed movements.

"You guys come here often?" I chuckled sarcastically.

"Yeah, you could say that," replied Stanley as he scrutinized his partner while he was attaching wires to something that looked like a plunger.

"What's that?" I asked, dropping the sarcasm.

"Plunger. It's how we blow things up."

"You're going to blow it up?"

"Yeah, it's the only way to make it safe," Stanley answered. "If it's blown up, it can't blow up again."

"That makes perfect sense. I just didn't think you were going to detonate something today, that's all."

"Yep, that's what we do. Blow things up."

"Hey, did you know this is part of ITSMUD Watershed lands?"

"Yeah, we've had an agreement with ITSMUD for decades," declared Stanley, who was busily double checking the wire connections. "We've been exploding things back here for years. Okay, we're ready, sound the siren."

Jackson moved quickly to their truck and activated the siren for a few seconds. Then he shouted, "Fire in the hole!"

"You want the honors?" asked Stanley as he stretched out his hand holding the plunger in my direction.

"Sure. What do I do?"

"It's easy. When you're ready, just push this handle straight down. I really don't think we'll get much more than a poof though. These explosives have been there since sometime back in the 1960s. I'm sure they're dead."

Standing about fifty feet back from the edge of the crater, I took hold of the plunger with my left hand and the handle with my right. With one last glance at Stanley, then

Jackson, I shoved the plunger down. A second or two went by, and then . . .

KA-BOOM!

The intense blast knocked all three of us off our feet and a yard or so backwards. Shocked, breathless, and in a near panic, I gazed wide eyed and straight up through the trees into the blue sky. I remember asking the Lord, "Is this the sign I've been waiting for?"

Once the three of us caught our breath, we stood up and began brushing off the dirt, most of which had been blown out of the pit and onto us. After having determined we were okay, we had a good laugh about the enormity of the completely unexpected explosion.

Stanley confessed this was the biggest explosion he had ever discharged in the pit. Walking to the edge, Jackson nodded his agreement. Noticing the crater now appeared several feet deeper, I too acquiesced to their evaluations.

At Watershed HQ late that afternoon, John pulled me aside and asked if it would be possible for me to accompany him when he went to testify before the committee. Having just arrived back from vacation, I was sure I wouldn't be allowed the time off. He understood and told me he would be back on Thursday, hopefully with good news regarding our guns and law enforcement responsibilities.

"Have you heard anything further regarding Henry's death?" I inquired in a whisper.

"Yes," replied John, motioning for me to step outside for the answer. "The more I snoop around, the more the evidence points to someone on the board. Remember those

272

two members that Henry called cop haters? Well, one of them has taken a six month sabbatical in South America.

"What's he doing down there?"

"Not he. She," advised John.

"What's she doing down there?"

"I don't know. She left under the guise of searching for some ancient water conservation method in a remote area of some place called Patagonia. If that isn't suspicious enough, when I asked a couple of the other board members about her, they didn't know a thing about the expedition. I tell you, Nick, I'm hitting a stone wall with those guys."

"It seems to me these utility districts are like little kingdoms, and the people who run them are the royalty dictating their every whim and fancy to us, the peasantry."

"Yeah," John agreed with a chuckle. "You may not be too far off in your assessment. Sometimes I feel like we're interacting with a dictatorship and not a democratically ruled water supplier. This must be what old John Muir had to deal with when they built Hetch Hetchy."

"You would think we would have learned from history."

"You have to be a student of history to learn from it," John stated plainly. "The District leadership doesn't appear to be interested in learning from history. They just do what they want."

"Yeah, no kidding."

"Hey look, Nick, someone may have planned to intimidate Henry, but I don't think anyone wanted to see him dead. You may consider me crazy, nevertheless, I really believe Henry's death was accidental."

"What?!"

"I do. Yesterday the limousine driver was arrested at a chalet on the outskirts of a town named Castle Junction, near Banff in the Canadian Rockies. The fax I ordered regarding his statement came through about an hour ago. He claimed he was paid to rough up Henry with the intention of convincing him to give up the case for us to keep our guns. The statement further says that he was paid fifteen thousand dollars, but it was wired into an account he opened in Switzerland. So we can't trace it to the payer."

"This is unbelievable!" I gasped.

"Yeah, I agree. Apparently, the driver, Jean F. LaGard, was picked up on a petty thief charge, but when the Royal Canadian Mounted Police discovered he was a person of interest in California they interrogated him. Here's essentially his story: He faked that his car was broken down in order to get Henry to stop and help him. As he approached Henry's truck, he claimed he saw a hornet fly in Henry's window, and it stung him on the neck. He stated that Henry slapped at the bee several times before grasping his neck like he was having difficulty breathing. Within seconds, he saw Henry slump down over the steering wheel. Fearing he would be implicated in the death, Mr. LaGard fled the scene. Evidently, he bolted all the way across the border and into Alberta."

"So do you believe his story, John?"

"Well, it does align with the evidence on the scene. Drake and I were the first ones there, and it all kind of makes sense. Maybe Henry was allergic to bee stings or something. Frankly, I think someone on that board ordered the limousine driver, Mr. LaGard, to threaten Henry, perhaps rough him up a bit. And that's the crime. The only criminal act Mr. LaGard committed was accepting the money. But obviously before he could accomplish his task, Henry had a heart attack and died. Now, the board member thinks her hitman did more than what he was paid to do, and she is desperately trying to hide her tracks—all the way to the southern tip of South America."

"But why would anyone want to bully Henry?"

"Because he was so insistent on the Rangers keeping their guns. I think if the board knew that Chief Bruckman supported our position as strongly as he does, they would bring some pressure to bear on him as well. Most of the members are dead set against us having guns. They don't have any idea why we became law enforcement officers in the first place. Nor do they care. They want our guns. Without Henry, they are most likely going to achieve their goal. It really sickens me. Now I have to drive there and somehow follow up on all Henry had already established. It's going to be a hard sell."

Thursday came and went with no word from John. Throughout the day, everyone kept asking if anyone had heard from him. At one point, just before four o'clock, Jill called his wife to determine if he had arrived home yet. She responded that he had not. Perplexed, I left work that evening not knowing what had become of John or our situation.

Friday morning, I arrived early hoping to see John before all the work crew folks arrived. But nothing. No John. Finally, just after lunch we saw a Ranger patrol truck making its way up the fire road where Phil, Stephen, Rob, and I were clearing some dead trees on top of a ridge. As the truck continued directly toward us, we turned off our chainsaws and slowly walked over to our truck and sat on the tailgate.

Ranger patrol trucks are rarely seen in the backcountry of the Watershed, which is where most of the work crews continually labor. So as the vehicle approached, we knew there was news, and most likely it wasn't good. The mood was increasingly somber as the four of us sat on or stood by our open tailgate, intently watching the patrol truck as it slowly crept its way up the ridge.

The glare on the windshield made it impossible to determine who was in the truck until it came to a stop. The driver's door opened, and John hopped out. He wore a bleak expression and deliberately shook his head from side to side as he walked toward us.

"Well, guys, here's the thing," John began sincerely, while taking off his Ranger hat and sunglasses.

"What happened, John?" interrupted Phil.

"Wait a second and I'll tell you, okay? First, I wasn't even allowed to speak to the committee. They claimed Henry had already testified, and they didn't require anything further. Second, they held a closed session. No one else, not even reporters were permitted to enter. Someone, somewhere wants this thing to be very quiet."

"Of course they want it quiet, John. They're taking away the guns of an entire police department!" shouted Phil, growing increasingly angrier. "Do you know what the public will say when they find out that there will no longer be any law enforcement protection out on these several hundred thousand acres?! They are going to be furious. That's why they're keeping it quiet."

"Cut it out, Phil," quipped Stephen. "You don't know that's what they're doing."

"Well, actually . . ." sighed John. "They voted yesterday. It was nine to three."

"What's that mean?" asked Rob.

"Yeah, John, tell Rob what that means," replied Phil in a sarcastic and irate tone. He shook his head in disgust as he kicked the dirt in frustration.

"Come on, Phil. It's not John's fault," pleaded Stephen. "He and Nick have worked harder than the rest of us combined on this thing. Well, except for Henry and maybe Chief Bruckman."

"Well, it's somebody's fault," Phil snorted.

"Yeah, well, what happened, John? Give us the bad news," chided Rob. "How did they vote?"

"They got our guns, Rob," breathed John. "Those clueless bureaucrats voted to take away our guns."

EIGHTEEN

When I heard the words leave John's lips, my body shuddered, my eyes turned toward Heaven, and I whispered, "Surely this is the sign I've been waiting for. It must be time to leave now, right, Father?" After a few moments, as hard as it was for me to believe, all I sensed was the thought to hold steady. But it was immediately flushed out of my mind when John answered Phil's next antagonistic question.

"So how long do I have to find another job, John?"

"Come on, Phil," pleaded Stephen. "It's not John's fault. He has been fighting for all of us."

"Well," continued John. "I received a telephone call from Chief Bruckman late last night. He called a meeting at the home office this morning at nine o'clock. All the sergeants, the lieutenants, and Drake and I, as FTOs, were invited to represent the Rangers. I came straight out to find you four as soon as the meeting adjourned. Whether you know it or not, you guys are the backbone of the WHQ based Rangers."

"Anyone else at the meeting?" asked Stephen.

"Yeah, two board members. There was a tall guy with grey hair and a shorter, thicker fellow who was nearly bald. I was in a fog though, so I can't remember their names. Look, here's the deal in a nutshell. Within the next ninety days . . ."

"Ninety days?!" shouted Phil. "That proves this whole thing was completely rigged. They couldn't care less about us, the Watershed, or the safety of the citizens that use it."

"Hang on a second Phil," begged John. "They are contracting with the local Sheriff's Departments in each of the six counties where ITSMUD has watershed land. These Sheriff Departments have agreed to hire over a dozen of our Rangers to cover the Watershed."

"A dozen?" scoffed Phil. "There's no way they can give the same level of service with only a third of the amount of officers patrolling. Besides, I don't want to be a Deputy. I'm a Ranger, and that's what I want to continue to be."

"Well, you can stay here at WHQ, but you won't be a Watershed and Recreation Ranger II any longer. And you won't have a gun."

"That's not right," stated Rob emphatically. "I'm not going to be a Deputy. Those guys have jail duty all the time. No way am I giving up this beautiful setting for that."

"If you stay, Rob, your new title will be Ranger Naturalist," declared John. "You'll be doing park maintenance, firefighting, interpretive stuff, and things like that."

"Will we still have the seasonal guys?" asked Rob.

"Nope, all seasonal positions will be cancelled, and no new positions will be created. Over the next few years, attrition will bring down the number of Ranger Naturalists to where they think it should be in the years ahead."

"What's ITSMUD's exact number?" quipped Phil sarcastically.

"Eighteen," acknowledged John.

"Eighteen? That's ridiculous! How can we be expected to maintain hundreds of thousands of acres with only eighteen Rangers?"

"No seasonal employees, John?" I asked. "Are you sure?"

"Yes, unfortunately, they made that point very clear."

"Uh, oh," mumbled Rob.

"Uh, oh, is right," I agreed. "I'm not going on any outhouse cleaning assignment. No way, no how. I'll quit before I do that."

The others all concurred with my heartfelt although benign ultimatum.

"We are professionals," barked Phil. "Not maintenance workers. This whole proposition is actually a demotion for any Ranger willing to stay at ITSMUD."

Then John, sensing the whole conversation was heading in the wrong direction, continued, "Guys, listen, times are changing. Whether we like it or not, our job is no longer going to include law enforcement responsibilities. I hate it too. But it's out of our hands now, and again, like it or not, that's the way the cookie crumbles."

"The way the cookie crumbles?!" jeered Phil. "You stink, John!"

"Hey, hey, knock it off, Phil," retorted Stephen. "That's completely uncalled for. We'll all have to choose at some point. And it appears that the fork in the road is just ninety days in the future."

"Yeah, that's right, well . . . kind of," interjected John. "For now, we have sixty days to decide if we want to apply for one of the openings in the Sheriff Departments. Then sometime after that a meeting will be called where the District will implement the change over to the Ranger Naturalist positions."

After work, I met Kristina for dinner at a café near the school where she taught. Our conversation lasted well past dessert as we discussed my options. She made the brilliant suggestion of contacting a couple of the deputies I had attended the Police Academy with to determine if I could ride along with them one evening. However, her most probing question was one that I had heard before and was all too familiar with in terms of its potential consequences. My ears perked up when she asked in her sweet, caring tone,

"Nicky, if you could have any job you wanted, what would it be?"

Secretly, I was afraid to answer her, realizing my response to this very same question had begun my journey along the path which led me to the very situation I found myself in today. She pressed me further, but I remained silent.

"Nicky, what's wrong?"

I whispered across the table, "Do you suppose this may be the sign God wanted me to wait for to turn in my resignation?"

"What sign?" she shrugged.

"You asked me the very same question years ago just before I discovered the job announcement for the Ranger position."

"Ooh, I did ask you that question, didn't I?"

"Yeppers. Same question, different situation. Is this the sign?"

"Okay, don't answer it. Just, uh . . . think about it, okay."

How could I not think about it? It was all I thought about. What if this? What if that? But as the weeks wore on toward the pivotal day when I would be forced to choose, the fork in the road became increasingly clearer. Having ridden on two shifts with my deputy friends, I had determined I definitely wasn't interested in becoming a Sheriff's Deputy. So, when the defining moment arrived, I chose to stay at ITSMUD and become a Ranger Naturalist. To my delight, Phil, Stephen, and Rob all remained as well. In fact, all but seven of the Rangers decided to stay. Less than a month later, while out on patrol, I received the radio call every Ranger had hoped would never come—the summons to attend the defrocking of the Watershed and Recreation Rangers.

Driving my Ranger patrol truck for the last time, I pulled into a spot in the parking lot at WHQ. Right away, I noticed an excessive amount of unknown vehicles. By the appearance of three vans, the media wanted a piece of this story too—a day too late and a dollar too short. Being the last one to arrive, I took my seat in the rear of the conference room and watched with undivided attention as the end of an era unfolded. All of the Rangers were in full uniform with guns, gold stars, and boots spit-shined. I had never seen us all gathered in one place before. Although short lived, it was an impressive sight. It truly was the saddest event I have ever attended as an employee in my entire career. I realized, as I glanced around the room, that I had but a few years invested in this role. But there were many men and women who had been Rangers for more than twenty years, and three Rangers had thirty years of faithful service.

The atmosphere in the room was one of tension mixed with coerced politeness. This actually had the effect of ratcheting my stress level even higher. It was extremely uncomfortable. Faint streams of sunlight filtered in through the four Venetian blinded windows. The heavy aroma of coffee wafted throughout the room as did the cigarette smoke, which clung to the ceiling. The air was stuffy, stale, and hard to inhale. The whole scene in the room seemed toxic, forced, and unnatural. I was disgusted with the whole situation. At one point, I wondered what old Captain Henry Cross would have thought of this charade. On the one hand, I could see him standing up before this board of injustice, cigarette hanging from his mouth, and barking out what a travesty this gathering was. On the other hand, I could also envision him sitting quietly, a wry grin on his face, giving me a wink from across the room. He was a good man, Henry, a rascal to be sure but a fine captain. I sure missed him.

The sergeants were cloistered in a small group, grousing about the authority they were going to lose in this transition to non-law enforcement jobs. Chief Bruckman, the only one of the Rangers seated at the long table toward the front of the room, gestured for them to settle down. He sat in the middle of the table with the ITSMUD President to his left and Jill to his right. She was obviously the designated scribe for this pretentious proceeding. There were two board members I recognized at the table and one man I did not. He sat all the way to the right with a large, empty box on the floor next to him. Would this be the so-called confiscator of our guns? I had never met him. He might very well be a pleasant person, but I was repulsed by his presence.

The buzz in the room quieted down when Chief Bruckman stood up. He introduced the others seated at the table with him and then addressed the Rangers.

"Ladies and gentlemen, this is the saddest day of my career as I know it is for most of you as well. Let me say here, for the record, it has been a great honor serving as your Chief. As many of you know, I was here when we implemented our change over to law enforcement. There were very valid reasons to do so. Well, evidently, those reasons are no longer important. There are folks who feel we no longer need guns to protect the people who use our Watershed lands or even ourselves. It's tragic really when you consider the millions of dollars spent these last dozen years or so, but that's change. That's what some people call progress."

"So today marks a new day, a new age for you, our Watershed and Recreation Rangers. From this point forth, you will be called Ranger Naturalists. There will be enhanced training for those of you who have decided to stay at ITSMUD, and Godspeed to those of you who are headed over to the Sheriff's Departments. Now, without prolonging this any further than we have to, let's get this awful day behind us, so we can move forward into our bright future. When I call your name, please come forward and place your gun belt, gun, and other law enforcement equipment in the box at the end of the table. Please ensure your gun is unloaded. Leave your gold star and Ranger identification card here with Jill. Once all the guns are collected, we'll have a short presentation before adjourning. You Rangers that were on patrol today get with your Sergeant, uh . . . I mean, your supervisor for your new assignments."

It was a pitiful sight, professionals being treated as if they were amateurs. It was as though all those years of training and experience counted for absolutely nothing. Each one, as our name was called, had to make his way to the front of the room, as if on parade, and be stripped of his law enforcement career. I witnessed grown men weeping. My mood was sour, my expression taut. Seated throughout the room, men and women I admired, and had risked my life with and for, were emotionally devastated. I could feel anger rising up within me. Trying to subdue the tide, I assured myself that once this miserable mockery of a meeting was over life could possibly take a turn for the better. Little did I know what was waiting for me just minutes away.

With the meeting adjourned, I made my way toward Sergeant, uh, supervisor Hamstead's office, still dressed in my patrol uniform. He was seated at his desk, head in his hands.

"You alright, Gary?" I asked, trying to sound sympathetic.

Shaking his head slowly from side to side, he didn't say a word. A minute or so passed by, then I inquired if he had a new assignment for me. Remaining silent, he simply held up a key attached to a key ring with the number 580 stamped on it. Taking it from his outstretched hand, I asked what vehicle it belonged to. He again said nothing, but waved his hand in the direction of the barn to the rear of WHQ. I thanked him and walked out toward the barn curiously examining the key. It was obviously the key to some sort of vehicle. Searching around the yard, I found no vehicle with the number 580 etched on it.

After trudging back to Gary's office, I told him I couldn't locate the vehicle. He made a gesture indicating it was all the way in the rear of the WHQ yard behind the barn. Trekking back out toward the barn, I slowed as I approached the corner of the structure and scanned the area. This was where the heavy equipment was kept, so I naturally thought that with my skill set Gary had assigned me to a bulldozer or backhoe. My eyes searched until I found the vehicle with the same number as the key in my hand. I was abhorrently shocked to discover it was the truck used for cleaning the several hundred outhouses in the Recreation Areas as well as across the entire Watershed.

"No way on God's green earth!" I shouted as I marched all the way back to WHQ. "I am not taking that assignment!"

Entering Gary's office in a huff, I threw the key on his desk and declared, "I'm sick today and I'm going home."

"Fine," mumbled Gary, "But it will be here for you tomorrow, and the next day, and for the next six months."

Storming out of his office, I slammed the back door to WHQ, quickly jumped in my vehicle, and sped out of the parking lot. This revolting assignment undoubtedly had to be the sign from God I had been waiting for. I mean, one minute I'm a law enforcement professional. The next, I'm cleaning outhouses. Easing my speed down to a safer level, I decided to pull into an overlook. From this spot I could see almost the entire south end of the Watershed. It was beautiful, so peaceful and serene. I loved the soothing effect it had on me. When first leaving WHQ I was furious. Now I was incredibly sad. Sitting in my car with tears in my eyes, I prayed and asked God if this was the sign I had been waiting for. I was ready to quit, and certainly now seemed to be the perfect time, undoubtedly better than after six months of cleaning outhouses. Upon telling Him I was prepared to drive back down the mountain and turn my resignation in to Gary, I was dismayed at the silence that ensued. All I sensed was that I should continue to wait. In my emotional state, it was brutal, and far from what I was desperately hoping to hear.

Later that evening, Kristina and I had a long discussion. It started in the kitchen, moved to the dining room, then to the living room before finally terminating in the bedroom when exhaustion overtook Kristie. Essentially, she had been correct in her counsel. However, I detested the ramifications for me. She had encouraged me to simply hold steady until God made the way clear because if I didn't, I might cut short all He had in mind for me along the way. There was also one other little piece of advice she had for me—be cheerful. She had expressed that while I may detest what I'm doing, I could still choose to be cheerful about it. Believing it was another one of those subtle forks in the road that could end up directing the course of my entire life, I determined to heed her words.

Cleaning outhouses was without question the most despicable job I have ever had the displeasure of accomplishing. I don't know about you, but raw sewage is not something I enjoy dabbling in. Having dreaded this assignment since I was first hired, I hated it all the more when I experienced it in all its colors and smells. It was as close to torture as I hope to ever be. Surely, without giving graphic details, you can somewhat conjure up the nauseating possibilities and therefore understand my revulsion. And try as I might to be cheerful, sometimes the whole nastiness of it all got the better of me. As I neared the end of my six month assignment, with every outhouse door I opened I declared sarcastically and in a loud voice, "Is this one the sign?"

Although, to be truthful, even with my career in the proverbial toilet I had taken Kristina's counsel to heart and was doing my best to make a dreary task as pleasant as possible. I even nicknamed the outhouse pumper truck. Its big tank reminded me of a spaceship I had seen on a television show. Also, I recommended and received a new perfume for the detergent that I used to wash out the interior. The old one smelled of formaldehyde. The new one was a bubblegum fragrance. I was learning to be thankful for the little victories.

The weekend before my last week on outhouse duty, Kristina and I were sitting in our living room having a cup of coffee together. On the end table lay my Bible. For no apparent reason, I decided to read it. Opening randomly to Hebrews chapter eleven, my eyes immediately fell upon the eighth verse:

> **"By faith Abraham . . . went out,**
> **not knowing where he was going."**

The words leapt off the page as if backlit by neon lights. Instantly, I knew that this was the sign, the message I had been waiting for. I jumped up, handed Kristina my Bible, and pointed at the verse. She read the lines on the page and glanced up at me with a perplexed look. I tapped my finger on the page several more times, indicating I wanted her to read it again, and again. After the fourth reading, she looked up at me again with confusion in her eyes.

"What is it, Nicky?"

"I'm free."

"What does that mean?"

"God just showed me something in this verse, Kristie. I've been waiting for a sign, a revelation, or something when all along it was right here."

"What was right here?"

"The answer. Not only the answer to my job situation but to my entire life. You see, I have been waiting on the right set of circumstances, the right economy, the right job, the right attitude, the right assignment, the right house, the right car, the right everything before making a move, you know, a decision, a choice. Well, Kristina, my love, He has showed me that I've been looking for the wrong sign."

"What?"

"Yep, now I realize I'm not supposed to be living by circumstances. I'm supposed to be living by faith. Faith is the answer that was there all along. If I had, way back before I got this Ranger job, been living by faith, maybe I wouldn't have had to go through this mess. Regardless, I know what to do now. I will never again turn my back on my faith to get a job, a promotion, a house, a car, or anything else. I commit to God and you that I will from this point forward try to live by my faith, starting with my resignation from my Ranger position, which I will turn in on Monday."

"Wow, Nicky, really? Are you sure?"

"Yes! You know something, honey? I always thought that a major decision in life was just a moment in time, a split second when the choice is selected. It's not. Now I can see that this turning point, this watershed moment, was actually the result of over six years of shifting and convincing my mind and my heart that I should always walk by faith and not by sight. The case for the verdict I reached today started way back before I ever applied for the Ranger job. God perceived I had a weakness in regards to my faith in Him. So He saw fit to lead me, or allow me, to experience the circumstances that would help convince me to make this pronouncement today. I am so very thankful that God is patient, aren't you?"

"Yes, I am, Nicky. More than you will ever know. Amazingly, I have found Him to be more gracious, patient, and loving than I had ever imagined He could be. While you have been going through your struggles with self-esteem, your job, and your faith, I too have been wrestling with my own issues. Was God big enough for even my problems? Absolutely! And I have a deeper appreciation for His care and a better understanding of His love. You see, I've been praying for you all along. I've been praying that you would one day reach this point, this decision. But as I was praying, our gracious Father did a work in my heart too. And He has shown me it was His plan for us all along."

It's been more than twenty-five years since I resigned from my Ranger position. Thankfully, I never had a visit from Victor "The Cleaver" Deaver, although he had been in my thoughts on occasion. About two years ago, Kristina found a newspaper article stating he had been arrested again, this time for armed robbery and attempted murder. He was sentenced to thirty-five years without parole but escaped while being transported to prison. The news confirmed he had been shot and killed days later in a gun fight with a homicide investigator named Lieutenant Shelby

Strictman. Confidentially, I was relieved to hear justice had been served.

More than a decade has passed since I've heard from any of the Watershed Rangers. So I can't give an account as to their whereabouts. Sadly, I've learned that nearly a dozen of the original Rangers have passed away and with them their stories. From all around our nation, they are a disappearing breed, victims of a society that craves the specialized rather than the jack-of-all-trades. Actually, this was one of the main reasons I decided to write this book. The story of the Watershed Rangers is so much more than a tale of individual rights. It is a reference to the continual struggle within ourselves to do what we know is right. This is the personal battle we must win on a daily basis. It is the fight of faith.

Although my tenure as a Watershed and Recreation Ranger was similar in length to that of a college student obtaining a higher degree, I was certain I had stayed long enough. The years I had toiled, sweated, and even bled over those lands as well as the many personal crises I had endured had done their work upon my heart. They had forever changed me. These are scars I still bear today. Yet with the passage of time, I have come to realize they were but lessons needing to be learned. I'm even grateful for the humility that was worked in my heart through cleaning those outhouses, hundreds if not thousands of times. Little did I recognize in my twenties, what I've come to understand as beneficial in my fifties. It would seem the old proverb is still true today "It is good for a man to bear the yoke in his youth."

Kristina and I are much older now and hopefully somewhat wiser. We have three children, two of whom are in college. Our youngest, Henry, is a sophomore in high school who, at times, can be just as ornery as his namesake. Amazingly, he too has the same endearing qualities as the old Watershed Captain. Sometimes he makes me smile when I see him interact with his siblings. Although I have yet to hear him say, "Good afternoon. What's your excuse," when greeted at the breakfast table. He's a good guy, Henry.

The day after resigning my Ranger position, I received a telephone call from my former framing partner. He advised me that there were many opportunities for us to start up our business again. The following week I returned to work as a Journeyman Carpenter. As the years have marched on, I have developed our business to include a custom furniture and cabinetry firm to complement our custom homebuilding company. Having found the design and building business to be a most satisfying and rewarding line of work, I have come to acknowledge that I wasn't created to be in law enforcement. Rather, I was made to design and build things for people. In fact, on a regular basis I still enjoy framing a house with one of our crews.

On one such day, more than a year ago, I was helping install the final rafters on the roof of a three story custom home. Resting upon the roof ridge, I could see a column of smoke rising above what I knew well to be ITSMUD Watershed lands. It was an indication of a wildland fire. My mind slowly drifted back to those emotionally charged days. And, for the first time in many years, I recalled the monumental realization which still remains absolutely true today:

When standing at a fork in your life's road—always, always, **always** decide in favor of faith. No matter how many days, weeks, or even years it might take you to make the decision, I highly recommend you choose faith. You may or may not recognize it at the time, but that junction, that choice, that veering of direction might be the most important, pivotal season in your life.

It could very well be your Days of Watershed.

About the Author

R.J. Graves, Jr. and his wife, the lovely Mrs. Graves, met on the mission field in 1978, he a Virginian, and she from Northern California. Working with their team on the construction of a church building for a missionary, they spent many evenings discussing life and future possibilities. Once back home, R. J. traveled to California for a visit and the two soon fell in love. They have been married thirty-eight years and have six wonderful children, one of whom has already arrived at his heavenly home. Three of their children are married and have blessed them, to date with four precious grandchildren.

Over the years, R. J. has held many roles in church leadership, including teaching and preaching. However, he most enjoys leading interactive Bible studies. He believes, "Come, let us reason together," is every bit as pertinent today as it was centuries ago. Storytelling and parables are two key ingredients he considers invaluable to discovery so he invariably has one of these ready to share. "Days of Watershed" is his fourth novel. He currently has two more in the works as well as a devotional he hopes to publish next year. Family gatherings and walks with his wife Susie, and their dog Pumpkin are two of his treasured delights. When he finds the time he likes to ride his bicycle and dabble in woodworking.

After college, he began his career as a carpenter's apprentice, quickly obtaining journeyman status. He also worked for a few years as a Superintendent and a Project Manager before opening a Design/Build firm. Having held numerous management and executive positions throughout his more than forty year career in construction, he now enjoys writing stories that both inspire and challenge. His gifts and calling are to exhort and encourage fellow believers to consider the greater possibilities of faith and the mysteries of a deeper life in our Lord Jesus Christ.

You can contact R. J. Graves, Jr. on Facebook at www.facebook.com/rojocci or at: www.therojoccipapers.com if you have any questions or comments.